Kill Radio feels like a classic Steph[...] around full, vibrant characters a[...] perspective. Downright claustrophobic and anxiety-inducing at times, the story breathlessly takes you into the occult and demonic which are made all the darker and larger by the warmth of the themes of family and support running through the work. I felt moved, and frightened, and hopeful, and angry, and heartbroken, and relieved, and enjoyed every minute of it. I suspect in time, Bolger's work will be many a reader's comfort horror read.

—Alex Woodroe, editor-in-chief, Tenebrous Press and author of *Whisperwood*

As a Horror publisher, I'm blessed with ample opportunities to immerse myself in tales of the occult. Hellhounds, warlocks and demonic possession are welcome tools of the trade, but a homemade radio that communicates with the denizens of Hell? There's a unique wrinkle; I'm all ears!

The real signal cutting through the noise here is Lauren Bolger's deft character work. All too often, writers lean on clever tropes at the expense of fully formed life. Not so in *Kill Radio*. Bolger's creations positively *hum* with life, rich with the song of profound existence and screaming forth from hellish speakers with crystal clarity. This is a tune you know from deep in your past, washing over you in contemporary surround sound terror.

—Matt Blairstone, publisher & founder, Tenebrous Press

Lauren Bolger finds the right frequency for horror with her absolutely frightening novel *Kill Radio*. Turn on, tune in and get ready to be terrified.

—Clay McLeod Chapman, author of *Ghost Eaters*

Bolger's *Kill Radio* is a throwback to those horrifying stories you heard from friends in cramped dorm rooms and those late-night 80s films you caught on local cable stations on the weekend. If you ever wondered where the voices on distant stations on your parents' car radio or the wooden set your grandfather owned, then Lauren Bolger has a terrifying answer for you. Images and scenes from here will remind readers of Bentley Little's work and John Carpenter's films. This book made me afraid to be alone in my car with the radio on!"

—Kyle Winkler, author of *The Nothing That Is*

Lauren Bolger has an unparalleled and utterly original imagination. *Kill Radio* is that rarely-seen combination of lyrical writing, breathless horror and captivating action that will leave you turning the pages long into the night. She effortlessly combines these elements with an understated wit that is a joy to read. I cannot think of any other author who can so effortlessly pull off this controlled combination of elements and *Kill Radio* stayed with me long after I finished. A brilliant first novel, it left me hooked on her style and eager to read more.

—Michael James, author of The Hotel trilogy

Kill Radio

KILL RADIO

LAUREN BOLGER

A novel

ISBN: 979-8-9874654-0-0

Cover design by Evangeline Gallagher

Published by Malarkey Books

malarkeybooks.com

For Hannah and Ryan

1

Rory burst out the back door and into the morning dark—the early spring kind that makes equals of sky and of earth.

The sky seemed to him to descend at night. To meet the ground. Today, it pressed heavily down on him, like a silent theater with no stage or spotlight. And Rory—the moving piece—was the focal point.

He checked behind him as he ran. Waiting. Expecting the thing to follow. Nothing came. But that probably meant it was still back there in the house, with her.

He turned as he exited his open yard. Saw the outline of the old playground with the broken slide and three dying ash trees. Bare branches reached from the base of the trunk, grasping at life the only way they could now. They were the only decoration in the wide-open field between neighboring houses a row of strong roofs and peeling paint.

He slowed again as an orange glow played across the darkness. He breathed in something familiar. Beyond the dead-fish stench of standing water. It was sharp and metallic. Stronger than a bloody nose. He could taste it. Rory turned. His own house was engulfed in flames. Flames bursting from the back windows; a pillar of smoke clouding over the smooth, black heavens.

There'd been house fires like this, many times. Except before, it'd never been his own. It had every characteristic of a real fire. The flames scorched his eyes with their white leaping brilliance. As the heat stung his face, that encompassing terror returned.

Angry house, he'd called it, for as far back as he could remember; probably since he could talk. Yes, the fire looked angry; violent even, with those orange thrashing flames. Consuming the wood, melting the siding. Hungry for destruction and desperate to escape, all at once. But ever since he saw that real house fire last year, the one his mom could see, he'd felt the big difference. That house was abandoned. Nobody inside. And there was no fear that time. No fury. And now, a new question was born. Was his house the new angry house because of what happened inside?

He couldn't go back. She'd forced him to run. His fear for her twisted itself up with the all-encompassing alien one. Confusing him.

"Mom," he choked. His eyes stung, and his nose started running. "It's not real," he whispered, then closed his eyes. Who cares about the stupid fire? He saw what happened inside before he left. The monster, and his mom. The bad screwing up the good.

He ran in the strange empty silence for a while, until a loud scraping sound made him jump. He looked down. A tornado of wet leaves danced at his feet.

His heart pressed against his throat and he swallowed. His hands were numb with cold. He stuffed them into the pockets of his pajama pants and continued on.

The leaves scraped each other again, this time more loudly. But when Rory looked down, the leaves lay still on the ground. Some protested in brilliant yellow. Others were brown and rotted from having been under the snow all winter.

There was no wind. Chills crawled down his back. It was like something borrowed the sound of the leaves and made a pattern with it. A harsh scratching, strung together by a softer dry brushing. Like speech.

Keep going, it said.

No. Of course it wasn't talking, Rory thought. He checked. Nobody there.

Straight ahead, it said.

He made it to the top of a hill. Up ahead, the pre-sunrise glow settled upon a parking lot. Weeds thrust their way up from underneath. Green raked across, choking the crumbled asphalt. The lot led to—and wrapped around—a small brick building with a wide back door and a dumpster. If it weren't for the cars and a light on inside, the place would have seemed abandoned.

Rory's gaze settled on a nondescript white box truck. A man hopped down from the cab of it, seeming impossibly miniature. A man with big shoulders and a beard. Rory glanced down at his feet, and began the quick shuffling steps that would bring him down the hill, to the lot.

Stanton Avery scanned the parking lot as he turned off the main road. Only two cars in the lot. One was the owner's. The other, an early-80s black Mustang with a cardboard window. He swung his truck around back and jerked the parking brake up with an angry quickness. He thought he'd known who'd be here at this early hour, and hated being surprised by someone different. But this seafood place was the best in town. And, therefore, his top customer.

To Stanton, early morning was the most tolerable part of the day. He imagined that the night—in all its stillness—refreshed the earth. He felt like all the bodies in the world heated it up and soured the air. Why else would the air feel so crisp and fresh in the morning, when the world had been quiet and still for hours?

Damned human emissions, he thought, squinting to himself, an expression that resembled a smile.

Stanton hopped down from the truck, eager to get in and out quickly. He shook his head at himself when he looked at the maybe eight better spots he'd passed up. *I wanna be where the people aren't.* In a few minutes, more people would be pulling in to start prepping for the day. *Better get moving.*

He loaded his first stack of crates off his truck onto a dolly. Clearing his throat loudly, he gave the back of the dolly a hefty shove with his boot and pushed it toward the propped-open door.

"Crabs are here!" Stanton called, craning his head toward the kitchen, competing with the blaring radio.

Some guy yelling for everyone to hurry up and come buy his cars before they float away and disappear. Stanton moved the dolly very slightly forward and back.

After some footsteps, a voice came from around the corner, "I hear you say you got crabs?" followed by a high-pitched, staccato giggle. Jimmy, the dishwasher, leaned against the doorway with one elbow, grinning maniacally.

"You're here early," Stanton said flatly.

"Yep, when I leave without finishing the dishes, they make me come in early with the prep guys to finish up."

"Gotcha."

"You aren't the guy who normally drops off. When Javier comes, he always laughs at my jokes."

"Does he really . . ." Stanton replied flatly.

"No. But he smiles politely." Jimmy grinned again, showing his long, surprisingly clean dentition. "So he gets more jokes outta me."

"Don't waste them all on me." Stanton mirrored Jimmy's exaggerated smile.

Very briefly, Jimmy fixed a blank gaze upon Stanton. "Where is he, anyway? He never takes a day off."

"Hard to say."

"I hope he's okay."

"I'm sure he'll turn up." Stanton gestured with his hand. "Where do you want this?"

***

Stanton turned and headed to the back of the truck to retrieve the rest of the order. He opened the roll-up door again and reached in, dragging more crates of fish toward the edge of the cargo area.

"Hey mister?" He thought he heard a voice. A frightened whisper. He turned, checking the rest of the lot. Nobody there.

He turned around to stack a third crate. Two small hands were wrapped around the edge of the second one. He tipped the crate to the side to avoid crushing the tiny fingers. The crabs shifted, and he almost lost his grip.

"Hey!" Stanton yelled at the kid. His voice came out hoarse and almost angry. He stopped, then stifled a laugh, observing the boy's horrified expression. He felt a little bad. He must have looked and sounded crazed. The kid hung back, staring at him with wide wet eyes, his face pink as though he'd been crying. He looked up at Stanton, shielding himself with one arm. *Is he crying because of me?* Stanton wondered. He set the crate back on the truck and turned to the kid.

He softened his voice. "Where are your parents?"

The boy's eyes widened. Then he shook his head—firmly and quickly—in response. The corners of his mouth turned down and he looked away, pretending to see something off in the distance.

"An emergency happened to my mom." He sniffed, and brushed the back of his hand against his nose. "I mean . . . she needs help. It's an emergency."

14

"What's going on?" Stanton's stomach clenched. "What happened?"

"A monster came in our house and got her. She told me to run."

"Can you tell me your name?"

"There's no time!" the boy reached for Stanton's hand, and then drew away again. "Are you going to help me, or no?"

Stanton never got involved with other people. *What's a little kid mean by monster? It could be anything.* He always felt getting involved was like picking up a mess nobody else wanted. He liked things simple. He didn't know many simple people. Here, though, it seemed the only possible option was to help.

"Yeah, I can help you."

"Who's the kid?"

Stanton and the kid turned quickly to Jimmy, who was leaning in the back door again.

"I'm Rory," the kid said nervously. Hands on his hips, elbows out.

"We ain't got all day." Jimmy's hands were palm-up in a disbelieving shrug.

Stanton stared hard at Jimmy for a minute. He felt the hollow of his cheek twitching ever so slightly, just above his jaw. He hated when lightweights acted like they had weight to throw around. But it wasn't worth it. He grabbed the crates from the back of the truck and hoisted them onto the dolly.

"Sorry, something came up. Gotta run. I'm sure you can wheel them in." He turned to Rory. "Can you tell me which way if we drive?"

The kid's eyes were dinnerplates. Dinnerplates with a little twitch in one corner. "I'm scared," he whispered.

"It's okay to be scared. You've got me a little scared too." Stanton tried to laugh a little. The kid's eyes did not get any smaller. He was breathing kind of funny, like he'd been running too fast for too far. He'd seen unkind gym teachers push a kid that way until they threw up.

I honestly don't want to go, he thought. But there was no alternative. They could call the police but he figured that'd take longer. No five-year-old could run very far on foot. The house had to be close.

"Just hop in," Stanton said. "She'll be okay. We'll figure it out."

Rory nodded and ran around the back of the truck, gravel leaping behind him. Stanton yanked his door open and climbed into the driver side. Rory was already inside buckling up.

He accelerated toward the main road. Jimmy still stood just outside the door, stuck in the same confused shrug.

Me too, man, Stanton thought. *Me too.*

2

"Rory! Babysitter will be here any minute! Where are you?"

"We don't have to go anywhere . . . why do you need to know where I am?"

Rachelle couldn't think of an answer, so she didn't respond. She was looking for her hairbrush while thinking of her lunch in the fridge, and whether it was too old to eat at work. Maybe it just needed to be thrown away. She rushed down the hallway toward the kitchen. She stopped when she saw Rory. He stood in the dark bathroom doorway, holding a handmade radio.

She gasped, short and weird. Like a hiccup. "Why do you have that—"

Rory's eyes widened at her reaction. "I just found it."

"Where?"

"In the back of the linen closet?"

Rachelle straightened her shoulders, and her expression. She pretended not to notice the inquiry in his voice. "Oh."

She turned away and stalked into the kitchen. She took some gray-looking meatballs out of the fridge and unceremoniously dumped the container into the garbage. Her thoughts followed her down the hall.

Just don't even ask. Let it go, and it'll end up ignored on the dining room table like half the junk in this house.

Rachelle paused, and leaned against the fridge, eyes squinting shut. After half a moment of quiet, she shouted without turning toward the kitchen doorway.

"What are you going to do with that thing?"

Silence.

Stop it. Just stop asking.

The quiet between her questions ushered the memories in. Nights spent lying in bed with that radio sitting on Chad's old headboard shelf, listening to callers tell "true" stories of the paranormal. A late-night program on some channel.

She tried to remember the station, but couldn't. Chad was the one who'd known about it. He was always finding stuff for them to listen to, or watch. She, usually leaving him at two or three in the morning, her brain a dizzy rolodex, flipping between horror movie scenes and carnal thoughts, windows down to keep awake until she got home.

Then she pictured the long trip East she took, away from Chad; Rory growing inside her. She couldn't remember packing the radio in the car, let alone the last thing she said to him. He hadn't known it was their last time. Rachelle'd never ceased to wonder at his opinion of her after. How long had he taken to forget her?

She shook her head. Something she'd pushed away and hadn't allowed for a few years now was returning; like a boulder in her belly. A meal that would never digest. She continued squinting against the quiet. She felt a void of sound and a loneliness with terror at the edges. A dread of what would happen if she allowed this feeling to grow. She opened her mouth to ask again about that fucking radio.

And then the static came in.

At first, the sound was like the transition between stations on any normal radio. But then the sound seemed to grow, to radiate. Before long, the sound was colossal, vibrating in her ears. Rachelle narrowed her eyes as if it'd help her understand the sound better. Waited for something to happen that would explain it. It seemed like it was coming from the bathroom. She walked slowly, cautiously, toward the source.

She stood in the mouth of the hallway. Rory sat on the floor at the back of the couch, radio in front of him. His face was contorted. He was covering his ears. He looked pleadingly to Rachelle with teardrop eyes, as if waiting to be told what to do.

"Rory?! Turn it off!" She screamed, covering her own ears as well. The sound was disorienting and she couldn't gauge whether he could hear her. The static was deafening now that she'd gotten closer.

Still covering one ear, he swiftly reached for the dial and switched it off.

The sudden silence swelled in Rachelle's ears. Relief washed over her. She smiled at Rory, bewildered. *It never made that noise when Chad used it.* Rory opened his mouth to speak.

"What—" he began, but then stopped, lips pressed tightly together, eyebrows knotted. He stared at the entry to the kitchen, then quickly back at her.

In that space was a large, mottled-brown coyote. It looked up at her with calm, amber eyes, as though it belonged there. Like it'd wandered in from the kitchen to investigate the sound.

Dread banged a single silent drumbeat in her skull. The coyote turned its head sideways, observing her with that disturbing stillness. Its eyes roved back and forth in quick, tiny motions, studying her face. Its fur was matted with dirt. *A wild animal. Why is it here? How?* Her stomach was suspended, frozen. She was still.

It leapt at her face. Bashed her against the wall. They slid together until they hit the ground.

She pushed and pulled with her lungs, and no reaction. Like she was broken. The animal was still on top of her. Heavy, like a furry sack of cement. As solid as it was strong.

"Rory," she mouthed over and over. Nothing happened. She couldn't get up. The pressure in her side, in her middle, caused everything in her to cringe inward. It was the only thing she could sense; the only thing she could focus on.

The creature had her pinned against the corner where the wall met the floor in the hall. A black nose in her face; two circles and three slits, just like a dog's. She had the strangest feeling like the nostrils were eyes that watched her. The animal's actual eyes were wide, round, and curious. Its eyebrows moved occasionally up and down, as though it were processing something. She felt its paws move off her chest and press down the fronts of her shoulders.

It sniffed twice, and pulled back its lips, slowly. A quiet growl started in its throat. It barked and lunged at her face, its teeth closing down on her cheek.

The pain was dulled and unreachable. Shock behind frosted glass. She pulled her head back too fast and it bashed against the wall. She took half of a labored, gasping breath, and shouted "Run!"

Its eyes flashed in challenge. Drilled the fear still deeper, into her. She couldn't make any more noise if she wanted to. She heard loud breathing. Was it Rory? Or her? Then Rory started making croaking sounds in protest.

"Please . . . just go," she stage-whispered to Rory.

Slow scuffling footsteps sounded from the hall. The back door clunked open. Rory was gone.

"Get off me," she pleaded. It watched Rory leave, and looked back down at her, considering the sound escaping her mouth.

She shoved the thing with all her strength, moving its body just enough to wriggle herself free. Scrambled backwards into the bathroom.

It followed. Crawling quickly on its haunches, claws ripped the carpet. Lips taut and teeth gnashing.

She kicked the bathroom door closed, but it bounced open again. Moving to her hands and knees, she crawled up and shoved her shoulder against it. The snout pressed its way in, six inches from her face. It was sniffing, searching for her. It caught her scent, then opened its mouth and bared its teeth again. With a horrified gasp, she shoved again. The nose retreated, and the door set abruptly into the jamb with a loud knock.

She pressed her feet hard against the door. Her mouth was dry. Her chest, hammering. She felt and heard a bang so loud, she expected the wood to crack. She slid back on her butt. The door bent inward from the center.

Rachelle gasped at the sight. The door stretched in about a full foot. The swirls of wood moved with the curve of the door. It looked fake, a cheesy effect in a B-movie.

Her feet still against the door, Rachelle reached toward the bathroom cabinet for a weapon, anything pointy or heavy. She tried to push away the knowledge that slamming a door on its face didn't produce any cry of pain whatsoever and just focus on finding absolutely anything to stab or bludgeon it with.

Nothing was there. Just a teak wood cabinet with a half-used toilet paper roll on the edge of the counter and a toothbrush she definitely wouldn't be able to reach without letting go of the stretching door. She let out a choked yell of frustration, and immediately panicked that the sound would further incense the creature.

She snapped back around to check the door. Her mind—a thing that'd wound itself to the precipice of a break—suddenly shredded to ribbons.

A normal door. A quiet house. Like it had never happened at all.

3

Rachelle was almost sure she'd heard footsteps go into the kitchen, then some kind of clinking sound. After that, nothing at all.

Did it leave? She stood up cautiously. She turned toward the mirror. A round, speckled blotch of blood stamped the left side of her chest. A thin line of it skipped across to her right collarbone. Gasping, she pulled open the collar of her shirt to check for a wound, but nothing was there. Just a small smear of blood above her bra; no broken skin.

She stared at herself, weighing her options. She couldn't afford to guess wrong. If it had already left the house, it was out there, like Rory was. But if she ran to find Rory with this thing still in the house, she—Rory's only capable parent—would be gone.

Maybe I have an advantage in the house. I can probably turn corners faster. Then if I beat it to the back door, I can shut it inside.

The mouth of the kitchen sat directly perpendicular to the bathroom. Their back yard had no fence. She'd have to just run to a neighbor's house to ask for help. She hoped to god Rory had done the same.

She tried the door, slowly.

Damn it! She wasn't going to be able to open the door soundlessly. The stupid thing always stuck, and made a sound of wood scraping metal as it jerked open. She pulled back against the door, tensing her forearm to create resistance. The wood groaned painfully against the frame, but didn't jump open until it was almost free of the doorjamb. Rachelle stood for a minute. Listening, breathing.

She pulled the door slowly in toward her, just enough to squeeze around it; then slipped out, padding her way down the hall into the living room.

The radio sat on the floor, plugged into the living room wall. The tiny red indicator light still glowed, but no sound came out. She looked left. One of the walnut-framed French doors stood open from when Rory ran out.

A loud sound like a dying machine gurgling oil came from the kitchen. An inhuman scream with something bubbling over the opening. She shouted out. Turned her body fully toward the hallway. She backed up toward the door in a rapid, terrified shuffle, stopping suddenly just between the couch and the door.

The fucking dishwasher! The mechanics of it were quiet, but it made a god-awful gurgling sound that expelled from the sink drains when pulling in more water. She gripped the back of the couch. Her heartbeat struggled to normalize itself. She continued—slowly now—

backward toward the door, arms out behind her for balance.

Her feet were bare; the ground cold beneath them. A gentle but icy wind bit her skin and she shivered. The sun provided scant light, though it had to be mid-morning by now. She held the door with one hand, and turned around to close it quietly.

Passing through the back yard, she looked toward the kitchen window.

Her blood froze.

A jagged hole in the glass, the bottom slathered in blood. It was just the size a large dog would make if it jumped straight through the window. This didn't look like the act of a confused or rabid animal. The house sat on a tall foundation, making the window about six feet off the ground. The thing would have to be adamant about getting inside, and unbelievably strong to be able to get up that high. To push its body entirely through the glass in a single jump.

I didn't hear him break through, Rachelle thought for a minute, and then realized the radio static had probably been loud enough to drown out the sound of breaking glass.

Rachelle looked down at the blood on her shirt. The stain was drying; the edges starting to cake up. She remembered the thing standing on her chest and realized it must have cut its paw and bled on her.

Rachelle's chest felt tight. Her mind was spinning. The succession of events swirled around her. Wild animal. Breaking in. Solid glass. And the attack. She kept seeing its snout in her face. Staring at her. Again, that mysterious air behind its casual expression.

"Rachelle!"

She turned toward the voice, heart hammering again. Palm to her chest. Rory was there. Her best friend Gaia was with him, standing between two neighbors' houses, holding a cinched paper bag and coffees.

"Rory!" she cried, wrapping him in a huge hug. His shoulders were stiff and set. He gently touched her arm with his fingers.

She sniffed and held him by the shoulders. He was pale. The corners of his mouth drawn down. It hurt her to see him that way.

He stuttered, trying to speak. His eyes were wet.

He tried again. "I thought it got you," he said loudly. She could feel him shaking now. He tipped his head awkwardly forward, sniffling into her shoulder.

"It's okay," she hugged him tighter. Again, like hugging a tree. A crying tree. "I'm okay. Are you—"

"—wait a minute. He 'thought it got you?' *What* got you, Rachelle?" Gaia shifted the paper bag underneath one arm, looking frustrated. "Can you hold this please?" she asked a broad-shouldered, bearded man standing on the sidewalk. He eyed them sideways, his discomfort apparent.

Rachelle watched the man for his reaction. "Gaia, who's your friend?"

She offered the man a small apologetic smile, and he returned it, reaching for the cup. Rachelle went back to appraising Rory. Offering him reassuring looks that he didn't reciprocate.

Gaia gestured toward the man with her coffee cup. "This is the guy who found Rory. He said he was wandering in the parking lot at that seafood restaurant on Clark. I got here, saw your car, and nobody answered the door. Then I saw him drive up with Rory."

The man cleared his throat quickly. "I'm Stanton," he said, holding his hand out to her, looking unsure of what to say. "Hope you don't mind, I parked in your driveway."

She shook his hand, looking toward her house at the white box truck. She tried to picture Rory wandering the field behind their house, all by himself, in the dark of the early morning. She felt afraid, even though he stood right in front of her now.

"I'm sorry . . . what's the huge truck for?"

"Oh—I'm a fisherman. I was covering for an employee who normally does deliveries." He rubbed the back of his neck. "I'm glad everything's okay. Your son seemed very concerned."

"I feel lucky he found you. You got him here so fast." The best she could manage was a tight-lipped smile. She looked at his mouth. It was set straight across, giving him a serious look. His beard was dark brown with some silver creeping up from the jawline. He wore a plain black baseball hat and a faded red hoodie.

"Thank you," she said, sniffing. "So much. I'm sorry, this is all just weird."

"Not a problem."

One corner of his mouth crept up. A smile, but barely. She looked quickly back up at his eyes, wondering if he'd noticed her studying him.

Gaia looked at Rachelle, then Rory. "Back to the reason we're all standing here. What happened this morning? And where the ff—I'm sorry. Where are your darn *shoes*, lady?"

Rachelle ran through the explanation in her mind. She wasn't sure where to start. None of the story sounded believable.

"A giant black dog jumped on my mom," Rory cut in, speaking quickly.

Rachelle looked at Rory, dumbfounded. "Honey, it wasn't a black dog. It was a coyote."

"Nope," Rory shook his head. "That wasn't a coyote. A huge black dog. It had fire in its eyes."

"Fire in its eyes??" Gaia looked incredulously at Rachelle, mouthing "*What??*"

Gaia shook her head. "Wait a minute. What were you doing outside though?" she asked.

"We were inside. It came in and it *bit* my mom," Rory explained. "So I ran out, and she must've followed me in a hurry."

Rachelle nodded at Rory slowly, in disbelief. How could he see something so different from reality? "Yeah. It bit me, but—" She touched her cheek and checked her hand. It was a little sore, but no blood.

"Okay then . . . What happened, Rachelle?" Gaia's tone grew still more demanding.

Rachelle shook her head slowly and shrugged. "Basically what Rory's saying. Except it was a coyote."

"A coyote broke into your house and attacked you?" Gaia's eyes narrowed.

"That's *not* what I saw," Rory insisted, shaking his head vigorously.

"Yeah. I know how it sounds. That's all I can tell you." Rachelle thought a minute. "I can show you the broken window."

As though on cue, the three of them looked at Stanton, who hadn't said a word. He looked uncertain. Like he was about to back away and leave.

Gaia aimed a leveling gaze at Stanton. "Don't worry. She's got issues, but she's not a liar."

He still eyed her suspiciously.

"Come on, don't tell me you're not curious," Gaia beckoned for Stanton to follow.

***

They stood in front of the window, surveying the jagged hole in the glass.

"What do you think?" Rachelle asked Gaia.

"I think it's increasingly strange what kinds of situations you seem to get yourself into."

Rachelle looked at Gaia angrily. "You know what, Gaia? Did we ask for this?"

"You may not have, but—"

"This has been a really shitty morning. We were scared. For a little bit, we both thought we were going to die. I don't *need* this from you right now."

Rory started to cry loudly. Gaia rushed to his side, hugging him.

"No!" he protested. "Mom!"

Rachelle rushed over and knelt down, holding him so he straddled her left hip, and stood up slowly with great effort. His tall five-year-old body bent her frame to a crooked shape. He leaned his head on her shoulder, quieting quickly.

"I'd better get back," Stanton said. He patted Rory reassuringly on the shoulder. "Hang in there, buddy."

"Could-joo-just come in for a *second?*" Gaia insisted between clenched teeth, gesturing stiffly toward the back door.

"What?" Stanton looked blankly where she'd pointed.

"You know, make sure there's nothing stalkin' around in there?" Gaia asked.

"Oh yeah, sure. Sorry." Stanton led the way as they entered the house.

"Thanks," Rachelle said quietly.

***

"Thanks for the coffee," Rachelle removed the paper sleeve and set it on the kitchen counter. She pressed both hands against the cup, warming herself.

Together, they looked at the hole in the kitchen window. "I'm not going to work today, obviously."

Gaia widened her eyes and nodded. A non-verbal "duh."

They heard the creak of the pane against the window frame as a strong gale pressed against and through the jagged opening. Their hair lifted slightly in the icy breeze.

"One sec." Rachelle headed to Rory's bedroom. "Hey buddy. Please put on your fleece."

"I'm not cold," he said quietly.

He sat on top of his sweatshirt while fiddling with some robot, trying to manipulate it into another shape.

She found Gaia in the living room.

"I gotta find a window guy."

Rachelle pulled her phone from her back pocket, tapping information in with her thumb.

"You'd better clean the blood off before he comes," Gaia said.

"And hide the body."

Rachelle laughed dryly and looked up from her phone. Her joke forced her again to think seriously about what they'd just been through. Her face fell. "I'd die for him, yanno."

"Sounds like you almost did," Gaia said. "What exactly happened anyway? Like, you guys were just standing there, and suddenly, a coyote jumped on you?"

"Well, I was in the kitchen doorway, looking at Rory. He had this god-awful look on his face. He was staring at something next to me. I looked down, and there it was. It looked like it thought it belonged there."

"Didn't you hear it break in?"

"No," she paused. "No. Rory was messing with Chad's old radio. The static was really loud. We didn't hear."

"You're giving Rory Chad's stuff now? What'd I miss?"

"No, I didn't give it to him. Rory found it in the closet."

"Yeah, but . . . why did you even bring the thing with you when you left? You barely talk about the guy. It's like you wish he didn't exist."

"I don't remember packing it," Rachelle sat flatly. She sat on the back of the couch, scrolling through her phone. She was approaching her absolute limit on this conversation topic.

"I have to admit I'm curious about him," Gaia mumbled cautiously, looking at Rachelle's face, which was still fixed downward at the phone. "Like, I'd always assumed he abused you or something?"

"No . . ."

"Well, I mean, mental abuse counts as abuse too. Did he say horrible things to you?"

Rachelle put her phone facedown on the back of the couch and held her hand there. She looked at Gaia.

"It's complicated." She paused. "He was a good guy."

"Then *why* did you cross the country to raise his son by yourself?"

Rachelle pressed her lips together, tight, and shook her head.

"I mean, don't get me wrong! I'm glad you did. You're my *best* friend. I love you guys."

Rachelle touched her fingertips to her forehead, and pushed her hands to her face. "Sorry," she said, her voice muffled. "I don't wanna talk about it. Not today."

Gaia sighed. "Sometimes I feel like I know you really well, and other times . . ." She walked around the L-shape of the couch and flopped herself into the corner.

"Maybe you should watch something really stupid to feel better." Gaia turned on the TV. Some movie apps popped up on the screen. "You know what, you didn't eat breakfast yet. I'll toast you a bagel. I bought onionnnnn!" She sang, playfully. She pushed herself back up and headed toward the kitchen.

"You can never just sit, can you?" Rachelle rolled her eyes and smiled. *What would my life be like if I'd never met Gaia?* she wondered. She closed her eyes and tried pushing away the thoughts from that morning. The sun streamed in now, tinting her lids pink. She tried to revel in the warmth and remind herself to appreciate it. Her path to this life had been dark and so, so lonely. The future at that time seemed swallowed by night, with no beacon.

4

"You know, without that radio? I'm a danger to you now. I'm damned forever, and you are as good as dead."

Rachelle's memory of her last moments with Chad wouldn't quit, no matter how many miles she gunned between herself and California. She was halfway through Illinois, and sweating. Panic gnawed at the bones of her fatigue. The truly disgusting gas station coffee did not help in the slightest.

Two in the morning was a thick, heavy black with nothing behind it. The Midwest yawned on; flat, uneventful, and indifferent to her struggles. A dull and endless drudge of strip malls and cornfields.

Her stomach grumbled fiercely as she drove on, deciding to wait until she neared Chicago before resting. However young it was, her pregnancy left her constantly hungry.

The wind strengthened to a frightening degree, making it hard to keep the wheel straight. Her wrists were sore and stiff. Every time she started to relax her muscles, another gust would blast into the side of her car. It was all she could do to keep from pitching straight into the oncoming lane.

Just when the thought occurred to her to pull over, another wall of wind came straight at the front of the car. A hard metallic bang sounded on the roof, then a thump. Her car lurched back violently, as though something huge was holding on.

She watched, stricken, as the needle shot back by about 10 mph. She gripped the wheel even tighter and tried to steer straight.

Her heart flipped, then flooded. "Ughh, the *mattress!*" she groaned, easing on the brakes and pulling over. It must have come undone in the front.

She inched toward the gas station at the next exit, careful not to disturb the giant slab of polyurethane fluff any further. Bright red letters hovered past the off-ramp, over to the right: "hell," they said.

"*Really* cute." She grumbled as she finally veered onto the ramp. She shook her head at the dead light bulb in the first letter of the gas station sign. The middle of nowhere, all alone, and the only light to be found was a glowing red neon siren, luring her to Gas Station H-E Double Hockeysticks.

After reattaching the bungee cords and wrapping twine around either end, she was sweaty and exhausted, her hands stinging and raw. She stood in the dim light, hands on her hips, gulping in the cool air until her mouth was dry.

Rachelle stared at the gas station attendant, turning to the side, sticking her belly out a little. She wondered if he'd realize he'd just let a pregnant lady sweat like beef jerky drying out in the sun and hadn't bothered to offer any help. Or maybe he already knew and didn't care. Too busy texting his mom asking why he has to wash his own bedsheets or something.

She stood like that for a bit. Trying to decide if she'd keep driving, or stop to get some sleep. She checked her phone. Still more than a full day of driving left. Fourteen hours, jesus. She'd been driving forever. Felt like it would never end.

"I need food, I need coffee. I need to pee." She pressed her hands against her neck. She slung her purse across her chest, adjusted her sweatshirt beneath it, and headed toward the gas station door, ready to side-eye the night-shifter.

The place was newer-looking, but dark. The lights shook, then kicked on by the door as she approached it. Motion sensor, to save electricity. She looked up as she reached for the handle.

Inches from her face was a girl in the reflection of the glass door. Arms out at her sides, bare feet vaguely pointed down.

"Whatthe—" she exhaled and stepped back quickly.

The paste-white face was blurry. The figure hovered and swayed, as though held by a gentle current. Its eyebrows were just a smudge across, joining two black circles as eyes. It wore . . . a tank top and shorts. A shock of hair hovered up and to the side, rippling with the same invisible tide. It tilted its head, pointing a blurry hand at something behind Rachelle.

"Nonono. No way."

Rachelle backed up faster, looking down at herself, touching her light gray sweatshirt. *It's just your reflection*, she lied to herself. She tripped over a concrete parking block and fell hard on her side. Standing up, she shielded her eyes and walked quickly back to the car, head down.

She gunned it out of the lot and crossed the bridge over the highway to the on-ramp.

Fuck this place, she thought. *I'll gas up somewhere else.*

She bit her lip and squeezed the steering wheel. The tires tugged at the curve of the on-ramp as she accelerated. At least she was away from that place. An annoying ad came on the radio and she abruptly turned it down. She was jumpy. Shaky. Agitated.

The sound of lapping water filled the car. Like she was in an aquarium. She twisted the volume knob again, but the noise persisted.

She clicked the radio off entirely. Still there.

"What now," she groaned.

"The radio," a voice rasped directly in her ear.

"What!" Rachelle shouted out, swerving the car wildly into the next lane. She righted the car, white-knuckling the steering wheel with both hands. It wasn't real. She didn't hear it. She was tired. That was it.

"The radio," the voice repeated.

"Fuck! What is it? Who *is* that?!" she growled. The adrenaline kicked on. She steadied the car and glanced behind her. Nobody there. Clearly.

The aquarium sound grew louder. Sloshing water in her ears. Brought her back to a memory. Years ago. An old friend she'd never see again.

She choked back a sob. "Daisy?" she asked weakly. Her eyes filled.

"Little seashell," the voice rasped.

"How are you here?"

Tears escaped the corners of her eyes, but her heart still pounded. She felt queasy. Something moved from the corner of her eye in the direction of the passenger seat. Over, and back.

She turned to check the back seat again. A face met hers in the dark. Like a Daisy death mask. Hair plastered to her head. Skin puffed up. An even darker contusion where her hair met her scalp. The skin at the hairline was torn and peeling back, just a little.

"No!" she exclaimed. "No, please, no."

"Shouldn't be here. Not allowed," the voice choked now.

"What can I do?" she sobbed again. "Does it hurt? Can I help?"

"The radio."

The thing reached for Rachelle, its fingers brushing her shoulder.

Rachelle glanced at the road. Her muscles were taut and shaking. "What do you mean? The car radio?" It took every ounce of strength not to recoil. The moment its hand moved back, her shoulder sagged. Her breaths came fast and deep now. She checked the road. She'd been drifting into the other lane. She righted it again.

"I can't stay. *Don't* turn it on."

"What? Why?"

She turned, and the figure was gone. She stared out at the endless road. Punctuated by identical gashes of yellow paint. Her eyes felt choked by the nothing. She tried to focus on her headlights. Searchlights, she told herself. Follow them and you'll get there. You'll settle in. Have the baby. Things can be good again. You'll make friends.

She hummed to herself, trying to vibrate her brain, shake it, make it forget what had happened. A tiny fragment of a song came to her. Maybe half a chorus. It felt like a strange lullaby; long notes with quick turns.

"I know that song," she found her voice again. Daisy was humming the same tune that night.

She stared, blankly, through the windshield. After two feet, the beams got lost in the darkness. She blinked, then focused at the area where they disappeared, her heart pounding. Bright, then dark. Like a solid line was drawn between them.

The wind blasted the side of her tiny car. Tugging it toward the road markings. She pushed back, flexing her muscles. Righting the wheel.

What on hell or earth am I supposed to do with this radio warning? She can't mean Chad's radio. She died before I met Chad. None of it made any sense. Everything back there had hurt her, body and soul. Almost killed her. *I left everything back there. Chad. The radio. All of it.*

What other way to leave all this behind than to say fuck it all? She felt herself smiling for the first time in forever. Smiling as her eyes stung. While tears ran down her face. *It can't touch me. It's behind me. And the distance only grows.*

Rachelle sat in that feeling of apathy until she fully owned it; until it dripped over her face, her body, and enveloped her. Cold, thick and heavy, like paint. The tears wouldn't stop. Everything was blurry. She finally pulled over and parked for the night at a motel. Slept for eighteen hours.

5

As night crept upon them, Rachelle struggled to ignore a heavy, nagging dread settling in her chest. Things had seemed mostly okay during the day once she'd found Rory, but now she felt on edge. Like the slightest unexpected sound would send her into hysterics.

Amid the waves of anxious energy, she'd hunted around for something she and Rory hadn't played with in a while. Their old charades game was the distraction of the hour.

They sat together on the living room carpet, embraced by the L-shaped sectional. Rachelle had pushed the coffee table back so it sat crooked between the TV stand and the open end of the couch.

She was sometimes impressed at how anxiety scripts could run like rampant crisscross marquees through her mind behind whatever activity she did with the kid. As she acted out the next card prompt, her list of regrets were: missing the sunset that was almost surely the most beautiful thing to ever set the sky ablaze, lamenting the impending darkness after the "accident," and not having asked Gaia to stay the night. She'd wanted to, but it just felt weird. Like asking your parents if you can sleep in their room. Only you're thirty-five.

I should just call her. It's not too late! She squinted, trying to read some faded pencil on a weathered piece of index card. She'd bought the charades game years ago, but many of the cards had been either lost or irreparably ripped over the years. She'd tried to replace some of the playable prompts from memory as she'd noticed what was missing.

"Spaghetti."

She stopped her pantomiming almost as soon as she'd started. "*Yeahhhh...!*" a little over-enthused. She realized this, and trailed off at the end.

Rory sighed loudly.

"What's wrong?"

"Mom, we've done that word a hundred times." Rory held his hands palm-up in exasperation. The motion still looked unnatural. A juvenile mimic. "You even always act it out the same way!"

"Well how many ways are there to eat spaghetti?" she scoffed playfully and swatted at him with the back of her hand.

"Can't we just go buy a new game?" he asked.

"Yeah. We should . . . We *will.* I've been meaning to pick up something new."

He looked away, then straight at her. "You're scared, aren't you?"

Shit, she thought. She was horrible at hiding her feelings. Especially from Rory. They were always around each other, and he was such a bright, perceptive kid. The older he got, the more he picked up on.

"We'll be okay, honey. That thing is long gone."

"Yeah but . . . what if it isn't? What if it comes back? We're lucky it even left when it did." He looked at her cautiously. "I mean, did you think about all those things?" Again with the hands.

Rachelle contorted her mouth into a reassuring smile. "Honey, if I thought it would come back, we wouldn't be here right now. It was a scared, confused animal. Coyotes don't even attack, normally. It was probably sick, and honestly, I'll betcha it went away to go be somewhere else."

"You mean like . . . to die?" he whispered, his eyes wide in disbelief.

Is that what I really believe? she wondered. *No. Not really. But it's the only thing that makes sense.*

"I mean . . . I wasn't going to *say* that, but yes, it probably had rabies or something. And after they get all violent, they are way too sick. Beyond help. Beyond saving. Then they eventually die."

Rory sighed. "What time is it?" He twisted his wrist around, looking at his blue plastic watch. "Seven o'clock."

He sighed again. Rachelle looked at his face. He looked pale. Little indents under his eyes. He wasn't old enough to have eye bags, but small half-creases rarely seen on a five-year-old made him look exhausted.

"Hey bug? Why don't you get started with your bedtime routine?" Rachelle suggested. "Tomorrow's a day care day, and you need your rest. Plus, I can stay out here in the living room with the lights on for a bit, while you fall asleep. That way you won't have to be scared."

Rory got up and stretched. "I'm not scared. I was just making sure you weren't."

Rachelle laughed. "Ooo-kay, buddy. I believe you."

"No, really!" He did a half-turn with his feet to redirect himself toward the hallway and ambled to the bathroom.

"You can admit it. I won't tell anyone!" Rachelle promised, joshingly.

"Maaaaa!" he whined at her persistence. He sped up as he neared the dark kitchen, practically running into the bathroom.

Rachelle watched the hallway leading into the dark kitchen. She was sure he was terrified. She thought about the coyote.

She'd tried all day not to focus on what Rory said he saw. Tried not to recreate the scene with *his* description of the animal standing over her. Watching her. The open wound in the glass of their house, breathing in the cold, cold wind.

Now that she was alone, she couldn't hold back those thoughts anymore. Where would a creature like that hail from? Something with fire in its eyes? As the burning fire focused on her, what would it want? And again, what would it have *done* if the door hadn't somehow prevented it from advancing on her?

Ridiculous, she told herself. She shook her head to try and release the thoughts from her skull. That wasn't the first time Rory claimed he saw things that weren't there.

She remembered the horror she first felt when her toddler began pointing to houses. His small body went taut in his car seat. He'd shout "Fire!" jabbing his finger repeatedly, as though desperately waiting for someone else to help. Once, she pulled the car over, got them both out of the car to show him there was no fire. That only prompted him to push her back toward the car and cry harder. Instead of reassuring, she'd end up asking "Where? Where? Not this house?" She couldn't help it. Somehow, she felt like telling him it wasn't there was making it worse.

These days, she knew he still saw it. His breathing from the front seat never failed to instill in her a ragged panic. A disbelief. She didn't acknowledge it anymore. She didn't want to push him into talking about it. He'd remain pale-faced the rest of the day. After, she'd ask if he was okay. He'd mumble that he was fine. He'd do something quiet like color, or look at books, but always very close by her. Eventually she stopped asking when he looked like that. It only extended his tortured pallor. She tried just being there. It seemed the best solution so far.

Rory issued a quick "g'night." He attempted to clear the hallway with a leap from the bathroom door to his bedroom. There was a thump as he slipped and banged into the door. "I'm okay!" he shouted.

Rachelle strained to listen to his movements. She heard the bedframe squeak as he lay down. *Why isn't he asking for a story, or to be tucked in?* she thought. *He's really leaning hard into pretending he's a grownup.* She often referred to him as her "little husband," to Gaia, and only Gaia. She was thankful she had someone to share her inane sense of humor with.

Rachelle picked up her phone off the floor to text her.

u up?
LH put himself to bed tonight.
so. weird.

He doesn't need you anymore!
Careful, lady.
He might find another mama.

Ha.
I am realllly creeped out now that it's dark.
can u stay the night? I'll sleep on the couch.
u can have my bed.

My brother stays in at night these days.
I'm afraid if I leave him alone he'll go
out and party again.

He's been sober for like a year tho...?

Exactly. Gotta make sure it sticks.
Maybe it's time you found one of those "adult companions" to stay with you at night. Don't want you to spontaneously combust now, do we?

Rachelle laughed.

so now ur a damn comedian?
btw, you're in no position to judge.
lucky your bro's there in case you need the
heimlich.

"btw," You'd miss me so bad if I croaked.
Read a book til u get tired.

a book...
have u met me?

Ok... put on Cake Boss til u get tired.
Go to bed
Ur worse than LH.

***

Rory lay in bed with his eyes closed. He felt more un-settled tonight than on other nights. As if he'd swal-lowed his food without chewing. It made him imagine a snake that swallowed a rabbit. Like he could feel that panic in his belly, and he could hardly wait until that panic died.

He did what he always did when that feeling came. He concentrated hard until all his thoughts melted. And then, like warm butter, he slipped out of the heavy thing that lay on his bed, and dripped up to the ceiling. He hung up there, looking down at his body on the bed. And beyond that, he saw the grid.

It started when he used to space out staring at the bathroom floor. He'd see a light green grid the same shape as the tiny white-and-yellow tiles, only the grid was underneath them. It was like a moving barrier with something else underneath. Like living in an apartment, feeling that presence below. He grew used to it. But the nights he saw the flames? The quiet after was extra hard.

Feeling for the grid was like checking to make sure he didn't leave his bike outside and then seeing it there in the closed garage where it belonged.

That, but bigger. And with his eyes closed.

There it was, in his room. It was doing its rhythmic dance. Floating, shaking a little, then settling back up again. But when he looked toward the corner by his door, everything was interrupted.

Instead of the grid was a turbulence. Like a vibrating black tornado. It stayed in one place, but it shook so fast, it made the grid all upset. It stopped that calculated rhythm of the grid and made its own new one, which was an angry quaking that wouldn't stop. The hole it made was big and jagged; a cracked-looking circle with soot-blasted streaks shooting around it. Like a black star with its insides all opened up. What if the strangers from downstairs would notice all that shaking? Rory felt like he was making it worse by knowing about it. What if they could see him, seeing them?

Rory tried to take slow, deep breaths. To coax himself into relaxing. As he left the area by his bedroom door in his mind, he heard a quiet growling sound. It sounded like it was coming from the tornado-ladder. He quickly backtracked, returning to himself. He turned his face toward his bedroom wall opposite the door, and squinched his eyes.

Breathe, he told himself. *Just breathe. You can sleep. You can sleep and everything will be fine in the morning.* His heart was banging the walls of his chest, trying to get out. He was holding on. He could. He could hold on until sleep greeted him. He was sure. He was tired. Very.

Rory didn't drift. He tumbled into sleep.

6

Rachelle sat in traffic in her black GMC Terrain, music on. She rubbed her thumb against the bottoms of her front teeth, humming absently with the riffs in the chorus, drifting in and out of paying attention to the song.

The light turned red again. The green had advanced nobody forward.

Rachelle groaned. "Always right before I get where I'm going, it slows down." She grabbed the steering wheel as though she were about to make a turn, released her grip, and sat back again.

Her gaze floated, then fixed on the cars in the right lane. They were moving—slowly—but better than her lane, which had been completely still for minutes. An old silver Honda Civic with her parking garage's permit hang-tag was turning into the coffee shop parking lot right up and over from her.

"Fuck it. I'm getting some coffee," she said out loud. She honked in what she considered a polite frantic staccato as she forced her way slowly across the right lane and into that same parking lot. One driver tried to lurch forward, but she forced her bumper into their space, imploring them to brake.

Pulling in, she saw the Civic sitting next to the only empty parking space. The person inside was just starting to open the door. She inched the car forward indecisively. *Should I be rude and pull in now, or be awkward and wait while they get out?*

Eventually, the man unfolded himself from the car. He noticed she was waiting, and sidestepped around the vehicle, twisting his briefcase and putting a palm against the front of his pale blue buttoned shirt, preemptively avoiding her car.

She didn't recognize him. He looked maybe half a head taller than her. He had pleasurably messy light brown hair, was clean-shaven, and looked to be in his thirties. She wondered which suite he worked at in the building. Maybe the family law office on the main floor? But those guys all wore suit jackets and ties. His dark green Carhartt jacket looked strange paired with the light blue button-down. A blue-collar worker's jacket paired with literal blue-collared office attire.

The man stared blankly at her for a moment and she put on a warm smile. As soon as she smiled, though, he looked quickly down. She realized he'd been staring toward her, not actually seeing her, apparently deep in thought. She reached up, pretending to be busy straightening her rearview mirror. He stood still a minute, staring at the ground, brows furrowed. Just when she thought she'd have to roll her window down and say something, he moved out of the way. She pulled in swiftly, offering a flat-palm wave that he didn't see.

She emerged from her car butt-first, dragging her laptop bag out from the passenger seat and headed toward the coffee place. It was called "Coffee" so naturally everyone in the office called it "the shop." She had the door half-open when she noticed the man was heading toward the office building instead of into the shop.

"Are you parking here for the day?" she called, reaching her foot out to catch the door. She gritted her teeth as it scraped heavily over her toes and stopped there, pinning them to the bottom of her shoe.

The man half turned his head to look at her, arms paused mid-swing. "Yeah," he said.

"I wouldn't do that. You'll get towed." She winced and relinquished her foot from the door.

"I was told it's okay when the garage is full."

"Uhmm, okay!"

He continued toward the offices, but turned back again briefly. "Thanks for looking out, though."

She shrugged and entered the coffee shop.

***

Rachelle set her coffee and bag down and hung her jean jacket on her desk chair. She rubbed her hands together and sat down. It was only early April, but the week before had been warm. She shivered, both from the cold, and from the thought that last year's mustard stain would probably never come out. *Note to self, take your coat off before eating a char dog with extra everything.*

"Hey, Rachelle?"

Kim, the digital marketing intern, stood uncomfortably close to her. Rachelle held her breath. The cloud of overly sweet perfume had preceded her by a few seconds.

"Morning Kim. What's up?"

"Is that your car?" she pointed slowly toward the big picture windows that faced the coffee shop across the road.

Rachelle let out an immediate huffy sigh. "Don't *even* tell me."

Kim's eyebrows raised. "Hey, don't look at me. I came as soon as I saw."

Rachelle hustled around the art department island to the windows. Some guy had already loaded her car on his tow truck. He spit on the curb and walked back around to the controls to operate the lift. He must have started the second she set foot in the building. And that damned Civic was nowhere to be found. Was it already towed? Or had that guy somehow moved it in time?

As if on cue, a door handle clunked down across the open office and the guy from the parking lot rushed in. His nose was pink. He was breathing heavily, still gripping his keys. He cleared the few steps to the reception desk quickly. He leaned over the front desk toward Sandra, the receptionist. Sandra turned and pointed to one of the meeting rooms.

Rachelle walked along the cubicles, toward the front desk. She glowered at him, her heart pounding. He didn't notice her. She narrowed her eyes, willing him to feel her contempt.

Asshole! she thought. He didn't know anything, but still, he corrected her. Someone who obviously comes here every day. Who would have possibly told him he should park there? This is practically the edge of the city. Nobody let you park anywhere if you're not a patron.

Rachelle furrowed her brow. She couldn't imagine who this guy was. They didn't have a lot of visitors other than their podcast guests. And when they had a guest coming in, everyone knew for at least a couple weeks ahead of time so they could prep for the recording.

Rustling clothes sounded next to her, and she jumped. Kim stood ungodly close again, watching the exchange with the stranger. Rachelle coughed. *Damn, I thought that was still the old perfume lingering, but it's a fresh cloud.*

"How long have you been standing there?"

"The whole time? Since James walked in."

Rachelle sputtered and then scoffed. "Who *is* this guy?" she finally managed. "And why am I the only one who doesn't know?"

"I'm assuming that's him, anyway. James is the new Content Supervisor? I think he's starting today. They didn't ask you to help interview him? I mean, you know your department best. You basically do it all. Especially since Garret quit."

"New Supervisor?" Rachelle whispered.

"Uh, yeah. I just overheard yesterday." Kim cleared her throat. "I assumed you knew."

Rachelle didn't respond. She strained to listen harder, as she hadn't heard the first part of his exchange with Sandra. Pushing out all the office noise, she could hear the rest of the conversation.

"They're in there now?" James was asking Sandra.

"They're in there now." Sandra replied with a single, slow nod. James turned away, pushing the door into the first conference room, which was partially ajar.

***

Rachelle had been trying in vain to focus on her outline for the upcoming episode they'd be recording later that week. Just when she'd started panicking a little on how behind she was, she heard the creak of the chair next to her.

"Rachelle?" her name was spoken in a gravelly singsong voice. Rick Norton, the producer, gripped the back of the chair. He always did that while he talked to someone. All white-knuckled, like he was losing control of his damn legs. Emphasis on "damn" today.

She took a discreet deep breath and held it as she turned to face Rick. "Hey Rick," she smiled as nonchalantly as her face would allow.

"Hey." He smiled kindly, his eyes clearly studying her reaction. "Hopefully it's been mentioned to you, but this is James Carroway, your new Supervisor."

Rachelle reached her hand out to shake with James. "It's nice to meet you, James." His grip was firm, not tentative, or . . . coddling, like most handshakes were. His hand felt warm, big, and rough.

He smiled and nodded, politely. She scanned his face for recognition, or remorse. Slowly, he released his grip, slipping between his desk and chair to set his things down.

She turned to Rick. "I just found out," she exhaled quietly, letting her breath leak out sideways like cigarette smoke. She bit the inside of her lower lip.

"I'm sorry," Rick said. The apology in his voice sounded genuine. "I planned to give you a heads up last week, but as you know, my lovely wife decided to fall off the roof of our house. And I was a *bit* preoccupied with her in the hospital."

The word "bit" had come out high-pitched. Rachelle furrowed her brow. She looked up at him, thinking. He sounded nervous. "I didn't know that was why you were out. Is she okay?"

Rick sighed, his eyes closed. "She'll be fine. No head stuff, just . . . fractures and bruises," he pantomimed, gesturing toward his forearm.

He looked relieved. Rachelle wondered if it was because his wife was okay, or because he realized she probably wasn't going to make a scene. He nodded awkwardly with most of his upper body, almost a bow, and walked back toward the front of the office.

After Rick's exit, Rachelle had to ask. "Did your car get towed, too, by the way?"

James turned his head toward her, his eyes seeming to flutter about the office before they settled on her. *Where the hell is this guy, if not here?*

His eyes seemed to clear for the first time. Then came those serious eyebrows, like in the parking lot.

"*Oh . . .* it's you," his eyes widened. The sentence seemed to be heavily weighted, somehow.

"Uh yeah. It's me." Rachelle looked at him quizzically.

"The girl from the parking lot." His faculties seemed to return to him. He flashed a toothy smile. "It's best not to listen to me. I rarely have anything constructive to offer."

The smile looked disingenuous, but his eyes seemed to be softly boring into her. Rachelle's heart pounded, annoyingly.

She ignored it. "Well I mean, I kind of have to now, don't I?"

"True. In a sense."

"Mm."

"I'll try not to disappoint."

***

"Soo, who used to sit here?" James broke the two hours of silence between them after Rick and the Network Manager had stopped coming and going from his new desk, helping him set up.

Rachelle leaned back in her chair and looked sideways at James, crossing her arms. "The last person who sat here, Garrett, used to swish mouthwash at his desk and then spit it into a little plastic cup."

"Wow. So I hope I'm an improvement over—"

"Jury's still out. He also used to let it sit there for days. It was impossible to quit looking at that cup. I'd stare and try to blank out the knowledge of what was inside."

"Okay, should I worry that there's even more to this?"

"One time we had fruit flies for like, seven weeks. I'm almost sure it was because of his sweet, spitty mouthwash cups."

"Done?"

She looked up at the ceiling, thinking. But that was about the worst of it. He was actually very nice otherwise.

"Yep."

James leaned in her direction from his chair. "Sorry about your car," he said evenly, quietly.

There was no response at first. Then Rachelle replied, "I know."

"Let me give you a ride?"

"I mean, yeah. I kind of need one. Thanks."

"No problem. Anything to make myself feel less guilty."

Rachelle looked up at him. He was smiling, cautiously. Looking into her face.

As she returned his gaze, she saw his eyes were a golden brown, and his eyebrows darker. The way they sat on his face seemed to shade his eyes and create an air of mystery, like he was in deep thought over something.

Does he just look like this perpetually? Rachelle found herself wondering what he could be thinking. A sick sensation spread across her stomach. Like hot honey.

7

She watched for James through the frosted coffee cup etched on the picture window, one cup in each hand. Sighing impatiently, she shifted her weight.

Feel stupid for buying him coffee.

He seemed nice, she assured herself.

Everyone seems nice before you find out why.

Careful, he's your new boss.

New boss. Let's not get started with that shit.

He crossed the parking lot. She turned around to face the counter, gathering herself, then sauntered casually toward the door.

"Hey," he drew out the "y," and broke into a wide grin.

"So—" She set down the coffees on a nearby table. "How was your first day?"

"Boring but . . . enlightening," he said, widening his eyes, fixing them on hers.

"Enlightening?" Rachelle felt hot. Was he flirting? Joking? Joke-flirting?

He nodded once without elaborating, tongue poking his cheek.

She grabbed both coffees and handed him one. "Ready to go?"

"What's this for?" He reached for it slowly, looking puzzled.

"Thought you could use something. First days are long."

"What is this, just black coffee?" James opened the lid and looked in. "Is it decaf?"

"Just regular. Plain black."

"No sugar?"

"No. I figured you could add it if you wanted."

He took the cup by the top edge. "Fine like this." He looked at her cautiously. "Thanks."

She eyed him sideways as she pushed open the door for him. "No problem."

"You didn't . . . piss in it?"

"Whaat?" Rachelle let out a short, disbelieving laugh. *That's . . . different.* "Nope. I would've, but *way* too hard. Small bathroom, two coffees, lids, you get it."

She turned to him as she held the door open. He wasn't smiling, but his mouth corners seemed turned down in amusement.

***

She sat down quickly in the passenger seat, rubbing her hands together to warm up. The strong, savory scent of sun-stroked leather greeted her. Behind it, lingered a slight cigarette odor. *If he smokes, he doesn't do it while he drives*, she thought. The car was tidy, but the sun reached across the dash and console, lighting a thin layer of dust.

He sighed loudly as he lowered himself into the car. He adjusted himself in the seat, then leaned forward, twisting the key in the ignition.

"You said this place is close by?" he asked her.

"Yeah, why? You have somewhere you need to be?"

James turned to her, mouth open in mock surprise. He backed up the car, spinning the wheel one-handed, touching the shoulder of her seat.

He bit his bottom lip before speaking. "All right, Charm School. Which way?"

Rachelle let out a quiet joking scoff and smiled. "You can turn right here. It's up four blocks and over two."

He turned onto the main road.

"Sooo," she asked, "did you move here for this job? Or have you been around here long?"

"I move around a lot." He paused. Rachelle wondered if he'd continue. "I came from New Orleans, most recently."

"Oh, cool! I've never been. I've heard that's a great place to visit."

"I was more than ready to leave."

"Yeah?" She tucked her hair behind her ears, turning back to him. "Why did you move?"

"I've been searching for something," he trailed off.

"Like, your dream job?"

"No," he exhaled quietly through his nose. "It's a long story, really." He stopped at a light, then turned and looked at her, studying her face.

She looked back at him. She couldn't tell what his expression was saying. Remembering the past? Deciding if he could trust her, tell her more?

"How about you?" he asked.

She hesitated. He'd changed the subject. "I came here from Crescent City."

"Is that where you grew up?"

"No, I grew up in Santa Ana. I moved when . . ." She paused again. "I moved a couple of times."

"Was a far move that last time," he commented, his pupils working side to side as he stopped at a light. He looked like he was processing the information. What could he be doing with it? She'd hardly told him anything.

"Yup." Now she was the tight-lipped one.

James smiled vaguely at her. Her heart stuttered. She took a big, silent breath in. They were so close together. She watched his profile as he drove; those studious eyes still working back and forth.

They drove on for a while. The quiet was occasionally broken with her speaking as she pointed out the turns.

The lot was marked by a big rusty chain-link gate. Gravel popped under the tires as James pulled in. Rachelle leaned forward, gathering her purse from the floor by her feet.

After paying the attendant, she got into her car, which felt exactly as cold as it was outside. She shivered and reached for her keys in her jacket pocket.

A quick rapping sounded on the window. She turned, expecting to see James.

An older man with wild hair and even wilder eyes stared at her.

Rachelle's heart leapt, and she moved back, away from the face.

"Run away, Chelle! Run away!" he shouted so hard his throat sounded raw. Spit had hit the windshield. He breathed heavily, looking absolutely frantic.

"What are you s—what do you mean?!"

"You killed her."

"What!! No—" her mind reeled. She felt dizzy. Her face was hot. She was far from everyone. From family. Friends. Everyone in that old life.

"She's *dead*, I said! And you should see what they're doing to your boyfriend!"

"My *boyfriend?*" Rachelle paused. "Do you . . . know me?" She looked closely at his contorted features. She didn't recognize him at all. *He's just talking shit*, she told herself. *Complete nonsense. The things he's saying . . . it's only a coincidence.*

He stared back at her, not answering. Looking confused. His jacket looked familiar. Heavy and dark blue with a red and white stripe on the arm. Was he . . . a mailman?

She yanked the handle and pushed the door open quickly, shepherding him away from her car. He staggered back, eyes wide in shock, and fell to the ground.

"Hey! Are you okay? I didn't hit you or anything, did I?" She knew very well she hadn't, but something in her head shouted "lawsuit." "What are you *doing?* What do you want?" She looked to make sure James was nearby in case the guy did something unexpected. James was *just* getting out of his car. She knelt down over the man.

The stench of something acrid overpowered her. Like burning hair, or something. She tried to suppress a physical reaction, though he wouldn't have seen anyway. He was lying, curled up, on his side, and his eyes were scrunched shut.

He looked like he was wincing in pain. She stared closer. She was completely sure he had fallen *after* she'd opened the door.

"What's hurting you?" she asked, feeling helpless.

The guy rubbed his eyes and looked tired. He sat up, slowly.

"Hello? You had a lot to say a second ago. I need to know if you're okay."

"I'm fine," he grumbled, waving her away.

"Here, drink some water." Her voice was all wavery, heart was still kicking her violently from the scare, but she pulled a half-drunk bottle of water from her purse. "I'm not sick or anything. I can try to find a straw."

James ran in through the big chain-link gates separating the front lot from the impound lot.

She set down the water bottle and turned to James, gesturing toward the man. "I don't know how he fell, or what happened. But he can't stand up. I'm calling 911."

She held her phone to her ear and looked down at the guy. She tried to think of something, anything else to do. All she could conjure were hospital dramas. CPR, defibrillators. But seeing as the guy was conscious, none of that was relevant.

The lot attendant rushed out with a thermal blanket. The guy took one look at her and bolted, kicking over the water bottle.

"Gary!" The attendant shouted. "You okay?"

The man's eyes widened like he'd suddenly woken up. "My route! I got sidetracked!" he shouted, running through the open gates. He took a sharp left turn and sped down the sidewalk.

"His route? So he's *actually* your mailman?" Rachelle asked.

"Yeah."

"That guy delivers your mail," she stated, trying to confirm. "He was . . . shouting at me."

"That's not like him." The attendant shook her head firmly, then sighed. "Seems fine now, though." She shrugged, folded up the thermal blanket and put it under her arm, then headed to check the mailbox.

"Okay." Rachelle shook her head slowly. She felt a hand on her shoulder. James'. "Why didn't you come over when he first came to the car?"

James furrowed his brow, thinking. "What do you mean?"

"I mean . . . he scared the *shit* out of me. No one was there, and then he was right at the window. At first I thought he was going to carjack me or something."

James started chuckling quietly. "He scared *you*?"

Rachelle felt exasperated. "What am I missing here? *Yes,* he scared me. Why is it funny?"

His laughing escalated. He was clearly trying to stop himself and couldn't. "Nothing," he said through his laughter. He closed his eyes and rubbed a hand over one side of his face. He looked at her. "I just, I wish you could have seen it from my vantage point."

"Please, enlighten me. I'd love to be in on the joke."

"I mean . . . did you *see* him? He's skinny as a rail!! And—"

"And what! He's probably stronger than he looks. A scrappy strength."

"A scrappy—" He shook his head, then shouted. "*Rachelle!*"

"Yes, what? I'm listening!!"

"You looked like you were going to *maul* him! And then you whipped open your door and he—he looked half scared of you, half 'I'm not dealing with this' and just slowly rolled back on his ass." James doubled over now, laughing hysterically, hands on his thighs.

"Rolled back on his ass? What does that even mean?" Rachelle chuckled a little. She looked over at the lot attendant, who stood at the door, bug-eyed, staring at James like he had four heads. Rachelle started laughing harder.

"*I'm* going back inside," the attendant spit out. She stomped through the brown metal door and into the squat brick building.

The moment the metal door shut, they were in hysterics. James put a hand on Rachelle's shoulder, as if to keep from falling over laughing.

The laughter eventually petered out and they looked at each other.

"You're sick, you know that?"

James smiled. "Yeah, and *you* were laughing too. What's that say about you, hm?"

Gary drove by in his mail truck and waved at them. Rachelle cleared her throat and James smoothed out his coat, erasing the evidence. They waved, their smiles just two pairs of gritted teeth. Rachelle snorting quietly, suppressing more laughter.

After he passed by, their breath came in short hiccups of laughter. Eventually, their breathing returned to normal.

James looked like he thought of something. "Hey, what was he saying to you anyway?"

Rachelle looked at him. She didn't want to explain how the man's words had resonated with her.

"Was he calling you Shelly?

"Yeah, so it's weird. My name is Rachelle."

"Yes," he nodded at her, still grinning. "I know that much."

She smiled and shook her head. "Take the R-A off my name, and it's Shelly. It was a nickname when I was younger. Nobody's called me that since I . . . since I was like nineteen."

He stared at her and shrugged curiously. "So . . . this guy knows you?"

"That's just it, I could swear I've never seen him in my life."

"And you're from California, so . . ."

"Exactly."

"Really unlikely he's met you before."

"Yep."

James looked concerned. He furrowed his brow. "That's not good."

"Well, I mean, it's puzzling, for sure. But I haven't made any sense of it."

"Mm-hmm," he was quiet. Eyebrows still furrowed. Forehead scrunched up.

Rachelle watched someone exit the lot. She looked at James, who still seemed deep in thought. Concerned about something.

"Do you think he just continued on his daily route? Or went home?"

James rubbed his face with his hands, looking stressed out, or exhausted.

She leaned in toward James. "What's wrong? Are you worried about him?"

"In a way," he said, vaguely.

A thought occurred to Rachelle. She looked at her phone.

"Shit!" she whispered. "I'm sorry. Thanks for driving me here. I gotta pick up my kid. I'm this close to being late." She gestured with her fingers, and then whipped around and ran back to her car.

James smiled a little. "Look both ways before you open your door."

She gave him a small wave as she drove past and smiled back, then paused and flipped him off.

His grin in reply lit up his whole face.

8

The waves heaved Stanton's boat as he tried to drink out of his thermos without spilling. He crooked his elbow to steady it. A good one; stainless steel and banged to hell, but kept coffee hot for hours.

Almost too hot, he thought, slurping it a little to avoid burning his mouth. He'd just left the docks but his dark hair already hung heavy at his temples, gathering flecks of the ocean as it spit toward the sky.

He watched the orangey-pink tinge of the sunrise as it crept up the horizon. He couldn't see the sun, but its essence illuminated the cloud cover. They glowed yellow, then reddish pink, and finally white as they pushed away the receding strip of night.

His thoughts moved to Rory. Something wasn't sitting right. He was sure it must be common for a child to see something scary and then get the facts wrong. But then, the mom's version of the story seemed farfetched, too.

He wished he could've seen what really happened. Was there something off about Rachelle? Maybe she abused him and Rory didn't want to admit it? Then she'd come up with elaborate stories to cover it up?

Stanton shook his head and leaned over the rail. He felt guilty for accusing her, even in private speculation.

"Hey, Avery! Can you help me out with these traps?"

Stanton looked up. "Hey, call me Stanton, remember? When you say Avery, I feel like I'm in high school." He smiled at Julian, but it was forced. Julian was a new college grad yet to start his "career," so he helped Stanton out part time for cash. Julian tried hard, but he was a suburban kid, still freshly away from his parents.

It showed.

"What's up with the windbreaker?" Stanton teased. "Got a tennis date after?"

Julian smiled back but his face was hardened. Clearly trying not to look hurt. "No . . . I forgot my gear at my girlfriend's house. This was the best I could find at my place this morning." He shrugged, running his hands down the front of the wrinkled nylon. "Could use a wash, too."

"Late night last night?" Stanton winked, and immediately felt awkward. He was trying to lighten the mood, not insinuate about the kid's sex life.

"Yeah . . . she needed help. Finishing up moving."

Stanton and Julian lifted one of the pots together. They were making good time. Stanton was hopeful they'd be able to get a good haul this morning, though everything was harder without Javi.

Javier was only three years older than Julian, but had seen more, lived more. He'd moved from New York City to get away from a cult his parents had joined when he was young. He'd had to secretly save up money, buy a car, and take off in the night. The operation took years of planning. Stanton had found him one morning at the docks, looking for work. He was good at everything immediately but lacked confidence. It'd taken at least six months for Stanton to glean these most basic details.

Stanton had gone everywhere looking for him. To no avail. Every time he went by the house, Javi's girl-friend's car wasn't there. He kept telling himself they must have gone somewhere together. He hoped there wasn't any trouble. He dreaded the idea that someone from his old life had come to find him.

Would they really go that far to find him? He kept wondering why Javier wouldn't just call him. For help, or to let him know he was okay. He worried if there was trouble, Javi would avoid reaching out to Stanton to spare him. The thought of it made Stanton sick inside.

Stanton was lost in his thoughts as they heaved the trap over the edge of the boat. As he watched its large metal frame sink into the water, he realized the trap hadn't been set.

"Goddamnit—" Stanton had to stop himself from saying Julian's name after.

"What," Julian said flatly, turning to Stanton, his face completely blank.

Irritated, Stanton scratched the side of his head. "Did you remember to set up all the traps?"

"I thought you were going to yesterday when we got back in?"

"Can you just double-check next time?"

"Okay, sure."

He stared at the pots waiting to be put out and sighed. He didn't mind the extra work required with one less man onboard but it became more and more daunting to try and keep the same quota. Javier was proactive. He didn't miss anything.

Stanton tried to sort out his feelings. One trap not being set was not the end of the world. They'd bring it back up, check the others, and put them back out. He grabbed hold of the rope and stared into the water until his worries grew silent. His vision blurred, then focused again. The waves bent and wiggled the frame of the mesh wire, distorting it. There was something strange about the way the squares shook. Not with the waves, but like they were moving independently. Shuddering. Sliding. And settling up again.

Stanton tried to blink it away and rubbed his eyes. He scanned the water. The mesh shape now seemed to expand across the ocean. A green grid with perfectly even squares. Perfect, until twenty yards off from the boat. There, the grid twisted down, as though the ocean were a bathtub with a drain. He followed the twisting grid down with his eyes. In that hole was . . . a twin horizon. A sunset that seemed to mirror their skyline, but with a starry blackness dominating the sky. He saw a beach, and a small blue house. He stared for what felt like endless minutes, completely still except for the boat's rhythmic motion.

What the hell am I looking at? he asked himself. And again, he thought about Rory.

***

A cartoon film soundtrack sang about how big the world was. Rachelle's head ached. She glanced at the car radio; turned the volume down. Rory protested.

"Better?" she asked, turning it back up one notch.

She'd barely made it to day care before it closed. Wearily, her mind shuffled through what she'd do when they got in the door. Coat off. Shoes off. Rush to make dinner. Force Rory to take a bath. Badger him about washing thoroughly from her seat against the wall in the hallway. Hang out. Make him go to bed. Forget what she did with herself before single motherhood while mindlessly staring at her phone. Sleep. Wake. Work. Repeat.

She yawned, stretching her mouth wide.

As she approached the house, she noticed a big white box truck in her driveway. Stanton's truck.

She pulled up slowly, looking around for him. Was he supposed to come back for some reason? Had she forgotten part of their exchange? As far as she knew, there was no reason why he'd need to be here.

"Who's that?" Rory piped up from the back.

At first, she didn't reply.

"Is that Mr. Avery?" he asked.

"Mr. Avery? What is he, your teacher?" she glanced at his face in the rearview, but it was too dark to see. "Why do you call him that?"

"When I met him he said his name was Stanton. But later he told me to call him Mr. Avery."

She leaned forward and tilted her head. She pulled in carefully; the box truck was wide. She had to avoid hitting that on her left and driving over the grass on her right.

She grabbed her bag and turned around to open the door. When she looked back, Stanton's face was right at the left corner of her windshield.

"Motherffff"—her eyelids drew wide—"fffatherrr." She pushed her fist against her teeth. He'd drawn back a little at her reaction, still waving awkwardly.

"What's wrong?" Rory asked, alarmed.

Rachelle inhaled big; staring at her legs, gathering herself. With an exhale, she offered a hand and a tight-lipped smile in greeting.

"I didn't know he was standing right there. He scared me," she told Rory.

She squeezed out of the car door and shut it.

"Sorry if I startled you," Stanton said.

"It's okay, Mister Avery," Rachelle said, smiling a little.

"Oh that. Uh, yeah. Growing up, I addressed all adults that way. I don't really know how things are these days."

Rachelle followed Stanton with her gaze as she opened Rory's door.

"Yeah, it *is* different now," she said quietly. "How can we help?" she asked him, trying not to worry about what a virtual stranger was doing at their house.

"Well, I mean, yesterday you guys seemed to be struggling a little." Stanton looked briefly back at his truck. His eyes flashed toward Rachelle's and then back down to the driveway. "I just wanted to let you know, I'm around if you guys ever need any help."

"Struggling?" she asked him, her eyes wide and unblinking in challenge, anticipation.

"I mean, he seems like a good kid. If you guys ever need a babysitter. Or anything."

Rachelle nodded, not in confirmation, but urging him to go on.

He looked down and held his hand, rubbing his palm with his thumb. "I grew up with a single mom. For us, sometimes, it kind of took a village. And other times, we needed help and it wasn't there, so sometimes, I just ended up . . . alone."

Rachelle blinked rapidly and scoffed. She shifted her weight and crossed her arms.

"Sorry for what you went through. Despite what you saw yesterday, though, I do not leave my kid home alone. I was attacked, and he ran."

"No opinion, no judgment." Stanton held his hands out defensively. "Just saying: I know for a fact it can be hard, and Rory seems like a good kid."

"Oh! You know it? For a fact? *Cool!* Listen, *Mister* Avery. I really appreciate you bringing Rory home yesterday, but we don't need you to save his life, or be the dad you both never had. It's a tough life, but we're okay." Her edge started to mellow at the end. "Mostly."

"Mom?" Rory said quietly.

"Yes, honey?" Rachelle winced.

"You kinda were just saying how hard it is to get to my day care in time after work. And you look really tired."

75

"Rory—" She paused, thrown off.

Rory was looking at Stanton instead of her. They seemed to be exchanging some kind of veiled somber understanding.

I was too harsh, she told herself. Also, she felt like she'd never get used to Rory's voice becoming one of reason. To valuing and sometimes needing his input on things.

"Sorry," she said quietly. "Why don't you come in?" she beckoned for Stanton. "We can talk."

***

Stanton waited in the hallway as Rachelle dropped her stuff off in the kitchen.

"Glad you got that window fixed." He nodded and smiled at her.

"How'd you know?"

"Oh, you know. Cold day, but it's warm in here."

"Ah, very true." She smiled back, pointing to the microwave. "Do you want some tea or something?"

Stanton laughed quietly and shook his head. "No, thank you."

This felt a little more formal than what he was used to. As he thought about it, though, he realized he didn't really visit people at their houses very often. He only went to Javi's house sometimes when business was quieting down. Javier and Corry would just tell him to help himself.

He hoped again that they were okay. Tried to keep himself from imagining the worst.

"Actually," he said. "Can I have some water?"

"Sure!" Rachelle grabbed a glass from an upper cabinet by the sink. She filled it with sink water and handed it to him. "Sorry," she shrugged. "Our ice maker's broken." She gripped her mouth gently with finger and thumb, then let go.

"Actually," she clarified. "It's been broken since we moved in."

"It's okay," Stanton said. He noticed a large group of pictures scattered down the hallway, all of landscapes at night. "You like . . . ah . . . nighttime, huh?" he asked, gesturing with his glass.

Rachelle laughed quietly. "Yeah, I wish we had a better view of the stars here. Too much light pollution."

Stanton squinted, looking closer at the pictures. "You like stars, huh? Oh, the moon, too. *Full* moon."

"Supermoon, to be even more specific." Rachelle's face seemed to light up. "I love a good supermoon." Her eyes met and locked on his. She dipped her head, as if waiting for something. Like she was checking if he recognized the term.

"Supermoon," he humored her. "I've never heard of that."

"It's the point when the moon is as close to earth as it can get." She smiled at him. "Kinda magical, I think." She gestured to Rory's room. "Whenever there's one, Rory and I try to take pictures, but we can't get it to look *anything* like this." She gestured toward a huge photograph of a big yellow moon that looked like it was sitting on the horizon, hovering over the end of a long dirt road.

Stanton turned back to Rachelle. She seemed to have disappeared into the photo, like she was there and not with him anymore. He didn't know what else to say. He always felt drained of energy after interactions like this. New people and places. His stomach hurt a little. He drank some more water.

He heard the unmistakable sound of a marble rolling across a hard surface. Something small bumped gently against his boot.

"Sorry," Rory was in his bedroom doorway, on his hands and knees. "I'm working on my marble run." Rory looked up at him, reaching for the marble. He cupped it with his index and middle fingers. "Wanna see?"

Stanton glanced quickly at Rachelle, checking in. She nodded him on.

"Sure." He followed Rory into his room. Kids were easier for him to talk to. They weren't bogged down by social niceties, and seemed generally more comfortable in their own skin. Silences weren't uncomfortable either, somehow.

"Look! This set came with clear ones with green inside!" Rory opened his palm for Stanton as he returned to his project. Three marbles sat together in his cupped hand. "It's kinda hard not to lose these guys," he explained. "My mom has me keep them in a coffee cup."

"That's clever," Stanton replied, observing Rory's work.

The wood paneling was painted a deep blue. He assumed Rachelle had this painted, or maybe did it herself. The edging was clean and the paint job, even. The bed had been dressed haphazardly with a blue and white argyle comforter. Toys were everywhere. A dark gray easy chair—a glider—sat in the corner. On that chair was an apparatus that surprised Stanton. He walked over to it, crouching down to look closer.

"Is this . . . a crystal radio?" Stanton asked, looking over his shoulder at Rory.

Rory walked up behind Stanton and crouched to the left of the chair, touching the wooden base of it with his index finger. "I dunno. Is *that* what it's called?"

"Looks like it," Stanton said, taking in the various items screwed into the base. "This is a good one, too. Whoever built this knew what they were doing!"

"How can you tell?"

"You can tell by what parts were chosen," Stanton said. He fingered the different pieces across the open-faced design. He loved how all the working parts were on display. Nothing hidden away by a decorative plastic cover. Everything just pinned down on a slab of wood. Weirdly beautiful. "A lot of people can build these using household items if they want."

"Like what?"

Stanton was quiet, searching the parts for the best example. "Like, you see this one, it has speakers, and big dials on it to adjust the volume?"

"Yeah."

"Not all of them even have speakers. A lot of them just have a little earphone connected so you can listen. Or some people even use an old landline phone to listen to the station you choose."

"What's a landline?"

Stanton laughed. "It's what we used before there were cell phones. We used to need a whole network of actual wires to be able to hear each other."

"That sounds old." Rory wrinkled his nose.

"I guess," Stanton sighed. "I don't have a landline either anymore," he admitted.

"I guess that kinda dates us." Rachelle chuckled, leaning against the doorframe. She'd put on an oversized fleece sweatshirt. She hugged herself and inhaled sharply like she was cold. How long had she been standing there? *Funny, I'm usually the quietest one in the room.*

"Yep," Stanton sat down on the floor, looking up at her. "Sometimes time passes without you even noticing it."

"It's kinda crazy." Rachelle shook her head.

"Did you build this?" he asked Rachelle.

She shook her head. "No."

"So where did you get it from?" Stanton wondered why she hadn't explained further.

Rachelle sighed, heavily. Instead of answering Stanton, Rachelle looked at her son. He had gone back to the marble run. He was lost to the world; tongue poked out to the side, trying to fit some pieces together to support the bottom without the whole thing tipping over.

She looked back at Stanton, as though satisfied Rory wasn't paying attention. "The radio was his dad's," she mumbled quietly.

"My wha—" Rory let go of the marble run. It crashed against the wood floor. Marbles rolled in all directions; debris from the accident. "My dad's?" he stared blankly at her. "How come you had it? How come it was in the closet?"

Rachelle's lips were clamped tight. Her eyes flicked back and forth, like she was rethinking what she'd said.

"Sorry, I'll be right back," she whispered. It sounded like a struggle to push the words out.

The bathroom light clicked on across the hall. The door was open. The toilet paper roll bumped against the holder as it was pulled.

Stanton looked at Rory. "Sorry, I didn't mean—" He didn't know how to finish his sentence.

Rory's eyes were wide. He stared at the collapsed marble run. He addressed Stanton in a whisper. "She never really talks about him. I didn't know she had any of his stuff. She said he's in California. She says it's like, twenty-hundreds of miles away." He spread his fingers apart to demonstrate what twenty-hundreds of miles looked like.

"Yeah, California is far from here," Stanton said.

Rory continued to sit there, his legs folded under him. Stanton looked around the room. Now this was an excruciating silence.

"You know what? I'm gonna go," he announced loudly, so Rachelle could hear him. "I can give you my number if you end up needing anything."

"Actually," Rachelle said, sniffing. She reappeared in the doorway. "Is there any way you could spend the night?"

"You mean, now? Tonight?"

"*Not* like how it sounds." Rachelle shook her head vigorously, holding her hands out to soften the blow.

"Just, yesterday we didn't sleep so great. It feels like things would be a little less scary somehow if you could stay. There's a room next to Rory's that we never use. I could make it up. Clean sheets and everything."

"I don't know," Stanton hesitated. "Can't you ask your friend? Gaia?"

"I already tried. She won't. Or, can't. Can you just think about it? Let me know. You could text me if you decide it's too weird." She lowered her voice. "I mean . . . I *know* it's weird. I swear I wouldn't ask unless . . ."

"Yeah, I get you." Stanton's jaw tightened. He'd offered his help but had never pictured a request like this. He needed more time. "I can't tonight, actually. I have some work things to sort out," he lied.

He stood up, pulling his phone out of his pocket. "What's your number? I'll text you about tomorrow."

They exchanged numbers. Stanton turned to Rory, who still sat cross-legged on the floor, looking at the ground.

"Good to see you Rory. I'll see you soon, maybe?"

Rory looked up at Rachelle as he answered Stanton. "I hope so." He smiled.

***

The sound of sloshing water surrounded Rachelle. Long vines of kelp danced in front of her, reaching toward the ocean's surface. The sea was a captivating blue-green. The sun above her grew rapidly brighter. Now, overpowering. She felt herself squinting. A voice spoke, unclear, muffled by the water.

Rachelle woke with a start. She was drenched, sheets stuck to her legs. It was 2:15 in the morning. After lying awake a while, she kicked off the covers. She slipped into Rory's room, stepping over the squeaky floorboard just past the threshold.

She stood there in the dark. It smelled like sleep. Like cozy blankets, and Rory. The scent was soft and familiar. She listened to his breath. Slow, relaxed, loud.

She closed her eyes and remembered when he was young enough to wake up crying in the night, to need her to cuddle him. He was a particularly fussy baby and toddler, but after he turned two, he rarely needed her comfort in the night. She remembered looking forward to comforting him after that change. She'd go in and swoop him up before he'd cried for very long. The ability to ease him just by her presence was unspeakably satisfying. Now he didn't need her like that. He hugged her plenty. He still wanted her company, but it was different, now. It'd never be as simple as it was then, again.

The old chair she used to use sat in the corner. It was still wide enough for both of them to fit in it, side by side. But it had been a year or two since they'd used it.

Chad's radio sat on the chair. She picked it up. It was big and bulky. She had to hold it with both hands. She slunk out of the room, and back to her own.

Rachelle set the radio on her nightstand. She pulled the small table away from the wall and plugged in the radio. Nostalgia reigned tonight, and it was all about Chad. Rory needed to know more about his dad. It would be hard to avoid addressing, or child-proofing the "why." The true reason was not something she'd repeated to anyone. Not even Gaia.

The radio had a big wooden base with something that resembled an old-fashioned light bulb. A copper coil he'd wrapped around a cylinder the size of an industrial toilet paper roll. *Maybe it* was *a toilet paper roll.* She couldn't remember for sure if he'd told her that. *Details, details.*

The copper coil still bore a small black marking. It pointed to the spot he'd set the tuner against to bring in the station their paranormal show was on.

It was 2:25 now. 11:25 on the West Coast. She doubted radio stations could be reached across the country, but still, she plugged the radio in and adjusted the tuner to the old spot.

Nothing but static. She adjusted the tuner very slightly back and forth in that vicinity. The scratchy sound of passing stations filled the room. Muffled voices were picked up, then dropped again.

She held the tuner still when she heard guitar. She quickly ID'd the song. "The Chain" by Fleetwood Mac. She let her head loll back and forth as the chorus reached its crescendo. It ended, and commercials set in. She turned the dial to quiet the noise, and laid back on her pillow, cupping her head in her hands.

Chad used to lay like this, she thought to herself. She closed her eyes, remembering one of the times toward the end. Before she left. Maybe the last night that things still felt mostly normal.

9

Chad's radio had been on that night, like always. It was left on their usual late-night paranormal show. Some lady was going on about how she knew when demons were in her house because it smelled like ferrets. The TV was on too; muted. The glow washed over their faces. Blue and then white. Fade to dark, then bright white again. The evening news. They lay on the couch in his living room, across from an empty pizza box on the coffee table. A couple of drained beer cans next to it.

Chad was starting to talk about his dad. Rachelle sat still and quiet, not wanting to interrupt.

Chad rested his head on his palms. Elbows bent. "I don't know what he was like before my mom died," he said. "I can't imagine he'd have been much different. Maybe he'd've been more interested in me? In raising me. Or teaching me things. If she'd have been around."

"What was he like with you?" Rachelle wondered. "You never talk about him."

"God, I don't know. As a dad, or as a person?"

"I mean . . . whichever."

"God," Chad repeated, rubbing his face for a beat. "Where to start? He got me to listen by humiliating me. He played mind games, laughed at me, called me names. Threw stuff at me."

"Did he ever hit you?"

"No. It's sorta like he didn't care enough. He never felt strongly enough about me to physically hurt me. Like, it wasn't his 'thing."

Rachelle rested her hand on his foot. Neither of them talked for a few minutes.

"I only saw him hurt someone once."

Rachelle refocused on Chad, pursing her lips to the side, waiting for him to continue.

"The one thing that used to put him over the edge was fear. It was like he couldn't comprehend a world where he could feel that feeling. He couldn't tolerate it. It'd send him into an instant rage. Like, if I was up at night walking down the hall and heard him up, I'd run and hide to avoid surprising him." He stopped and stared at the TV, which at that late hour had changed to infomercials.

"What did he do?" she prodded him quietly.

"He used to drop off his car at the mechanic's for an oil change the night before. Then we'd get a cab home. One night, he picked me up after a school trip. It was late. Like 11 or so.

"We'd drop the car between an old warehouse and another building with these big garage doors. Fire escapes. You know, creepy dark-alley shit. It always smelled. Sour garbage water in the cracks of the street. I hated it there. I hated waiting for the cab. Technically, it wasn't a bad area or anything, but it still felt like . . . I don't know. Like something was there with us.

"Anyway, when my dad turned off the car, I could hear two girls laughing. Mean laughter. High-pitched and nervous. Then, loud whispering. I kept hoping they were laughing about something besides us. Maybe they just left a place where something funny happened. But I had a really bad feeling. Sometimes I think I know what's about to happen. Not the exact happening of it, but the mood of it. How I'm going to feel about what happens next. Like an alarm going off in my head. But, silent." He paused again, staring at the ceiling.

"So yeah, they were laughing loudly, then they got real quiet. We heard their footsteps get quicker and softer. They were definitely getting closer. We were kind of just sitting there. Tuned in. Waiting to see if they'd just pass, or if they were going to do something. I was watching my dad. I remember he was so still, I was like staring at his chest, wondering if he was even breathing.

"Then suddenly this ear-splitting sound came. Two girls' faces in the window. A flash of red. Then they screamed. Like a crazy squeal mixed with fear. And they ran."

"What was it? What happened?"

"It was an air horn. It . . . scared the shit out of my dad. I've never seen him that surprised. He shouted out, then like, punched the horn. He grabbed the steering wheel and gritted his teeth. Like he was trying to ride out the feeling. Then he whipped the door open and took off after them.

"At first, I just watched him from the car. I didn't know if he was going to just yell after them, or what. But he like, grabbed one girl by the backpack. Pulled her down to the ground. I remember she dropped immediately. Her feet were up and she was just . . . down. The other one kept running, left her there on the ground."

Chad took a deep breath and caught his lip with his teeth.

"She lay there for a few minutes, I think," he continued. "Really still. Really quiet. Maybe she hit her head. Or was just shocked or something. I don't know. My dad just stood there, like he was waiting for her to do something. Then she started to scream.

"He started, like, yelling at her. Gesturing with his hand. Like shouting and shaking his finger at her. Like he was scolding her or something. But she just kept screaming over his voice. She tried to get up, but he pushed her down. He covered her mouth with his hand, and kept shouting. Like he wouldn't stop 'til he got finished with what he wanted to say.

"I still had no idea what he was going to do. But at some point, I got scared he was going to hurt her again. Or maybe even kill her.

"Finally, I got out of the car and started running toward him. I was yelling at him to stop. Telling him we had to go. When I finally got to him, I pulled on his arm and he came with me really easily. Like he'd been just waiting for me to come get him. Like his work was done there or something. He was satisfied.

"We moved kind of quickly to the car. I heard her get up and run off. She was crying and stuttering something. Like the word fuck or something. She sounded really mad and scared, but it felt like she stopped just short of saying 'fuck you.' Like she didn't want to set him off again.

"He basically launched that car out of the alley. He seemed excited. Probably full of adrenaline. I think he said something like 'I don't think she'll be doing *that* again,' and laughed. Like he'd just stopped some hardened criminal. And at first, I'd assumed they were older? But when I saw her up close, I swear, that girl was not much older than me. Maybe fourteen at the oldest."

"Oh my god," Rachelle breathed.

"I still remember her face when he let go of her, too," he sighed. "She was like a scared animal. Just her eyes darting back and forth. The way she looked at us, like she thought she was gonna die. Even when I was pulling my dad away. Like she couldn't believe we were going to let her go or something. It was terrible."

"Did anything happen after?"

"You mean in response to what he did? No. I don't know if she called the police or told her parents, or what. But nobody ever came to us, so I don't know what happened after. I assume that fucked her up, for sure, though."

"So that was what he did when he got scared?"

"Mm."

"That's horrifying. But, like, he never did anything like that again? Hurt somebody else?"

Chad grabbed the remote and started running the volume up and down. Each time he turned the volume back up, he brought the peaks higher and higher. By the third time, Rachelle had to resist the urge to cover her ears.

She took a breath and held it. "Actually, maybe we should be done with this topic for now."

"I need another beer."

Chad returned from the kitchen, can tipped completely back, already finishing the last dregs of it. He lay back down and held the can against his chest, plinking his thumbnail against the tab.

He continued. "With adults, he was just . . . methodical. He'd challenge people, get them to submit to him. Say things loudly that everyone knew was a challenge. If they had too good of an answer, if they didn't seem, you know, verbally beaten down, he'd amp it up. Do really over-the-top shit to them. Orchestrate situations where they'd be stuck, or stranded. Inconvenienced. Embarrassed.

"And he always needed an audience for it. That was the only time he'd smile at me. Try to relate to me. When he was fucking with someone else. He'd laugh, and laugh. And he'd look into your eyes and basically keep it up 'til you laughed with him. Like, he had to have an enthusiastic witness. It made me sick. But I always laughed anyway."

He watched her for a reaction. "It got lonely having nobody to connect with," he reasoned. "Sometimes it felt like I was all alone in the world."

"How did you get through? How do you seem so . . . able to cope with life after he raised you like that?"

"I don't know, he kinda always left me alone when I went in my room. Like I said, he wasn't . . . interested in me. In what I was doing. I was basically a housemate. If I did something he didn't like, it pissed him off and he messed with me. If I stayed out of his way, it was at least quiet. Though a lot of times, I don't really feel like I cope that well."

"No?"

"Nuh-uh." He crumpled the can. His hands seemed to have short little scrapes all over them. *Do I remember any of these?* she asked herself.

As he crushed the can, the heel of one hand pressed down on the opening.

She immediately reached for him, clasping her hands around his wrists. "Chad, be careful!"

"Thhhh!" He pulled in air rapidly through tongue and teeth and flipped his hand over.

His fingers curled in protectively, the skin on his palm creased. She caught a thin crack on the heel of his hand as the blood rose within it.

"Aah!" he exclaimed, holding it to his chest.

"No big deal. I'll get you a bandage." Rachelle moved to get up.

"Don't go!" Chad grabbed Rachelle's forearm.

"Don't go to the *cabinet*?" She felt dizzy and confused. "Chad, Why?"

"I don't like blood."

"Okay, I mean, that makes sense. But then, just don't look at it, right? I can cover it up for you."

"In a second." Chad sat up, holding his arms out to her. She leaned into him and they lay back down. The sour smell of beer hit her in the face. His chest rose and fell quickly. At least twice as fast as her own.

"Are you really that scared?"

"I just told you. I hate blood." His voice came out choked. "Can you stay the night?"

"You know I've got work tomorrow. I'd have to get up in like four hours!"

"I know, I know. Just for tonight. I really, really want you to." Chad wrapped his arms tighter around her.

"Hey-hey-hey!" Rachelle pushed on his chest, breaking their embrace, and sat up quickly. "Okay, not to make this about me, but like, you probably just got blood on this shirt." She pulled the fabric and turned her head, trying to inspect the back. "I love this shirt."

"Sorry," he said quietly. "Your shirt looks okay."

Rachelle stood up. "It's okay. I do have to go, though."

The corners of his eyes were turned down. "You don't."

"Just call your little pseudo neighbor mom. She can mosey over like old times." Rachelle didn't realize she was basically jeering at him until it was too late.

"That was shitty."

"I'm sorry." She covered her face. "Fuck. I'm really sorry. That was selfish. You're just being so weird. It upset me."

"It's okay." He stood up too. "You'd better go then, I guess." He stood up, arm behind his back.

"You really hate blood that much?"

"Yeah."

"Maybe it was that plus you talking about your dad?"

"Maybe."

10

Rachelle dreamed of a man strolling casually down a sidewalk late at night. The man's face was a blurry paper white. His eyes were black socks stuffed into sockets. All interrupted, like her head, by the growling inside.

What's wrong here? She cleared her throat. A strange action when trying to see something better.

Somehow, it worked. She could see now that his gait was wrong. His legs bent in front of him as he walked, instead of behind.

He turned toward her, his eyes closed. The growling stopped, but whispers replaced it. They were sharp, like peppermint. They stung her ears. The whispers told her the man was walking backwards. Her breath was stuck, like chocolate, pooled, then hardened inside her.

He opened his lids, and his bright searchlight eyes cut through her and kept moving. She held her breath. After a few moments, he closed his eyes and continued his backwards walk.

He crossed the street and continued down the sidewalk. She watched him pass some overgrown hedges on the corner lot.

He passed a driveway lined with dahlias. They hung dead. The slightest hint of frost, and their leaves had shriveled like cooked collard greens. Dried-up flower heads tipped down, mourning themselves.

Dead dahlias. I know those. He's on my street, two houses from mine.

She knew he could feel her eyes touching him. Her fear was visceral. It scratched her insides. Sandpaper grit swelled across the skin of her organs.

The moment he rambled up her driveway, her house grabbed her. Brought her inside itself. His eyes couldn't touch her here.

But oh, god, that's him from the front now. Coming up the walk. My front walk!

He was so close now. So goddamn close and facing in her direction. Just one inch over and he would see her. Her damn body was just standing in the window, dumb and paralyzed.

Why didn't I hide myself?

Because I am the sentinel and nothing will stop my eyes from touching him.

"Monster, monster, monster," growled Rachelle's head.

He was nearing the front door. *But monsters don't use front doors.* As he approached the house, her eyes thrashed out, grabbing nothing but the corner of bricks before the porch.

***

Rachelle opened her eyes quick, like a gunshot. She looked at the clock. 4 a.m. She had a sudden urge to check on Rory. She slid herself to the end of the bed and sat up, her head bowed with sleep. Laughing quietly to herself, she realized she didn't feel like walking; that it would be preferable for her to crawl to his room.

She was typically easily spooked by the dark, but she didn't bother to stand up and switch the living room light on. She crept quietly on hands and knees, giggling, thinking of the terrified reaction Rory would have if he came across someone crawling toward him in the dark. She tried to stifle it, but it was like a dry cough. The more she resisted it, the harder it came out. She doubled over for a minute, feeling slightly like she might piss herself. Then she continued, still shaking with quiet laughter, sniffing in and out rapidly.

She held that empathized feeling of fear inside herself. It made her cringe, and laugh some more. She pressed her mouth closed, until her lips were hidden, trying to hold in the sound. She had better control of it now. Her breath escaped more quietly out her nose.

He probably wouldn't realize who it was at first. Maybe he'd think she was a stranger who broke in and would do awful things to him.

Or maybe he'd think she was a ghost. Someone who'd died horribly. He'd wonder: who is that, why are they crawling. Then she'd look up at him, and their eyes would lock, and all would be lost. Maybe he'd be afraid she would reach into his body for his soul.

Rachelle made her way down the hall and turned left into Rory's room. He slept crooked across his double bed, splayed across both pillows, one arm extended out like a ballerina's. A slip of moonlight crossed his face. It had stolen in via a crack in the curtains, illuminating a peaceful closed eye. Continuing across his forehead.

She was still on all fours, like a dog. She brought herself to stand. *I was crawling just now. It wasn't a dream. What came over me?*

A sound issued from the opposite corner of the room, at the foot of Rory's bed. A long, loud sigh.

She stared, shaking in anger, in fear.

"Who's there," she hissed. Blood throbbed in her ears.

The corner was silent and dark. No sound came.

Rachelle began to doubt herself. Maybe it was nothing. Maybe Rory was sighing in his sleep and the sound was displaced. She shifted over again to get herself up.

A quick movement, and her eyes caught it. A shape. Like black paper cut out of the moonlight. The shadow of a person. It crawled silently out from the corner, like a dog. Like she'd done. It headed straight toward her. Darker than the dark room. She scrambled backwards on her elbows, heading for the bathroom.

She heard the frantic sliding and thumping as it scrambled after her. It grabbed her by the ankles. Its hands were solid and strong; her feet were held fast against the unforgiving ground. She twisted and bucked, but her feet did not move off the floor. Again, she could see it easily against the dark hallway. It was darker than the dark. Complete lack of substance. It crawled across her and grabbed her by the collarbone, pressing her flat against the floor with its shape. Her head clunked against the wood. Big white bursts flashed in her eyes.

Six times, a rapid hammering rocked the front door in its frame, the knocker slapping the door on each return.

A light; a glorious light clicked on in Rory's room.

The shadow was gone in an instant. All that remained was a humanlike shape that seemed burned into her retinas. As though she'd stared into a bright light. The weight disappeared off her. Rachelle gasped in relief.

"Mom?" a scratchy whisper came from Rory's room.

Emboldened by her sudden ability to move, she scrambled to her feet and banged out the few steps to the kitchen, where the coyote had escaped. She slapped on the light switch. It was definitely gone. She looked at the kitchen window and remembered the hole was gone, wondered if this thing could just disappear and reappear at will.

"It's okay, Rory. I'm here."

She returned to the kitchen entryway, into the hall. He was standing in his bedroom doorway, in gray sweatpants and an oversized t-shirt.

"What happened? Who's here?"

"I don't know . . . I'll go check." She turned to go, then stopped. "Do you . . . feel okay?" She wondered what that creature was doing by his bed.

"Um, yeah," he paused. "Why, what's wrong? Why were you up, anyway? What was going on in the hall?"

"It was just me. I couldn't sleep. I came to check on you."

"I was really scared. I thought I heard stomping. Or crashing. Then a voice whispering. Right outside the doorway. It was a really weird voice."

Rachelle hesitated. She was sure she knew what the crashing was, but she hadn't heard any voice.

"What'd it say? I mean . . . are you sure you weren't dreaming?" She despised lying about the crashing sound, but what was the alternative?

Rory sidestepped the questions. "What woke you?"

"I don't know." Rachelle sighed. "Stay here. I gotta check the door." She held up a finger and padded quickly to the front entry.

She crossed quickly through the dark living room, took a deep breath, and swung it open. Two empty rockers faced her, half-encased in shadow. The knocking hadn't continued past that first time, so she wasn't surprised to find nobody there when she opened up. Her porch lamps were on, but they were shit. Just little yellow circles of light that radiated straight back onto the siding.

She squinted in the scant light, and saw wet shoeprints from the morning dew on the wooden deck. Some pointed toward the door, curving up from the grassy lawn, and then the rest trampled back over the same set, pointing away from her door.

Rachelle stared at the pressed-down blades of grass. They unfolded slowly. She thought about her dream. Backwards men. Bending dahlias. She jumped when Rory touched her shoulder.

***

"What's the problem?!"

"Rachelle! He talks like an old man!"

"What do you mean?"

"How did you not hear? Just now, when I asked how he was doing."

"What?"

"I don't even want to repeat it. First of all, he *rhymed*. Remember? The thing he said that rhymed with 'missing screw?'" Gaia whispered, her eyes bugging out.

"He's *not* an old man. He's *three* years older than me. And I'm not . . . mothering his children or anything, I'm just . . . having him over!"

"You know what I mean. He *acts* old."

"Who cares?!"

The toilet flushed. The sink ran. Stanton came out, pressing his hands against his jeans.

"Hey, so were we thinking about dinner?" he asked.

Rachelle and Gaia looked up expectantly.

"I was going to cook something," Rachelle offered, starting to walk toward the kitchen.

"Sure, what were you going to make?"

"Oh I don't know . . . fish fry or something?"

"I love fish fry, that sounds—"

"Tickety-boo?" Gaia choked, then burst out laughing.

"Yep, exactly. That'd be just fine," Stanton put his hands in his pockets and lifted his eyebrows at Gaia, looking mildly confused.

"Sorry, Stanton. Gaia thinks we can only use idioms invented in the past twenty years." Rachelle shrugged at Stanton, rolling her eyes. "She's easily amused, and not always in the best way." She flashed her eyes at Gaia.

"Is that true, Gaia? Are you trying to 'harsh my mellow?'" he asked, elbowing the air in her general direction.

Gaia opened her mouth to speak but Rachelle cut in.

"Hey Gaia, I wanted to show you this new decorative pillow I bought for my bed to see what you think," Rachelle said lamely. *God, I should've thought of a better excuse.*

"Decorative pillow? Have you *seen* my house? Rachelle! My bed and my couch are the same piece of furniture."

"Actually, you *never* invite me over. But I thought of you when I bought it."

"Get it? It's a futon."

"Yeah, I figured." Rachelle gestured wildly with her head when Stanton tipped his head to scratch his beard. "Stanton, we'll be right back, okay?"

"Uh, okay!" Stanton wandered to the hall by the bathroom and observed Rachelle's wall art.

"Get over here," Rachelle whispered between gritted teeth. Gaia followed her, but slowly. She swiped at Gaia's arm, but Gaia moved it away.

"Ow!" Gaia held her hand protectively.

"I hardly touched you," Rachelle hissed.

They padded into Rachelle's room. She turned the handle, quietly shutting the door.

"Why so careful with the door? Is there a slumbering giant in your house?"

"Jesus! No, Gaia. It's a bear, and I wish you'd quit poking it!"

"Sorry! I feel like you're setting me up on a blind date or something! You invite me over, sounding all weird and nervous. *No* explanation, and then our weird coyote wrestler just shows up at the door, like five minutes after I get here."

"Okay first of all, he didn't *wrestle* a coyote. And I asked you over because you know I need someone to spend the night with Rory and me. I asked Stanton and he said he would."

"What?"

"I'm not asking, I'm telling you. And if you feel like you could—"

"—No, I told you. My brother needs me. He needs normalcy. Routine. You're my best friend but he's my family." Gaia shook her head.

"I was saying, if you *feel* like you could," Rachelle cut back in, "even one or two nights a week, it'd be really nice, so Stanton could sleep in his own house some nights?"

"Why are you having a guy you *don't know* sleep in your house? How is that safer than just you and Rory bundled up in your beds with all the doors locked?"

"Didn't help us when a coyote broke through the window."

"Uh yeah, what is making you think something weird like that will happen again?"

"Uh, well, because something weird *did* happen again."

"What now?"

Rachelle explained her dream and the shadow figure.

"So, what does this mean?"

"It means I'd be dead right now if that pounding on the door hadn't happened right then. I don't feel safe in my own house. And I don't know what else to do. I'm in real danger. My son's in danger. So I'm looking for options, wherever they may be."

"Ok, well . . ."

"If you can't come sleep here, can we go there, by you?"

"I don't know—"

"See?!" she pointed at Gaia.

"See what?"

"I gave you all my ideas. If you have nothing to offer, I'm going to accept Stanton's help."

"Okay, so if this is what you expected, are you just like, trying to get my permission to do what you're already planning to do? You don't need my permission."

"No." Rachelle pulled on the edge of her sleeve. "I mean—I don't know. I just want you to understand. I want you to stay here so you can see what I see when this . . . craziness happens."

"Sorry. I just don't get it. I try but it doesn't make sense."

"Well . . . try harder, I guess." Rachelle swung her bedroom door open, effectively ending the conversation.

A heavy sigh issued behind Rachelle. *At least she's walking with me.*

"Hey roomie," Gaia grumbled as they made their way back to Stanton.

"Oh, you're helping too?" Stanton smiled warmly.

"Uh, nope. You're the only roomie. The night watchman."

"Ahh gotcha. Yeah, we'll make it work. Hopefully we don't see anything else weird and it all blows over," Stanton offered. "I'll say 'tickety-boo' again if it'll make you feel better." He grinned at her.

"Jesus, you're good-natured," Gaia scoffed. "I'm trying *not* to like you."

Stanton shrugged.

11

A throat cleared at the desk next to Rachelle's. She ignored it and kept typing.

Double throat-clear, two sniffs.

Ah crap, lost my place.

"Rachelle," James' voice came from the next cubicle over.

"Yeah," she said, eyes still on her screen. She didn't want to turn toward him, on account of her cheeks burning. *C'mon face. Work stuff. Get over yourself.*

"How am I doing?"

She turned toward him. At some point he'd unbuttoned his sleeves and rolled them halfway up his forearms. They were bigger than she'd pictured. *Wait, when was I picturing his arms? Ugh, stop.*

"Wouldn't I normally be asking *you* how you're doing?"

"Oh, right. Sure." He smiled. "Go ahead, ask me."

She laughed. "How are you doing, James?"

There we go.

"Well, I'm really proud of myself. I did a *very* good job parking today, which I definitely couldn't say about myself yesterday."

"You know what they say. Every day's a chance to be better than you were yesterday." She turned, cross-legged and tapped a pen against the desk gently. "So, why did you ask me how you're doing?"

"Mm?"

"Like, are you asking me how I think you're doing at your job? A performance review?"

"No, I meant how am I doing as your desk neighbor? Last I heard, the jury was still out."

"Oh, that." She chuckled; raised herself slightly off her chair, peering at his desk. "Got any mouthwash cups?"

"I specifically made sure to spit my mouthwash into a sink this morning." He grinned. "I was very afraid of upsetting you."

"Well that's a good start." She sat back in her chair. "I'd hate to have to get you fired like I did Garrett." *Why'd you say that? What a weird, random joke. What if he thinks you're serious?*

She looked up. James looked serious. Dreadful serious. His eyes were practically smoldering. "I *hope* you don't get me fired."

"Yeah?" She raised her eyebrows. Searched for a way to show it was a joke; just in case.

"I'd miss you."

To her, the sky had opened up and dropped the words on her. She was silent for a beat. "Yeah?" she asked, her voice softer now.

"Yeah. I was thinking." James looked down at his hands "Would you want to take me out tomorrow?" He squinted up at her, as though insecure of her answer.

"Take you out? What do you mean? Where?" She played dumb and tried not to smile, while her entire head prickled and smoldered.

"I hadn't decided yet. Can I let you know?"

Rachelle wanted some confirmation this was more than platonic, but didn't know how to coax it out of him.

Think! She shouted to herself. *Something to help him along. But don't be weird.* She released a breath she'd been holding. "Yeah, I'd love to take you out." She smiled, her heart jackhammering.

He smiled back. His eyes glimmered, but he quickly cast them down. "Nice. All right, then."

She heard something small land, saw movement near her purse. A charm was in there, face up, glinting in the halogen. The leather cord nestled between her wallet and hairbrush, as though it'd been there all along.

She furrowed her brow. *That's odd.* Her purse sat right at her feet. How did the necklace get in her purse from where James sat? "Hey you dropped this," she said. She couldn't picture how the necklace could have landed that way.

"Oh yeah, oops," James smiled again. "That was my sister's. You should keep it."

"Aw no, not if it's your sister's. I couldn't—"

"No really. I'd like you to have it. She gave it to me. I wouldn't wear it anyway."

"Uh, okay?"

"You should wear it. It's not technically for luck, but I feel like it's brought me luck."

"Good luck? I could use some of that." She took it from her purse and put it on. She looked down at it. A strange eight-point star housed partially inside a square, surrounded by rings with more writing inside each one. "Hey, isn't this like a Satanist thing?"

"Oh no, it's not a pentagram. It's an astrology medallion."

"Astrology? Aren't there normally twelve zodiac symbols or something? Twins, fish, scales, stuff like that?"

"Yeah. This one's essentially the Middle Eastern version. You ever see the Chinese one? Different animals; by year instead of by month?"

"Yeah, I guess."

As she swiveled back toward her desk, she saw another black leather cord behind his shirt collar. She shook her head and went back to work.

***

They walked slowly together, trailing a half-block behind the tour group. A cold gust of wind carried the sound of voices and occasional laughter. It played with Rachelle's hair. She breathed in at the same time, and the chill felt like it touched her bones. The second bar seemed like quite a walk already from their original meeting point. Rachelle hugged herself, walking along next to James.

"The only thing I can think of right now is how we're walking further and further away from where we parked," James commented.

"I feel like you read my mind," Rachelle said. "Though *you're* the one who chose a ghost-tour pub crawl in early spring to get to know your new town."

"Yeah." He squinted playfully at her, rubbing the back of his neck with his palm. "I really want to see like, a Redcoat on horseback, or something." He watched her, his eyes smiling. Let his hand drop and swing at his side. "You think they have one of those on this tour?"

Rachelle laughed a little. "You never know!" She cleared her throat. "You'd think they'd change it to an indoor thing when it's thirty degrees out," she complained.

"Oh yeah," he put his hands under his arms. "Just let me know if you want to get out of here."

Rachelle didn't want him to feel bad "No, it's okay," she assured him. "The tour guide seems cool. She really knows her shit."

"Yeah," James agreed. "She's a great speaker."

"I just wish the friggin' group would shut up while she's talking," Rachelle complained. "There's no doubt they pre-gamed. We only just left the first bar, and they're already so drunk and loud."

"Really? I was impressed by them. They're full of life! And *so* outgoing."

"Bullshit." Rachelle laughed, then looked over at him. "Really?"

"No, I'm with you," James smiled. "I meant that's what they think about themselves."

"They probably don't even feel the cold with that whiskey roaring through their veins." Rachelle shook her fists in the air, growling playfully. "Maybe I *do* wish I was drunk."

"Yep. We're the only crazies out here totally sober in this weather."

A loud chime pierced the quiet street. Rachelle crashed into James' shoulder, heart slamming wildly in her chest. A bike rushed past, its ring still echoing in her head.

She realized she was not only holding James' forearm, but also squeezing it with all her strength. James gripped her wrist gently. Once she unclenched, he removed her hand from his arm. He was looking at her, laughing quietly.

"You okay?"

She took her wrist in her left hand and held it to her chest. Her face was burning hot. "Yeah," she laughed too. "I guess we *aren't* the only crazies out here."

"Maybe he's riding drunk," James said. "It's pretty fucking bold to stealth-speed your way past someone and then ring your stupid bike bell the second you're next to them."

"Yeah, what the fuck!" she agreed, craning her neck to look at the cyclist again. "It's not like we were in his way!"

"We've got your plates, asshole!" James shouted, shaking his fist at nobody. Rachelle realized the cyclist must have already turned right two blocks ahead of them. Everyone in their tour group stopped walking and turned in unison to stare at them.

"I didn't really get his plates. Did *you* get his plates?" he asked Rachelle. That mock-serious expression had returned.

"No, I didn't catch them in time," she said. "If we run into that Redcoat ghost, we can send him after the guy. I bet he can ride like the wind!"

James did a double take at Rachelle. He grinned. "You know, it's starting to feel like I'm not even new here."

Rachelle wasn't sure what to say. "Yeah, I definitely don't regret leaving the house tonight."

They arrived at the second bar a few minutes behind their group. A big old red brick structure set along a row of other shops and restaurants. Dark brown awnings decorated big storefront windows.

The floor groaned under Rachelle's feet the moment she stepped into the place. It smelled like garlic, lemons, and old wood. James came in behind her and walked to the bar. A big intricate semi-circular thing of dark wood, a band of deep ridges chasing down the curve to the opposite end. Rachelle stared at the rings in the wood, which were probably considered a handsome detail to a woodworker. For some reason this large wooden furniture reminded her almost everything in this place was essentially tree carcasses. She imagined the dark rings as being scratch marks. The soul of the tree trying desperately to escape.

A middle-aged man came over and set his hands on the bar top. "What'll it be?" he asked.

Rachelle continued staring at the bar. She hardly heard him.

"Dark 'n' Stormy," she heard James say, resting an elbow on the bar.

"What?" Rachelle inquired.

"Mixed drink. Rum and ginger beer."

"Hey," Rachelle looked around. "Where did the tour group go?"

"Does it really matter?" James was looking at her, sipping his drink.

"I mean, not really," Rachelle adjusted a small standing drink menu on the counter and eyed James hopefully. "Are we just ditching them, then?"

A loud collective whooping noise came from one of the other rooms of the restaurant. A male voice yelled "Ow oww!"

"It is a tough choice, but it is the right choice." James teepee'd his hands and bowed slightly. He nudged the space next to Rachelle's elbow with his own. "So, are you drinking something or what?"

Rachelle raised her eyebrows and pursed her lips playfully. "Yes, I was going to. Why? Are you trying to make me drink?"

James snorted into his drink and took another sip. "Oh you know, you could put it that way." He set down his glass and made a mock sweeping gesture of invitation. "Or you could say I'm inviting you to join me." He leaned back in his chair like a mobster about to set terms. "Coke? Pepsi? Water with lemon? Go crazy. I'm paying. But um, they might only have one choice between Coke and Pepsi."

"Ah yes, thank you. I feel very welcomed now." Rachelle smiled, shook her head and ordered a light beer. The bartender poured it from the tap and slid it over to her.

"So . . . I have some questions for you."

"Okay—" Rachelle was hesitant. She had started this under the assumption James was interested in dating her. Now she worried there was a pretense. An agenda. *I really wanted him to like me.* What if she made herself believe something was there, when there really wasn't? Maybe this was how he worked things in the business world? Getting to know employees so he could get the social lay of the land at his place of work?

"I can't help but feel like I'm about to be interviewed or something," she tried. She wanted to address her worries and gently press for an explanation.

"No, definitely not," James insisted.

"Okay, well, what did you want to ask me?"

"I'm seriously just making conversation." His laughter sounded too gentle to her. Nervous, even. "I was going to ask you more about that homeless guy. When you said he knew your nickname. What did he tell you to do? To run away?"

Rachelle sighed. Some tension evaporated. Maybe he just really liked a mystery. *Maybe he'll ask me my birthday and give me my horoscope.*

"Yeah, he told me about how I always leave people." Rachelle blinked at James and smiled, not continuing. Chiding him, forcing him to ask more questions.

"So, you felt like this comment applied to your life somehow?" James asked.

"Yeah. It's just weird. I sort of ran away from two big situations in my lifetime." Rachelle spun her glass slowly with both hands, eyes cast down to the counter-top. "I obviously left Rory's dad. And before that, I left my parents' house abruptly. When I was in community college. A friend and I ran into hard times."

"I remember when I first met Daisy Kelly," Rachelle said, staring at nothing. "We had a lot in common. We were both nineteen and already tired of most people."

James smiled. "I feel like that some days. I'd imagine most nineteen-year-olds felt the same."

Rachelle shook her head. "I mean, everyone wants more. They dream of it. But we were actually going for it. You know those people who act like something's owed to them simply because they want it? And if they don't get it, there's always something or someone *else* to blame? *That* is what we were tired of. What I'm *still* tired of. People, being . . . well . . . *people*."

"World-weary. I get it." James smiled, knowingly. "Go on."

"Yeah, so we were at different tables in a study area. I was trying to keep to myself. Some guy came up to me, trying like hell to induct me into some organization. I can't remember what one. I was kind of incredulous. I started . . . roasting him, I guess."

***

The guy with the severely straight side part splitting his smooth brown hair was *really* still standing there, interrupting Rachelle's precious quiet time before her morning classes. *Fuck it*, she thought. He thinks he's got all the answers after I've said no in six different ways. He's got this coming to him.

She let out a short, loud sigh. "You've really got yourself in a catch-22 there, don't you?"

"What do you mean?" The man-boy nervously readjusted his manila folder, then tried to smooth out the gesture by holding the thing awkwardly in front of his chest with both hands.

She rolled her eyes. "What do you *mean*, what do I mean? What's a catch-22? Or what's *the* catch-22?"

"I *know* what a catch-22 is." His lips looked thin when he pressed them together.

"Well, you apparently aren't happy with the number of members you are made of, but you have your reputation to worry about, too."

"My reputation?"

"Yeah. Your group's reputation is important in order to increase membership. So your challenge is, getting the word out, without letting the world know you interrupt fellow students from studying just to fulfill your selfish obligations."

"Well, I—"

"Oh!" she interrupted, clapping her hands with glee. "*I* know! You should get a booth! Then that way, people can come to *you!*"

"I'm just fine with how I'm doing things, thanks."

"You can't mean that. You get the poster boards. I'll buy the glitter!" she shouted as the offended party stormed off.

Daisy came over and sat down at Rachelle's table. "*So*, how's being an asshole working for you?"

Rachelle looked down, scratching something out on a piece of paper. "I was being helpful." She glanced up casually, changing her mind and deciding to try erasing the pen scribble she'd just made.

"No, you weren't. But it's okay. They were bothering everyone."

She sighed. "Yeah, he was one of those types. You know, lawyer parents or something. Probably taught him he can't take 'no' for an answer." She shrugged. "I was nice at first, but then he wouldn't shut up."

"Rachelle Harrison?"

"Yeah? How do you know?" Rachelle swept the eraser shavings off her paper.

Daisy set a pinkie finger on the corner of the sheet, looking down at it. "It's at the top of your paper."

"Oh," Rachelle paused, then smiled. "What's your name?"

"I'm Daisy."

Rachelle snorted quietly, still smiling. "Like the flower?"

Daisy rolled her eyes. She leaned back in her seat and crossed her arms first, then her legs. "And you're Shelly? Like a seashell?"

"Not before. But I guess I am now."

"Okay, Chelle it is."

***

"So we got the 'Chelle.' But why did you leave town?" James asked. "It sounds like you two would get along really well."

"How do I explain it?" Rachelle looked at the ceiling, thinking. "I sort of realized one day that I was going out of my way to please her. To please everyone. But I decided I couldn't do it at my own expense anymore. That was when I moved to Crescent City. I moved there by myself."

"Crescent City? Why there?? Isn't that, like, a thousand miles away?"

"It's weird that you know that."

"I told you. I get around," James said, tipping his head forward slightly.

"I just drove."

"You just . . . drove."

"Up the coast."

"Until you got tired?"

"Sort of, yeah."

"Did you pack everything? Did you just bolt?" James' eyes were locked on hers. Like he was processing every word.

"So many questions." She laughed quietly. Her heart sped up.

"Just trying to get my head around it."

"So I sort of just bolted. I packed what stuff I really needed. Some small furniture from my bedroom and all my clothes. Told my parents I was leaving. They were sad, but I mean eventually they got over it." She shrugged. "A lot of time has passed since then. It's funny," she said. "I haven't talked about this, really."

"They just let you leave?"

"I was nineteen. I was saving up to move out anyway. So it was getting to be time. They were going to start

116

charging me rent if I didn't move out soon. I was going to community college. Taking pre-requisites. I never ended up finishing."

"Did you work at the time?"

"Yeah, I had to. To pay for my classes. I worked at a local radio station," she said. "I *hated* it."

"How come? You don't like music?"

"No, the problem was that I *do* like music. Very much," she said. "But they didn't have the license to play most of what I liked. So we had to play the same shit over, and over, and over again. I didn't even bother to put my two weeks in. I found another small AM station to work at in Crescent City. I took things more seriously there. An opening came up for morning producer, and I got it after a few months working there."

"Wow, so it sounds like broadcasting is really your thing."

"Yeah. How did you get into the business?"

"Oh." James sighed the word. "Do we *have* to talk about me?"

"You can't *seriously* still be wanting to listen to me talk about myself," she asked. "I mean . . . *can you?*"

"Oh, I guarantee you're way more interesting than I am," he said. "I'm kind of new to broadcasting, to be honest," he said, seeming to wince a little. "I hate that I got this position though. I sort of get the sense that you'd really be the best one for the job. Way more so than me."

Rachelle blushed. A little forward, but he had a point. "Thanks for saying so. How did you get the job, anyway? I didn't know it was even available."

"I guess you could say I got lucky."

"Well that's vague," she stated aloud to herself.

"Yeah, after I move to a new place, I kind of just look around 'til I find something that sparks my interest."

"Ah. Did you travel a lot for work before?"

"Yeah, I don't really stay in one place very long."

As much as she liked him, she didn't really want to hear more about his path to the job that might've been hers. "I'll tell you why I really left Santa Ana."

"Oh, okay!" James responded, looking puzzled.

Rachelle took a deep breath. "I don't really tell people this story. Something really bad happened with Daisy and me one night. Most people blamed me for it."

"Sorry," James said quietly.

"It's okay." She pressed her lips together, and continued. "So, not long after we met, Daisy and I hung out together practically every day. She had an infectious personality. She was frank about everything, to the point of being offensive. But she somehow also had this undeniable gift of getting everyone to like her. To want her to like them. She could get them to do anything that struck her fancy at any given moment. And not always in a good way.

"She liked to do a lot of reckless and crazy shit. And she liked to have company when she did it. Like, if something looked tall and rickety, she wanted to climb it. If someone looked morose and dangerous, she wanted to be friends with them.

"She once went up to a towering half-drunk biker who had gotten thrown out of a bar and started talking to him. They sat on the curb together. I had refused to go with her, so I was watching from the parking lot she'd left me in. Within minutes, they were laughing. Within ten, she called me over. They had somehow unearthed their fascination with watching peoples' model trains on the internet. They'd been talking about how it calmed them down.

"So anyway, we were walking barefoot on the beach one night, just talking." Rachelle looked down at her feet, wiggling them against the barstool footrest. "We did this often. We walked onto a pier and sat down on the end of it. We were watching the sun set over the water. It felt like the most perfect end to the best day ever, at the time. I remember she said 'What if we just stayed here all night?' I told her no way, I can't sleep on wood boards all night long. So she suggested driving my car to the end of the pier and sleeping in there with the windows open.

"Not that this makes it any less stupid, but I had a pretty small car at the time. An '82 Ford Escort. She explained that the pier was wide and sturdy. We'd park at the end of the pier and roll down the windows. We'd get to fall asleep to the sound of the waves, and have a cushy surface to lay on.

"I'm sure you can guess what happened next. Everything felt okay at first. I drove out very slowly. Like, as slowly as the car would go. I kept braking until she told me to stop because it kept making the dock wiggle. We sat there for, I don't know, five minutes. She was talking to me, trying to distract me, because I was scared.

"My heart was beating so hard the whole time. I started to feel those sick sweats. You know, like when your face gets cold and your body's really hot, and your shirt feels glued on? And then, the wood didn't make any noise, but I felt kind of a sliding sensation. Like the posts coming loose in the dirt. Or sand. Or whatever was holding them there." Rachelle swallowed hard.

"At the time, I remember Daisy looking so focused. So intent. And I was almost sure of what she was thinking. She forced me to drive the car out there. She was hell-bent to help get us out of this.

"She even knew what to do. But it still went wrong." Rachelle's voice wavered, but she didn't cry. She paused, squeezing her eyes shut, holding it in, and then continued. "I remember she said we had to open the doors and get out now, because the pressure wouldn't let the doors open once the car fell in. But when we went to open the doors, they were locked. I turned to get the locks, and the pier collapsed. The car just plunged in, nose first. Then it was too late to get out."

"How did you get out?" James asked.

"When the car hit the water, it threw Daisy into the windshield and started sinking, fast. I was buckled in. And on impact, she was unconscious, I think. There was a . . ." She swallowed. Her mouth was full of spit. Her eyes felt all prickly. "A car battery I'd bought that I'd left in the fucking back seat. I was supposed to get it changed out but hadn't gone to the shop yet. I'd been having to jump my car every few starts for the past week. I don't know if the battery had hit her. I really don't know if she was already dead or just unconscious. There was no time. But the windshield was starting to break. It was so scary watching that crack spread and make more cracks. I crawled out of my seat, put my weight on the dash and waited for the whole thing to break.

"It finally broke. There was water rushing in. I *had* her. I was getting her out, but then the car hit the ocean floor. The pressure of the water rushing in, and the car stopping suddenly . . ." Rachelle shook her head and pressed her fingers to her temples. Her mind was thrashing. She felt panicked, existential, like she had that night. She opened her eyes and James was watching her steadily, calmly. She got ahold of herself, and sighed. Her eyes were wet now. "Sorry." She sniffed again. Grabbed her beer and took a long drink. "I lost her," she whispered, but her voice didn't join the movement of her mouth. She cleared her throat and tried again. "I lost her."

"God, Rachelle. I'm sorry." James put his hand down on the counter. Comfort from a distance.

She sighed. "Thanks. Anyway. I was out of the car, and she was still inside. The water was ungodly strong. Pressing me down. Trying to suck me in. Literally all I could do was hang onto the frame of the car and wait until it was filled so I could swim back up. I can still taste the salt. Feel the water just lodged in that unnatural place where it didn't belong; between my nose and throat. That feeling of choking. The godawful sting. All my muscles telling me it's wrong. It's wrong, but they can't help me get rid of that feeling."

"Wow," James replied, rubbing the back of his neck.

"I was so mad at myself for not going back, even though it was physically impossible," she said. "I was furious at Daisy, for being dead and not being there to blame for it. And I was mad at myself again for being so easily influenced. That I would go so far, do something *that* stupid, just because someone pushed me to do it. To the point where she *died*.

"I was stuck in this avalanche of horrible feelings, and I actually didn't leave town right away," she realized. "I don't know why I didn't remember that right away. I mean, obviously I was devastated about Daisy, but this voice in my head was just ripping me to shreds. Telling me I was nobody. I had no identity. I did whatever others told me, I had no personality. I was a chameleon. A fucking dog who followed around anyone who gave me any attention. How could I be so stupid, so naive?" She bit her lip. "Sometimes I wished *I* had died, so Daisy would have to deal with the guilt instead of me."

She paused. "God, this is so heavy, James. Maybe I should've just called my therapist or something. Are you sure you don't want to run off?" Rachelle eyed him cautiously. *Ugh, lady, you just got him alone. Don't give him these ideas.*

He joined his hands in front of his mouth again. "God, no, I don't want to run. I sort of can't believe you're telling me this." He said it gently, then let out a laugh that sounded like a cough. "I feel horrible this happened to you. And also, kind of honored. I didn't think this was how our first date would go but it feels like you really trust me. I'm just hoping that means I did something right."

A warmth spread across Rachelle's face; a huge grin chasing that feeling. All of this felt good, somehow. And he hadn't freaked out. Really, he'd done the opposite.

James faced Rachelle now, fully. "So the thing about wishing you'd died. Do you still feel that way ever?" He was squinting at her, reading her. His eyes were soft. Not with anxiety, but empathy.

"Ah, right back to it, Dr. Carraway." She grinned sarcastically. "Yeah. So for a few weeks after, like I said, I was depressed and not coping well at all. Sometimes I had dreams that I *did* die. The sweats would come back. I'd wake up with that choked feeling like I'd had that night. Most of the time I felt like whoever I was actually did drown in that car. But at some point things slowly got a little easier. I realized I could get rid of the parts of myself I didn't like. I could learn and grow, and live on my own terms instead of someone else's. That's when I finally left home.

"Sometimes that feeling comes back, of not knowing who I am. The mom thing really threw me for a loop, too. Living for another person, and on top of that, being relied on for everything. Not having Chad around makes it harder, too. I've been working on it, though."

James shook the ice in his drink. "That's so funny, the impression I got from meeting you was that you're insanely driven and self-sufficient. I know you shouldn't really peg people you don't know, but, ya know. I thought you were cool. So at first, I wasn't sure I should ask you out."

"How so?"

James' eyes traveled around the room like he was trying to recall. His gaze centered on her again. "Oh, um," he put his fist to his mouth.

"What?"

"Nothing, like, that morning I was going to ask you, Rick saw us talking, and he caught me fixing my hair when you looked away for a sec. I guess I looked really intent. I didn't admit to him I was interested, but he said something weird like 'Careful man, she keeps things close to the chest.'"

"What? Why would he say that?"

"I don't know. Maybe you just put off that vibe like you know who you are, you like your life as-is and you . . . have things covered, I guess?"

"I have my moments?" She laughed and glanced at James. He was looking right at her. His hand sat on the counter, nearer her arm, his fingers tapping the wood softly. Seeing it felt like reading an invitation to somewhere she really wanted to go. The hot feeling spread from her face down her throat, to her chest, her arms, her middle. She inhaled sharply, quietly, her heart trying to beat its way out.

The bartender walked closer to them to wipe a bit of countertop. James cleared his throat, moving his hand away.

The tapping became a drumming against the bottom of the bar.

12

James rolled over in the back seat of his car, trying to get comfortable. The buckle dug into his inner thigh. He shoved it back into its alcove with his knee. The hard plastic hit the side of his kneecap just so. Pain hurtled up his leg, launching him into a swearing mess.

"She's going to find out about you" a voice rasped, loud and quick. Hardly audible over his own shouting.

"What?" James asked, quieting quickly, but the voice was gone.

"Disembodied voices," James grumbled to himself. "Par for the course, I guess. Been here long enough without any crazy visitations yet." He rearranged his three fleece blankets over himself. The bottom one was always bunching up under the two heavier ones. He tried to pretend he wasn't cold. He closed his eyes and pictured himself in Rachelle's living room. Warm and sitting on her couch. In his imagination, she entered the room. Invading his reverie. Wearing a long black t-shirt. Her shorts were so short, he could just barely tell she was wearing any. She was walking straight up to him.

She didn't slow down when she got close. His breathing quickened, and he sighed.

"That's what happens when you people get off the drugs." The voice was back. "You start looking for someone to stick it in."

James sat up in the back seat and leaned forward, running his hands through his hair. His chest, his neck, his face was hot. He was covered in sweat.

"That's besides the point, isn't it?" he asked weakly. "You *know* you don't belong here. Just tell me what you're doing, or what you want."

All he heard now was a quiet breathy laughter.

He pressed on. "You can do this the long and hard way, or—" The laughter became a roar at "long and hard".

"Fucking *grow up*," James growled.

"I can't," the voice said between chuckles. "Literally, I can't. And who wants to, anyway?"

"*Anyway*. We can have this take forever, or you can tell me what you want. Do what you're gonna do. But I *promise* you, there will be repercussions."

A rattling groan shook his car. James steeled himself, maintaining his composure.

Parlor games. Just bullshit parlor games, he said to himself. *You've seen it before.*

"You think so?" the voice replied to his thoughts.

You are fucked James. Fully, fucked. Your tools are in the trunk. You'll never make it. Now you know they'll be a step ahead of your every move. Shit. Still, he wouldn't let himself visibly react.

"I'll show you something," it hissed. "We know more of pleasure than any of you fleshy insects with brief life-spans."

"If I'm so unimportant, I can't see why you're deigning to waste your time with me."

"Do I need a reason? No. It's great fun crushing bugs."

"Then do what you're gonna do, I guess. What choice do I have?" James braced himself again. The dread was inescapable now. He didn't protest. That'd only make the inevitable that much worse.

***

He couldn't see, but he heard his car door shutting. His heart was jumping in excitement. Right behind the yawning hole inside. The aching chasm that light wouldn't touch. Only the gray stuff that longed to get in and warm itself inside his body.

It's not me. This isn't me. I don't need drugs. I left that life behind. But something was pushing the words, the will, down. Deeper and deeper, to somewhere in him. Hiding it away. Behind his spleen or something. All he could feel was the want now. The want and the helplessness. They were almost as one. Like a twisted cord that scratched his flesh and opened a hole within. A hole that needed filling.

It hurts, he couldn't help saying to himself. *Where is it? Are we almost there?* he asked the voice. He knew it was inside him now. Though he felt alone.

127

It was dark. He stood there in the grass, trying to blink something into being. It was cold. So cold he felt naked. He wished he'd brought his blankets.

He saw a window. *Rory's window.* James was standing in front of it.

No, he was crawling up inside himself from deep within. *I will not go in there. I will not.* His insides curdled with fear. At the thing standing in front of Rory's window. At the fact that that thing was himself. And the dread of what was going to happen next.

The window was growing a little bigger.

Why? and he realized it was because his right foot had moved a step closer.

No, he said again. His left foot moved forward now, and that's when his mind stopped knowing.

***

Rachelle was awake, but a happy awake, thinking about the date. About those damned long fingers. He'd counted out the bills with quick flips of his thumb and pointer, like a seasoned cashier. What is it about the way he laid the stack on his palm, then turned the bills back over to rest on the edge of the counter? So effortless. Those mannerisms, that absentminded regular shit would be her undoing.

He hadn't come to work the next day. She hoped it had nothing to do with her.

Either way, her stomach was doing flips. She wondered when she'd see him next. She caught herself smiling at the ceiling.

The back door slid shut.

She sat up, stiffly. It wouldn't be like Rory to up and leave, especially in the middle of the night. That made her think about the coyote.

In seconds, she was standing in the kitchen, in front of the sliding door, trying to catch her breath. The breathlessness soon gave way to terror, as she realized she had no idea who or what had moved the door, and whether it was inside or outside of her house.

Deep breaths, she thought, steadying herself. Opening the door.

That was quiet enough, right? She leaned her head out to check the yard. Nothing at first. Just darkness. Then, a short hunched-over form interrupted the smooth lawn, not ten steps away from where she stood.

Her heart started galloping again.

It's just a bush, she insisted, though she had no bushes in that spot.

The bush moved. It was large. She heard grunting and a soft scrabbling sound. Something digging in the dirt.

The fear of unknown dropped away. She was still scared. But now it seemed she might need to scare off a large animal. Rachelle reached inside the kitchen door behind her to turn on the light.

"Hey!" she shouted, flipping the switch up and down.

ON

A person kneeling and hunched completely over.

OFF

ON

His fingers were claws. Curled and stiff. He was raking up the dirt in her garden. Desperately. Ferociously. Like a dog after a chipmunk. She let out a quick scream, but he kept going. Maybe flickering it would interrupt his focus and he'd leave.

OFF

ON

It was eating a handful of dirt, she realized. It turned sharply to look at her. The light illuminated its eyes like a camera flash.

She gasped.

OFF

She covered her mouth in disbelief. The bright eyes were gone. But now it was just her and that person in the dark. She fought to reach back for that light switch again. It could be anywhere now that it'd seen her. She couldn't let the darkness hide it. It could be upon her any second.

ON

The person was still in the same spot. The white light in his eyes was gone. He sat back on his haunches in the dirt, still looking at her.

She realized who it was.

"James!" she shouted. "What are you doing? Are you okay? What are you . . . eating?" The questions were coming out of her too fast. She looked down, quickly making her way down the steps and over to him.

He just stared up at her like he'd been caught doing something embarrassing. He had no shoes or socks on. His mouth and cheeks were smeared in dirt.

"Did you *walk* here? Where do you live?" She realized she'd never asked him that. James seemed to always bat away any questions about his past or, well, almost everything.

He still didn't answer. He looked confused. He stared at her like he knew her but wasn't sure where from.

"I just realized I hardly know the first thing about you," she said.

James' eyes grew suddenly wide as he was looking into her eyes. Like he'd just filled a vacancy. Or woken up. He gasped, then closed his mouth. He turned away from her, hunched over, and started coughing, gagging and spitting in the grass.

"What's happening to you?!" Rachelle reached to put a hand on James' shoulder and then brought it back to her side again. Then sadly, she said, "You didn't come here to see me, did you? You're here by accident."

James stopped retching after a few minutes. "Are you . . . have you lost your *mind*?!" James shouted. Rachelle sat back, shocked at his outburst.

"No, why? What's *your* problem?!" she shouted back.

"You just found me shoeless in your back yard in the middle of the night. It's like, thirty degrees. I'm sure I still have fucking *mud* on my face. There is clearly something wrong with me. And you're beating yourself up because I might not be here for a visit?"

"Get over yourself! All I said was I don't know the first thing about you"

"Why would you even *want* me to like you—"

"I do . . . *not*. I—"

131

"I just—I'm damaged, Rachelle. Beyond repair. You don't want this."

"Whatever," she mumbled, standing back up. "Come inside. You need to wash up."

***

Rachelle returned from Rory's room to a frigid kitchen. The sliding door had been left open. She crossed the room to go close it. James was at the kitchen sink, splashing water over his face. It felt weird being with him in her house in the middle of the night.

Rachelle set a tiny toothpaste and toothbrush on the counter next to James. "Luckily, Rory went straight back to sleep when I checked on him."

"Glad he's okay." He moved his face toward her, but stared down at the counter. "Is the bear still sleeping?"

"Uhh, the what?"

"You know, your salmon man."

"Um, Stanton? You're new here. It's crabs, not salmon. And he's *not* mine."

"Heh, guess I knew that." James' voice was quiet, weak. He turned the water back on. "Sorry. And thanks for the toothbrush."

"I guess it's a good thing he's hibernating. He might've mauled you if he heard what you said."

James snorted. She watched him as he brushed. His movements were slow and labored. The scratchy scrubby sound of brushing continued for a few minutes. Eventually, he spit, turned the sink off and faced her, holding a wet paper towel. Big blobs of blood ravaged the crumpled white.

"Wait, where are you bleeding?"

"My hands," James replied, squinting and uncertain.

"How," she asked without inflection.

James shrugged slowly. "I can't remember."

His eyes were cast down, eyebrows furrowed; he looked like he was struggling to recall what happened, or maybe wrestling with how. She reached toward him to take the paper towel and threw it away.

"Show me."

He extended his hands in front of him, palms-up. He uncurled his fingers. Short little scrapes climbed haphazardly up his fingers on both hands. One longer, deeper scrape reached across his right palm. She puzzled at them as they wept.

"Was there something sharp in the dirt? Did you touch barbed wire or something?" Rachelle brought her hand to her chin. "I don't have any gardening tools that could do this."

He shook his head, eyes squeezed shut in frustration. "I didn't touch barbed wire. Well I mean, I don't remember. I just, I don't know."

All was quiet for a beat. A full two minutes passed, and he looked up at her. "Did I get all the mud, though?" he asked her, twisting his lips as if it showed her more of his face. He still looked tired but the hardness in his eyes was softening.

"No." She curled her lip in mock disgust. "Well, most of it," she offered, smiling cautiously.

She was trying to be okay, but she kept feeling nothing was okay. "So . . . something weird is going on. Are you ready to tell me what that is yet?" she asked him.

No response. He stared at her.

"This isn't easy for me, James. To show a new person I care. To ask them to let me in after they've basically refused to. But then you keep showing up or at least seeming interested, so I keep trying again. I can't. I can't keep—"

"You just—"

"I what, James? I what?"

"It's too much to unpack. You wouldn't believe me. You *really* don't wanna know."

"I wouldn't ask if I didn't want to." She closed her eyes and inhaled sharply. He really wanted something from her. Maybe she'd never find out what it was. But whatever it was, it probably wasn't what she'd hoped.

"Rachelle?"

"Yeah." The reply was a barbed statement instead of a question.

"I respect you. I'm just trying—"

"If you respected me, you'd trust me to be able to handle whatever the *hell* is going on. I told you what I've been through. I obviously can handle it."

"I'm sorry. I'm just not ready. It's—" He paused, his eyes searching, plucking the words from thin air. "It's a leap."

"A leap." Rachelle lowered her eyes, fighting the urge to scoff. She crossed her arms. When she looked up again, he had closed the distance between them. He was reaching for her forearm.

He placed his hand around her arm. His fingers were warm. The warmth crept through her flesh, branched out through her bones. Everything. Was warm.

"Meaning, I'm scared"—his voice was low and gravelly—"of how you'd react."

He guided her arm open as she uncrossed them both. She left them open for a minute, awkwardly. Palms down, fingers wilted. Waiting. Watching him. His lips were parted and his breath was growing heavy. He seemed to be staring at her chin.

He pressed his lips together and let them go again. He bit his lip and slowly placed his hands over her hips. He looked up and smiled at her, his eyes hooded in sadness and desire. He looked apprehensive, like what he was doing was forbidden.

"It's okay," she whispered.

"It's okay," he repeated.

Their lips met. Soft and dry. Behind that familiar mint she knew, he tasted of earth. Like coffee and mushrooms. It was weird. Remembering how she found him. The circumstances she kept finding him in. The strange things he said. But he was more real than most people she knew.

Her blood was churning itself. She clenched her fingers into his shoulder blades. She wanted to hang on. To have him. He walked her backwards, their feet stumbling over each other until they were against the fridge. His hand traveled up to hold her head. His lips softened as he kissed harder. Her head bumped into the freezer door and she cried out in surprise.

James eased back and laughed quietly. She looked at him. His eyes were alight and he was smiling at her. Looking at her again.

She smiled back. "Cool."

He laughed again. A quiet throaty laugh. "Yeah." He kissed her and bit her lip gently. He cupped her head again, inhaled and sighed into her neck. He groaned, hoisting her up. She gripped his waist with her legs. They teetered away from the fridge and then he pressed her against it again.

Rachelle laughed quietly, resting her forearms on his shoulders, looking away and then back at him. "Uh—we should probably go in my room."

He leaned his forehead against her chest. "Was waiting for you to ask," he whispered. "Would rather not meet your kid 'til morning."

***

"Hey," a voice whispered sharply to her in the dark. Something tapped her arm.

"Hhhh," was all she could manage as she struggled to wake up. She reached out, hanging on to the dark form. "Wha?"

James replied. "You fall asleep fast."

"Actually, I never do," she whispered, still trying to make herself more alert.

"Even if I don't want to tell you things, will you still let me help you?"

"Help me how?"

"Like, I could . . . be here. Help out. Take shifts."

"I hardly know what I've even told you about these problems."

"I mean . . . it must be serious if some guy is staying the night in another bedroom."

"Ahh." Rachelle got the gist. It was nice to feel like he cared enough to take stock of Stanton. "Yeah, that'd be great. Scary shit's been happening, though."

"I think I can handle it," James said.

"Uhhhh-*huh*." Rachelle rolled over to go back to sleep.

13

James stood on the crumbled concrete steps of a dilapidated duplex in Lafayette, Louisiana. The building sat along a line of weather-beaten housing hugging the street. The street technically accepted cars, but was really more of a strip of chewed-up asphalt than a true road. James stared up at Gavin's place, thinking about how—from said street—the whole structure sat kind of crooked, almost as though slouching.

He banged out a third set of knocks at the door. He'd saved this variety of hefty pounding for pseudo-emergencies like this. The door groaned and rattled in its metal housing; a wooden geriatric. *We're running out of time before the meeting starts.*

Normally, being late to this thing was no big deal, but he'd worked a night shift at the gas station last night. It was evening, now. He'd only just woken up and hadn't eaten all day. His stomach was eating itself. *If I don't get one of those pre-meeting donuts before they're eaten up, I'm gonna barf.*

He stared at the deep scrapes around the lock. *Why does he bother locking up? He's always too loaded to unlock it when he gets home. Anyway, there's nothing in there to steal.*

A muffled shout issued from deep within. Then quiet, followed by heavy sliding footsteps.

A sleepy, shadowed eye surveyed him from the crack, then the door opened fully.

Gavin Hammond wore a pair of faded basketball shorts and nothing else. He was slight of frame but carried the beginnings of a gut. Gavin squinted at him. "You took the last of my shit, didn't you?"

"No." James chuckled nervously.

"Yeah. The bag I keep in the toilet tank? That was the last of it."

"Nuh-uh." James shook his head vigorously. "You have more. I saw it on the kitchen counter."

"I don't leave that stuff on the kitchen counter. That was for those flowers my sister's boyfriend bought."

"Oh."

"You didn't snort some of that, did you?"

"Maybe."

"And how did that work out for you?"

"It didn't." James bowed his head. "Just got a headache."

Gavin shook his head. "So, we're going now to get more."

"We don't have time now. We have to go to the thing."

"No. Nope. Ranger Rick's gonna leave for Hawaii tomorrow. You gotta replace what you took."

"Hawaii. Must be nice."

"Well . . . we're the ones that keep him fat and happy."

"I'm not responsible for him being fat, or for his god-awful street name."

"No one said you were."

"Seriously. I'm going to the meeting. You don't have to come. But I'm going."

"Yeah, I'm not going to that anymore. Those people are a bunch of Flanderses."

"That's what I like about them." James smiled with his teeth. "They're a good influence on me."

"Yeah? And what's that make me?"

"Well, you're trying to force me to go buy drugs with you instead of go meet with my . . . my weekly . . ."

"Your coven?"

"I guess you could call it that?" James rubbed the back of his neck and kicked at a chunk of concrete.

"That's what it is. And I'm not pushing you to do drugs. You do that already. I'm pushing you to replace what you took that was mine." Gavin's voice was growing louder. His eyes were slitted in contempt.

"Jesus, man."

"What," he spit out.

"Take it easy. You look like a damn bull with a hernia," he scoffed, looking down at his feet. He looked up again. "All right, I'll go with you. Just let me text them." James tapped a quick message in his phone. "Remind me never to do anything wrong in front of you again."

"I just don't want you to take my shit!" Gavin sighed. "We'll meet Rick by Anderson's Deli."

"You gonna get dressed?"

After Gavin got clothed, they walked around the back of the house, crunching through the dead grass in the empty yard.

The rain started down just as they reached the gravel path of the alley. James looked up. Water showered down on him from a dark gray sky, mottled by dirty-looking clouds, and chewed-up orange-brick rooftops.

"Shoulda gone to see my peeps." James raised his voice to be heard over the rain. "It's closer!"

"Yeah, I'd rather walk in the rain, thanks. I didn't know when you dragged me there they just like, pray to trees and nature and shit."

"Really? What did you think it was? *Real* magic? Like *The Craft* or something?"

"No," Gavin answered, a little too quickly.

"Ha!" James laughed and checked him with an elbow.

They turned through alley after alley between overgrown grass and shitty beater cars until James felt lost. It grew harder to see. Streetlights floated in from the main roads, filtering through dead branches. Slender black shadows sliced through the light before it reached the ground.

Gavin slowed as they reached a burned-up garage with soot blasted across the front panels.

James' neck was all tingly. The place felt weird. Haunted. He hesitated. "You said he'd meet us by Anderson's?"

"Yeah, that's around the corner. We're meeting him here."

"Oh." James folded his arms. He stared into the garage, letting his eyes adjust to the darkness. The wrecked skeleton of an old 80-something Oldsmobile was still inside. The whole top of the vehicle was missing. The seats, blackened; burned down to the frames.

"Who the fuck lives here?"

"Ranger Rick."

"What happened here?" he asked, his voice low.

"You folks talkin' about me?" a gravelly voice issued from behind the garage. A light came on in what looked like the kitchen of the house. Then the porch light. The rain pulled back to an intermittent drip. Wisps of black fog twisted in slow spirals, seeming to penetrate the darkness in the veil of the porch light.

"Uh, Gavin was just telling me you live here." James gestured at the house just past the blackened garage.

"Ah, no. The people that live in there? I call them my neighbors." The man emerged from behind the garage. He was heavyset, but muscular. He wore a dark blue pajama set with white piping. He held a strange piece of fabric strung round the back of his neck. James tried to study it without being obvious. It looked like an old waffled blanket with frayed silk edges. He offered an odd half-smile and cocked his head to the side.

"Okay." James waited for further explanation. "He lives in a burnt garage?" he whispered to Gavin.

"Yeah, so?"

James rolled his eyes. "What's with the nickname?" he asked Ranger Rick.

Rapidly, Gavin "psst'd" him and smacked him in the shoulder.

The man stepped out from the garage, grinning. "If I told you, I'd have to kill your whole family." He doubled over, laughing. Then took a long dragging breath in, holding his tongue between his teeth. "No. No, no, no. I'm kiddin'. Real name's Anton."

"Oh. So, how'd you get the nickname?"

"Childhood name. Ever heard of the kids' magazine? About wildlife?"

"Not exactly, no."

"Ranger Rick's a raccoon character. And the name of the magazine. I spent a lot of time outside. Like, I even slept outside. Called it camping when kids started spreading rumors."

"Uh."

"My parents are crazy."

". . ."

"Well. *Were* crazy. They're dead now."

"I'm sorry."

"No, it's good."

James looked at Gavin. He didn't know this guy, and wasn't sure if Gavin even *really* knew him. Gavin was fidgeting with his sleeves. His upper lip looked sweaty. Maybe it was just rainwater.

"You guys look scared-like. Like you want to leave. Am I keeping you from something?"

"Nah, we're fine. We were supposed to meet with my coven tonight." *Feels weird to say out loud.*

Anton's eyebrows shot up in recognition. "Oooh! We've got a warlock in our midst!"

James laughed sheepishly. "Yeah, well, Gavin thought we did *real* magic."

143

"Real magic, huh?" Anton bit his tongue again, nodding. "You wanna see something real, boys?"

"Uh, no, that's—" James started.

"Yes. Yeah," Gavin cut in.

"Come in here with me." Anton beckoned them with his hand.

James and Gavin stayed exactly where they were.

"Aw c'mon. That's where the stuff is, anyway. You think I just walk around with it in my pockets?"

They looked at each other. Gavin shrugged and started toward the garage. James followed.

They filed in behind Anton, who sidestepped his way between the garage wall and the car. *Where the fuck are we going?* James asked himself. He walked slowly, assuming they were going to stop at the back wall of the garage.

Anton flipped a switch, and a big rectangle of light jumped on at the back of the garage, behind the car. *Another room?* he asked himself. *How would it fit back there? I thought that house wrapped around behind the garage.*

James stepped into the box of light. The light stung his eyes. A firework exploded inside him. A burning, like an electrical charge, bursting from the center. *What the fuck? It's just a hallway. What's wrong with me?* He stopped short, moving a hand to rest against the wall. His hand swiped at nothing. Mind spinning wildly, he stumbled, then reoriented and steadied himself.

"What—?" The wall was right there. An old dusty wallpapered thing; visceral purple background stamped with faded yellow fleur-de-lis. He swiped at it once more. Again, his hand went straight through. He could just make out his fingers on the other side. *Wait so, the wall is a ghost?* James' heart vibrated. That charge smoldered in his chest. *Am I having some sort of medical emergency?* "Hey, uh, guys?" James hurried down the hallway after them.

A room sat at the end of the hall, maybe six or seven yards ahead. A floor-to-ceiling chest of drawers took up the whole wall to the left. A life-sized black carousel horse stood in the back right corner, the pole still extending through its middle. The horse had an intricate mane of twisted golden vines and roses. Its head was twisted wildly to the side; teeth bared. One leg curled up in midair.

More of that energy radiated from the horse. He didn't want to look at it anymore. Gavin and Anton gazed at him casually.

James took another step. His stomach flipped. A heaviness settled in his gut.

"I call this 'layering.'" Anton held his arms out, gesturing at everything, and nothing in particular.

"Layering?" James asked, hesitantly.

"Layering. I made the name up myself. Like, borrowing a sheltered space."

James rubbed the back of his neck. "Are you still talking about magic?" he asked, lamely. His brain was still trying to piece itself back together after the ghost-wall.

Anton looked around him, as though jokingly checking if others were listening. "I'm *always* talking about magic."

Gavin made a kind of croaking sound.

"What the ff—?" James tapered off.

"My 'magic' room is located in their office, which they barely use. That works best for me. Sometimes they come in here, and I think they see me. But I'm transparent. Like a ghost. I know cuz that's how *I* see *them*." Anton laughed. "They think the room is haunted, so I get it mostly to myself."

Almost immediately, a taut, thin voice came from the dark hallway. "Did you hear that?" The shrill echo that had asked the question shivered about the room like leaking gas. An opaque form like a human-shaped pitcher of watery milk stood in the mouth of the shadowed threshold.

"Jeez-us!" James shuffled back and away from the ghost, startling himself further as he crashed into Gavin.

"Watch it, man!" Gavin yelled, then gasped. "Fuck. Mygodwhatisthat?" Gavin grabbed him roughly by the bicep, shuffling them both back to the corner of the room. *He must've seen it too.* Anton stepped gracefully out of the way, wearing nothing more than a bemused smirk.

Another lower voice came in just as echo-y as the first. "I told you, keep that door closed!" Clear as day came the metallic clicking sound of a door being shut. The figure disappeared.

Anton returned casually to the giant set of drawers. "Always a shock the first time you see that." He smiled at them, his eyes shimmering in amusement. "I normally don't let anyone else in here. I'd hate for them to figure out my arrangement." He wiggled his fingers, scanning a section of drawers. Slid one of the larger ones open along the floor and peeked in.

A loud hissing sound filled the room. Gavin and James clambered behind the twin bed. A flash of light shot out of Anton's fingers, and the drawer slammed shut. The bright light made no noise, but James' ears popped.

"Wrong drawer." Anton held his fingers to his mouth and raised his eyebrows.

***

James was deep in the ether when the vibrations began. Vibrations, then a slow and deafening crack, like a house being wrenched in half. A black shadowed figure stretched out across the trunk of a towering tree. Its voice was low and loud, but muffled. Like a barely overheard phone call.

Another voice now. A low groan. Slow, and labored. His throat tightened. He heaved, trying to open it back up.

"Something—" he coughed out the word. He had to get these words out, whatever it took. "Something crawled—" He strained harder to focus, pushing the pain in his head to a far back corner. Slowly, the rest of the words spun themselves from nothing.

> *Something crawled up*
> *those dry dead roots*
> *and got in from underneath.*

Flames danced in front of the tree. James' head ached. His muscles tightened, then burned. He tried to listen harder, but the vibrations grew stronger.

Real muscle-clenching jaw-breaking tremors shook him awake. He lay there for what felt like a half hour, afraid to move, other than occasionally rubbing his jaw. Eventually, he sat up. He was on the floor at Anton's place. He picked up the flower he'd eaten from and spun it between his palms. Five spines were missing from the coneflower. Five very potent spines. The almond-shaped purple petals folded downward, plaited around the spiky center, like a skirt.

"You have to check this out," James said, stretching his aching muscles.

He was still grinding his teeth. He was sure Anton could see him shuddering.

"I haven't messed with that shit for years." Anton watched James, his eyes hooded. "Eat ten of those things, and your heart will fucking explode."

James raised his eyebrows. He hadn't known that. He felt like this should bother him more than it did. But he continued.

"There was a . . . signal. And a figure. I tried to learn more, but it shook me awake."

"What did it feel like?"

It felt like something made by us, but in some other-worldly language. Like some type of alien Morse Code."

"Are you sure you didn't snort those bath salts again? That doesn't make any sense."

James sighed. "Yes, I'm sure."

He'd been staying with Anton for a few weeks now, ever since he'd come back to town. Had learned a lot about what Anton called psychedelic scrying. James already knew how to differentiate "seeing" from a drug-induced hallucination by that point. "That stuff's pretty basic. I don't need your help with that anymore."

Anton laughed bitterly. "You came for the bath salts. I showed you that magic shit, and now, buddy, you're having one of everything I've got. I think you need more help than I can give."

"What's that supposed to mean?"

"You're on it for hours a day. You should pace yourself."

"Are you sure you're not just being selfish with your supply?"

Anton shook his head. "I'm not your dad. I'm only eight years older than you. You've got problems. I can't help you."

"Are you kicking me out?"

"Not right this second, but yeah."

"Fuck you."

Anton didn't appear fazed. "We're not family. And you have vomit on your face."

James rubbed it off gently with his knuckle and looked down at his hand.

"You think it's nothing." He blinked rapidly. His eyes stung. "I don't care what you think. Something's going on and I'm going to find out what it is."

"Yeah? Then what? You're gonna go save the world?"

"Maybe I will."

"You should start by saving yourself." Anton shook his head and laughed. "You've been doing this for five minutes and you're acting like you discovered the beginnings of the apocalypse."

"Whatever."

14

Rory tipped his head back in bed to look out the window above his headboard. Dawn crawled pale yellow up the gray sky. He shuddered. He brought the covers back up to his chin, and tried settling back down to sleep. After a few moments, he realized he was wide awake.

Rory slung his comforter over both shoulders like a cape, grabbed two mismatched socks from the foot of his bed, and kicked his way inside them.

He walked toward his mother's bedroom. The door was shut all the way; usually it was open a crack. As he walked closer, he heard a strange voice inside, muffled by the door. His heartbeat quickened.

Who is that? He knocked on the door and the voices stopped abruptly.

A beat of silence, and then his mother's voice came from inside.

"Rory, is that you?"

He froze and didn't respond. The voice wasn't as deep as Stanton's. Did she have a sleepover? She didn't have very many friends, and he knew all of them. Also, she never had boys over to sleep. *Stanton doesn't count,* he told himself. *Stanton is my friend, not hers.* He considered sneaking back to his room.

The floorboards creaked. He ran the other way down the hall, his comforter trailing behind him. A sharp turn into the kitchen brought him to safety.

Rory leaned against the wall, panting a little. He walked over to the sliding glass door and looked out. Stanton sitting on the stoop, smoking a cigarette. Rory's stomachache disappeared. He didn't realize he'd even had one until it was gone. Like that feeling of finally coming home after a bad day of school. He knocked at the glass, then put his nose up against it. Stanton twisted around. He smiled and waved. Stanton only seemed to smile at Rory. He wondered if Stanton would smile at the man from his mom's room when he saw him.

Rory dragged the door open slowly, and was forced to retrieve and re-situate a corner of his makeshift cape blanket.

"Are you sure you can wear that outside? It might get dirty." Stanton eyed the blanket from top to bottom. "Nevermind, I think you're good."

"What do you mean, I'm 'good?'"

"Well, I mean you will be okay, outside, with the blanket," Stanton explained.

"Why?"

"Well, because I don't know if it can get any dirtier," he said. "I mean, you could try, but I don't think that fabric is designed to hold one more crumb or piece of dirt," Stanton's mouth was serious but his eyes still smiled.

"Ew, you think things are *supposed* to be dirty?" Rory wrinkled his nose and inspected Stanton's wardrobe. Everything looked like it had been washed.

"No, I'm just saying, if we lived in a world where things were supposed to be dirty, you would get a lot of compliments," Stanton replied.

"Oh, you're just teasing," Rory stated. "I keep asking Mom to wash it, but she keeps telling me what other things she has to do, she tells me she doesn't have time." He rubbed one foot on the stoop and squinted up at Stanton. "She says it's because I take it with me around the house and in the yard that it's so dirty."

"So why are you out there getting it all dirty?"

"I like to dig," Rory said with a deathly serious glare. He opened his mouth to speak again.

"Oh yeah?"

"Yeah. I use sticks and rocks."

"Okay, that's good." Stanton was smiling again. "No shovels?"

"Nah, my mom uses a shovel though. She's a good digger!" Rory opened his mouth to speak again and then covered it quickly. His belly suddenly hurt again. He couldn't tell anyone, could he?

"Is there something you want to tell me?"

"Well, one time, mom was digging in dirt and I was watching from inside?" Rory's voice lilted up at the end, almost asking himself if he was going to continue.

He looked at Stanton, who was watching him intently. Like he was really listening.

"And yeah, she dug this big hole to put some flowers in, and went to go get the plant from the front yard. I thought the hole looked real big, and I thought if it was big enough, maybe you could see the other side of the world. So I went outside and just laid on my stomach to look into the hole."

Rory held out his hands, palms up, shrugging as he spoke. "It was the biggest hole I'd ever seen. So I had to look."

"And did you see anything?" Stanton was sitting on the stoop, arms crossed over his knees, squinting in the sunlight. Still expressionless, waiting until the end of the story.

"*Yeah,*" he whispered. He had told almost the whole story and now wasn't sure if he could tell the rest. He felt very scared just thinking of retelling it.

"I saw, like, people being mean to people. Like . . . down there. In the hole."

"You saw that. In the hole," Stanton repeated, dipping his head, waiting.

"Yeah. Like . . . there were guys who were stuck to the ground by some ropes. They weren't wearing any shirts. And this big guy on four legs came. It looked like a horse but the top was like a person. And he had a bunch of thin horns on his head. Or maybe it was a crown. They were reaching for him like they wanted him to help. Only instead of helping, he started biting them! He bit their hands, then their arms, and he kept eating them, like, all the way, eating them. I got really freaked out and didn't feel good after seeing it. My mom called to me and I turned away. Then, it felt like the hole was just sitting there, open, waiting for me to look again. I was kinda scared something would come out of it. The whole time I had my snack, it was hard to eat it because my stomach was all bothered. I checked the hole again right after, and it was like that biting thing had started again from the beginning. Like it was a real life show on repeat."

"Hmm." Stanton scratched the back of his head slowly.

"But, like, it turns out they didn't know I was there, up above, and could see them."

"Well, that's good."

Rory nodded. He gathered both ends of his blanket with one hand. He leaned over, picking up sticks, tossing them further across the yard.

"So anyway," Rory said while sighing. "I won't be doing *that* crap again."

Stanton laughed again. "You're probably not supposed to say that."

"Oh yeah, sorry!" Rory smiled. He felt bad but didn't feel like he was in trouble. He liked Stanton's laugh. It sounded like it came directly out of him, not like it had been attached to speakers to be made louder. Making Stanton laugh felt like getting a trophy.

They sat there for a while, quietly. The sky started to lighten some more. Stanton opened his mouth to speak, and suddenly the door slid open again. Rory and Stanton twisted around to see a guy leaning out the door, in a white t-shirt and black basketball shorts.

"What on *earth* are you two doing out here?" James asked loudly.

"Uh . . . are those mine?" Stanton asked, nodding toward the shorts.

"Oh yeah." James chuckled quietly, lowering his head. "Sorry. I'm a boy scout, normally. Always prepared. Besides last night—er, besides today."

"I really don't think Stanton wants to know," Rory said, shrugging. Both men laughed quietly.

"It's okay, just a little weird is all." Stanton turned back around, squinting his eyes shut and putting his hand to his head.

Rory looked back up at James, agape.

"What's the matter, guy, you look like you want to ask me something," James coaxed.

Rory stared a little longer, trying to form words.

"Go ahead, there's nothing to be scared of," he teased gently.

"Who the heck are *you?*" Rory asked him, squinting, awaiting an answer.

"I'm called James. I work with your mother. We had a . . . slumber party," James said, with knees bent, hands on his knees so he was closer to Rory's level.

"You slept over because you like her. I get it, I'm not *four*." Rory laughed, then whispered "*Not anymore*" and turned back around, like Stanton had.

"I don't think he likes me," James laughed to Stanton, standing up slowly. "Rachelle's making oatmeal, she sent me here to tell you that." James popped his head back in the door and began to close it. "What a little shit," he chuckled quietly.

"Did you hear that?!" Rory said.

"No—what," Stanton said, after gritting his teeth.

"He said shit! That's even *worse* than saying crap, you know."

Stanton laughed, trying to change the subject. "I've never heard of someone making a mass bowl of oatmeal. Do you guys have cereal or something? Toaster pastries?"

"What's a toaster pastry?" Rory squinted, mouth hanging open.

"You've never had a toaster pastry? That's just gruel."

"I dunno what you're talking about, but I'll ask her if there's any cereal."

"*Ahh*, let's not. Actually, I just thought about it, and I decided I'd love some oatmeal. You hungry?"

15

Something crackled, then buzzed, as Stanton passed by Rory's room leaving the kitchen.

"Can I come in?"

He knocked three times, tipping his head through the doorway. He shook his head at himself. Knocking on an open door. Reminded him of his mom. Made him feel annoying.

"Sure!" Rory's eyes lit up in response. "Are you done with the dishes? I have a question for you."

Stanton smiled. "Sure, what is it?"

"What's this thing that looks like the Eiffel tower?" Rory asked. He pointed to the apparatus screwed on top of the crystal radio.

"Good question."

Stanton kneeled down next to Rory, who sat on the bed of a large yellow dump truck toy. Rory squinted at the dial as he turned it some more. More crackling. Conversations severed by more buzzing, folding into screeching instruments. More static showering in.

"Well, that's the funny thing," Stanton said, rubbing his face. "It looks like a tiny version of a transmitter."

"Transmitter, like the thing that gives the signal?"

Stanton nodded slowly. "Yes . . . very good!" he squinted his eyes in appreciation. "Are you sure you're only five?"

Rory laughed. "My mom says I'm an old soul."

"That would explain a lot of things." Stanton smiled, looking back at the radio. "But yeah. A normal full-sized transmitter is usually gigantic and sits on top of a radio station or something. It puts out a very strong signal that radios can pick up. So that's why it's weird this thing is on here."

"And the signals are invisible!"

Stanton chuckled. "Exactly. There's a whole electromagnetic spectrum we can't see. Kinda like real-life magic."

"Cool," Rory breathed.

"What are you guys so intent on?" James leaned in the doorway, tipping his head to see better. Rory pursed his lips at him.

"Oh, Rory's just asking about this radio he found," Stanton responded, still touching the wiring around the apparent miniature transmitter, following it with his fingers. "I couldn't figure why this small thing looks like a transmitter. They're normally very large, and typically put out a strong electromagnetic signal."

"*I* know a bit about electromagnetic energy," James nodded.

He said that too quickly. Stanton thought. "Oh yeah? You know about radios?"

He turned to James, his jaw set.

"Not radios exactly." James ventured into the room, distracted by a marker drawing taped to the wall. "Is this . . . a purple pickle . . . with eyes?" He smoothed the tape back over the bottom corners, his tongue pressing his upper lip.

"Yah," Rory said softly.

"Any more details you can share on the radio thing?" Stanton suppressed a smile. He motioned toward Rory with his hand. "It's been kind of an impromptu teaching moment here."

"Not sure if it's anything you two would believe." James put his hands in his back pockets and flared out his elbows. "I used to use something like a meter, or machine that picked up something on the electromagnetic spectrum called infrared light." James turned to Rory. "Different energies give off infrared light. Heat is one."

Rory glanced back at James periodically while he talked, but mostly just stared down at the radio, his fingers on the dial, not moving it now. He seemed to be focusing hard, absorbing James' words.

"What, for work?" Stanton raised his eyebrows, disappointed he had to concede before the fun even started.

"No, it was a recreational thing, really."

Stanton left his eyebrows up and dipped his chin, waiting for more.

James caught Stanton's eye and laughed quietly. "It was sort of uh . . . a ghost hunting group."

"Ghost hunting, huh?"

"Yup." James popped the "p" and rocked up on his tiptoes. He changed the subject. "Did you know remote controls use infrared to change channels on the TV?"

Rory's mouth fell open. "No."

"It's true." James nodded. "Soo, can I get a look at this thing?"

Stanton scooted over. "Be my guest." Rory rolled himself backwards on the dump truck.

James crouched down and ran his fingers across the wooden base of the machine.

"What's this?" He pointed to a small green board with tubes and connectors.

"Oh, that's a circuit." Stanton furrowed his eyebrows at it, bringing his face closer. "Funny though. The radio itself is essentially a circuit. I wonder why there's a separate, smaller circuit added here." Stanton tapped it, then brought his hand to his chin.

"That's bizarre." James looked at the circuit.

Stanton looked up at James. "You said it was something we wouldn't believe."

"Huh?"

"The thing you knew about electromagnetic energy. You said we wouldn't believe you."

"Hhh—" James laughed quietly again and shook his head.

"So it's not that hard to believe you went ghost hunting."

"No?" James chewed the side of his lip. He didn't elaborate.

***

From a deep sleep, Rory's mind swam to a flickering light.

The glow of his lamp painted his lids an orangey-red. Then, another flicker of darkness. The bulb flickered and clicked. Like it was struggling to hold the electricity or something. He opened his eyes and the light went out. The crystal radio sat there next to the lamp.

That's funny, I thought Stanton took that out of my room.

It was dark without his lamp. The blinds were shut, but some moonlight crept in between the slats. It looked almost blue. Something about the dark and the blue moonlight made his stomach jump around in his body.

He heard a vague whispered voice. It sounded like scraping metal. His mind reeled in panic. It sounded like it came from the foot of his bed.

He opened his eyes. "Who's there?"

"Dozz eet heer," the voice said.

"What?"

"Can it hear?"

"Me?"

"Yes."

"I can hear, yes"

"It is young?"

"Me?"

"Yeeees"

He sat up quickly. A shadowed head crested the foot of his bed. Then came shoulders, arms, and a torso. It was big, like a grown-up.

The floorboards moaned as it crouched back down. Rory leaned forward to try and see it again. Its head reappeared. He felt the bed depress by his feet, the mattress coils squeaking. It hoisted itself up and crawled toward him. The whole thing was a shadow, darker than the night. The contours of its face were chiseled, like coal. Crevices sat where the eyes should be. Its mouth, a chasm that hung open.

It pressed down heavy on his legs. Brought its face over his. That metallic smell entered his nose, just like when he saw angry house. But it was extra strong and sharp, and it crept into his mouth. When it was this strong, it tasted exactly like the time he tripped and fell and tasted his own blood.

All he could do was stare and try to breathe. His breathing was fast; his heart even faster. Its face almost eclipsed his, blotting out the blue light from the windows. He felt it looking. Its head tilted to the side.

Something brushed against his shoulder. An immense pressure crushed the back of his neck. Gradually, the pressure grew and grew until he thought his eyes would pop out of his head.

He cried out. "You're hurting me!"

"Yes."

"Stop!!"

No response. But the pressure stopped growing.

"What do you want?" he breathed desperately.

It sighed loudly. "Not the boy. Leave him. Machine matters more."

"What machine?"

"It's *so* young," it dragged in another breath.

"Who are you talking to?"

"The boy."

"Me?"

"*Yeeees.*"

Rory could hardly move his head, but he turned it to the right as far as the thing's grip would allow it. Maybe an inch.

"Moooom!" he called. His voice was choked. He doubted she'd hear him. Even if she were right outside the door. He brought in another breath. He held it a minute, gathering his energy. "Moooom!"

"Moooooommm," the scraping metal voice whined loudly, mimicking him. It started out quietly, and repeated the panic in his voice back to him, growing louder and louder.

There was no answer to such a sound. Rory's breath came in gasps. He lay very still. He listened, straining his ears, reaching through the silence. He searched for someone familiar stirring; anyone who could hear him.

He squeezed his eyes shut. *Help, help, help.*

He heard the shadow figure shift as it moved, and he opened his eyes again. Its head was tilted the same way as his, toward the door.

The scraping metal sound spoke again. "Whattt . . . is this?"

Was the figure talking to him again? Why was it looking at the door?

"Wha—" Rory started to ask. Maybe it didn't want him. A machine, it said. *What machine does it want? I'll give it anything. Anything to make it leave.*

The door handle rattled slightly, but didn't open. Rory stared hard into the dark. The knob twisted back and forth, not fully turning. The door was already open just a crack. An energy was there, more familiar than the alien energy of the shadow figure. It felt like the energy of a person.

Just as he had the thought, a pale translucent face pushed straight through the solid door; one sunken eye was open wide, rolling around wildly in the cavernous socket, orienting itself with the room.

Rory gasped, focusing harder. It made no sense.

"Yyyou," the shadow thing said.

It quickly adjusted itself like it was going to crab-walk backwards, away from Rory. Then it leaned forward again tentatively, watching.

Rory looked back in that direction. The transparent figure now stood—in full—to his right. It resembled a human, though part of its face looked blasted apart. A crater shone in the scant moonlight where one of its eyes would have been. It wasn't looking at him. Its attention was fixed on the shadow figure.

The shadow figure slipped off the bed, moving between Rory and the disfigured ghost. It reached toward the door, as if to wedge its hand in and pull it open. The ghost reached in the same direction, and it clicked firmly shut.

"Go away!! Go somewhere else," Rory told them, his tiny voice not convincing anybody.

A shuddering sound rattled the quiet room. Wood squeaking against wood. Rory's window opened slowly with quick jerky motions. It finally stopped when it reached the top of the frame. The shadow moved toward it, limbs moving in quick jolts. Immediately after, it slammed shut.

"Are you going to hurt me?" Rory asked the specter.

Its mouth stretched wide; an oblong oval. It fed its despair to Rory like a punch to the chest. He couldn't stop staring.

"You're sad? Is that how you felt? When you died?"

The ghost nodded.

"How did you die?" he asked, fear still prickled inside his skull, but curiosity gripped him harder, now.

It put its index and middle finger together, pointing into its mouth.

"What's that? Did your mouth get shot?" he asked, incredulous. They didn't even do that in the movies.

It nodded.

The fear gripped him harder, encasing his throat. A human adult, anyone he'd ever encountered, would never tell him something like that.

Still, he had to learn more. "How come you're here?" he asked.

Immediately, the figure vanished. It was so sudden, Rory wondered if it had even been there at all. Everything felt exactly like it always did. The quick return to normalcy felt almost more alien to him than everything that had just occurred.

Rory dropped back onto his pillow, waiting for his heart rate to return to normal. He placed his hands on his chest. His head was still tilted up, looking around, watching for anything else to appear.

The feeling of normalcy remained.

***

Stanton woke to three soft knocks at his door.

A whispered voice spoke: "Are you up?"

Stanton rubbed his face and dropped his hands again. *Am I dreaming?*

The voice spoke again, sharply. "Hey!"

Stanton turned his head. It was dark, but clearly, a small face was an inch from his own. He heard an inhale, an exhale, and then smelled horrible morning breath. He sat stark upright.

"Hey! Did you brush before bed?"

"Yup."

"Are you okay?"

"Scared."

Stanton turned fully toward Rory. "Yeah? How come?"

"I saw something. A shadowy person. Or like a person, but not. They came on my bed. Then a weird ghost saved me."

"Soo . . . a bad dream?"

"Not a dream. The ghost was scary too, but the dark shape was hurting me. Can we go in the living room and turn on the lights? I wanna get away from there."

"Uh, sure." Waking up whenever a kid can't sleep. This is what it's like. Just this once was kicking his ass. The clock said 2 a.m. and his face felt melted with sleep. He shuffled to his slippers and rubbed his face again. He turned and Rory was still standing in the same spot, staring at him. Stanton gestured lazily. "Go ahead, I'll follow you."

167

They walked into the dark living room. Rory crossed the room, heading toward the light switch by Rachelle's door.

At the last second, Stanton saw someone standing next to the light switch.

"Rory!" he hissed. "*Come back here!*"

"Why?" Rory whispered back. He flipped the switch.

"Ah!" Rory and Stanton breathed in tandem. James was there, standing right next to Rory.

"Shh!" James held his finger to his lips. "Shut up! Rachelle's sleeping. I mean, your mom's sleeping."

"You don't tell a kid to shut up!" Stanton hissed. "What are you *doing* standing there in the dark?!"

"Something's in this house."

"It's okay," Rory said. "It was two things. They're gone now."

"What?" Stanton felt like an outsider. His heart started pounding. "Rory! You just had a dream . . . right? Nobody's here?" he started to turn toward Rory's room. Would be better to investigate.

"Not a dream. I told you. But they're gone. *Really*," Rory assured him. "James? How did you know they were here?"

"I uh—" James eyed Stanton before he looked at Rory. "I heard a noise."

"I didn't hear anything," Stanton said.

"What did you see?" James ignored Stanton.

"He said a shadow thing that wasn't a . . . thing? And a ghost," Stanton reported.

"Shit," James whispered sharply.

"James!" Stanton rasped, incredulous. "The *kid!*"

"I know they're gone," Rory repeated. "I know they're gone because the ghost like . . . made the shadow thing leave. Like it was helping me." He shuddered. "But they both *really* scared me, and now I don't want to sleep."

"Do you know anyone who died recently?"

"No," Stanton and Rory said.

"Okay, disappeared, then?"

"Why?" Stanton's stomach dropped. He thought about Javier. "*Why?*"

James continued. "Someone good? Who would see a kid in trouble and try to help?"

"What the hell is going on here?" Stanton felt his face getting red. "Last I heard, these things don't happen. Now you're talking to a kid like his weird dream really happened."

"Sorry, I've seen too many things to not believe him."

"What? Like shadows in abandoned buildings with your ghost hunting? Imagined disembodied voices? You're gonna scare the kid."

"Stanton."

Stanton rubbed his face. His voice was weak. "What?"

"You asked me why when I mentioned a disappearance. Your face went stone serious for a sec. Can I ask *you* why?"

Silence settled over the room. The furnace turned off and the air was still. *Fucking hell.* Stanton jutted out his jaw. It wasn't like him to avoid things. But this was fantastical. This was nonsense. *Right?*

"Stanton, come on, man. We need to talk about this."

"I just . . . I got the worst feeling when you asked if someone disappeared. My friend's been missing for a week. I have to check on him."

James sighed now. "Need some company?"

"Whatever. Yeah." Stanton headed to the coat hanger by the door.

"What are you guys doing?" Rory asked.

"Just taking a quick trip, kid." James' voice sounded unnaturally kind. "We'll be back soon. Why don't you go in your mom's room? Try and get back to sleep."

Rory looked to Stanton, who nodded toward Rachelle's room. Rory pivoted and headed in, gently shutting the door.

16

They approached a ranch, midway down a wide street with double yellow lines.

It was a neighborhood that could easily be mistaken for Rachelle's, 60s-style houses, impressively well-kept for how tiny they were. Some had obvious little additions, a craftsman door, or windows flanked by custom shutters. Flat mailboxes sat next to everyone's front doors.

Here and there were hints of original outdated embellishments. Square glass blocks decorated bathroom windows. Detached garages sat over and back between houses.

James parked in the street. They both stepped out of the car and headed up the drive. The siding glowed powder blue in the moonlight. Stanton walked along Javier's black pickup truck in the driveway and peered in, head tilted down, checking for clues.

As they turned up the front walk, something glinted in a nearby bush. A set of keys caught the moonlight. A pack of Parliaments in the mulch underneath.

Stanton poked the pack with his toe, and it made a scraping sound against the small cement stoop. He turned toward James, staring at the blue-and-white box as he spoke. "Last week, I came and knocked a few times. Back when he first stopped showing up to work. His car was here, but nobody answered. I didn't see these when I was here." Dread gripped Stanton's throat. His mouth felt hot and he swallowed his spit. The feeling, the horrible flavor, remained.

"Well, I'm gonna call the police." Stanton took his cell phone from his back pocket. "If you want to go home to get some sleep, I'm sure someone would give me a ride home."

"I mean, let's just go in and see what there is to see."

"What if there's someone in there?"

"C'mon. It's been a week. Nobody's there." James walked up the step next to Stanton. He pushed the door gently with his fingertips and the door swung open.

A sick smell rushed out at them. It wrapped itself around them, beckoning them in.

James gagged and pulled the door closed again. He breathed the outdoor air, trying to dilute the smell.

"*Fuck.*" Stanton covered his mouth and turned away.

"I never get used to that," James said as he inhaled again.

Stanton was still turned away. "Used to it?" he asked James, facing the wall.

James didn't answer.

"Something in there is dead," Stanton said flatly. His chest was tight, like his heart was being squeezed. *Knew I should have assumed the worst. Should have just walked right in the day after the kid went missing. Could've done more. And now, this.*

James nodded slowly. "Yep," he said quietly. "Nothing else smells like that."

Stanton let out a long sigh. "Well, I can't wait for the police. I gotta know now. So we're going in."

The room Stanton had visited so many times felt unfamiliar now. The warm yellow walls, the floor-to-ceiling gray wood bookshelves, the pictures Corry had put up. Blue agave. Purple and green succulents. Everything was just as he'd remembered. And now this dark heaviness that blanketed the furniture. The room. The air around him. That was new.

He wondered if it had anything to do with whatever terrible thing was waiting, in some unknown room, to be found. Not a who, but a what. Just an object now.

A matter of perspective, blackening this place.

Something drew his eye down near his feet. A dried puddle of vomit.

Did Javier get some kind of fatal food poisoning? But where was Corry? Had they both eaten the same thing and died somewhere in the house? He wished he'd come in here earlier. What if Javi was still alive when Stanton had come by? He could have called an ambulance. He could have helped.

"Let's check the kitchen," he said reluctantly to James.

James was just stepping in the door. "Oh, wow," James breathed as he entered. "It doesn't feel great in here."

Stanton nodded stiffly, lips pressing tight together.

"Just take your time. And brace yourself," James instructed.

Stanton walked slowly. He'd never felt fear like this before. The moment before he entered the kitchen was excruciating. He pictured Javier, dead. Doubled over next to the sink. Facedown at the table. Lifeless for days, the sun rising, then setting, his vacant body completely still and alone in the pitch black. No one to observe, or find him.

Stanton's jaw was tight and twitching. He took a deep breath and stepped forward, peering into the kitchen.

A body lay there, next to the stove.

Stanton flipped the light on and stared. His brain wouldn't allow the reality of it.

That's him, he thought, and explained out loud to himself. "It's Javier."

He lay curled up on his side. His posture seemed relaxed, like he was sleeping, his face turned away from them, toward the stove. He still had his coat on.

"God, Stanton. I'm *sorry*, man."

"Thanks," Stanton said the word slowly, feeling the sounds in his mouth. He stepped in gingerly and leaned over the body. "I mean . . . I think."

Stanton recoiled. "Part of his face is gone, but it's him. This is his coat, too." He grimaced. That sour taste was back in his mouth. It almost seemed to mimic the smell of death. Of Javi.

"Who would do this??" Stanton shook his head, his face cast down to the floor. He felt like he'd lost a kid. *What was all this for?* He was born, taught how to walk, speak, be a person. He went to school. He revolted from his upbringing. Escaped their poisonous influence. All to be snuffed out in his early thirties.

Stanton worried that someone from that cult had found Javier and punished him for leaving.

"Uh, Stanton?"

"Yeah," he answered with a statement.

"I mean, the gun is next to his hand. Was he struggling, mentally?"

"No. He was fine! Why? What are you saying? He doesn't even own a gun."

"Okay, maybe it's not his. Maybe he borrowed it?"

Stanton straightened his shoulders very slightly as he turned to glower at James.

James met his gaze nervously, his eyes shifting away and back, away and back. "I mean, all I'm saying is what it looks like."

Stanton's stare continued. "He didn't kill himself. He wouldn't."

Stanton stared at the body some more. "Hey." He hit James on the shoulder with the back of his hand. "The crushed cigarettes. The keys outside."

James nodded. His eyes glinted in recognition.

"He fell down or something outside and dropped stuff. Then he went in the house. He's still wearing his coat. Something weird happened here. Who comes in from being out and then runs into their house to off themselves?" Stanton said.

"Yeah." James rubbed his hands together, looking down, thinking more. "He would have seen something, or someone who he didn't expect. There's another layer here. Something big is missing. I think he killed himself but didn't act alone."

"First of all, how could he kill himself without acting alone? And secondly, I don't know how you could know that." Stanton left the kitchen and checked the whole house for Corry.

"She's not here. Corry's not here," Stanton said quietly.

It was quiet for a minute.

"Stanton?" James asked.

"Yeah"

"I'm going to tell you something that you're not going to believe, or like. Then I'm going to do something that will make you believe me, and dislike me even more."

Stanton looked at James warily. "What are you talking about?" He shook his head, exhausted.

"Do you trust me?"

"No. But now you've gotta tell me what you were going to say."

"You're *really* not going to like it. Will you go with whatever I do?"

Stanton leaned his head back wearily. "What are you going to do? Burn down his house? He's dead. What could *possibly* make this worse?"

James laughed quietly.

Stanton glared at him again.

"Sorry."

Stanton continued glaring.

"It isn't the situation it's—"

"*Yes, I know.* I get it, okay? Do what you're gonna do. Tell me your weird secret."

"It's kind of a life cheat, I guess you'd say."

"You're going to bring him back to life?"

"Stanton, I'm going to temporarily revive your friend."

"James, what in the *fuck* are you into?"

"Hear me out. We want to find out what happened, right?"

"*Yes.*" Stanton's tone was urgent, impatient.

"So, this is my thing. This is what I do."

"What? Playing God? *Magic?*"

"I mean, *yeah.* To the second thing. Magic."

"You know that's crazy, right?"

"I *knew* that's what you were going to say—"

"Because you're clairvoyant, too?"

"No. Let me finish. I knew, because you are fucking dreadful-serious *all* the time. But most of all, because I've heard people tell me the same thing. *Exactly* that same thing, every time I tell them this."

"Is this going to hurt him?"

"Probably."

"But we will find out who did this to him?"

"Again, *probably.*"

"And things will go back to the way they were? Him, dead, and not in pain?"

"Yep."

Stanton rubbed his palms together, standing quietly. After about a minute, he nodded, slowly. "Okay, let's do it then."

James slipped his hand into the collar of his shirt, and pulled out a necklace, bringing it to the outside of his shirt. He let it drop. Stanton glanced at it. A silver talisman with a star set inside a square, and rings drawn around it with writing, pluses or crosses in between each one. It hung from a thin black leather necklace.

James saw him eyeing it. "For protection," he explained. James looked around the kitchen, pulling some drawers open, pushing utensils around.

"What are you doing?"

"I need a long thin object, for the ritual."

"The ritual. Right." Stanton rolled his eyes.

After a minute, James headed to the living room. Stanton waited, watching him through the kitchen entryway. James stood at the spot where the living room began. He looked around, and finally shrugged, walked to the fireplace and grabbed a poker from the hearth.

"What are you going to do with it?" Stanton asked when James walked in with it.

"I'll show you." James closed his eyes. He stood with his arms out. One flat palm over the body, and his other hand gripping the poker, he began to speak in a loud voice.

"By the mysteries of the deep, by the flames of Banal, by the Power of the East and the silence of the night—"

Stanton sighed. "No offense, but is this needed?"

"If it wasn't, would I be doing it?" James pressed his lips together, then continued. "By the Holy Rites of Hecate, I conjure you, distressed spirit, to present yourself here. Reveal the cause of your calamity; why did you offer violence to your own life? Where are you now in being?"

Nothing happened. They watched, and waited. Stanton shifted uncomfortably, crossing and uncrossing his arms.

James took the poker and tapped the body with it gently. Stanton counted nine times. As he tapped it, he continued.

"I conjure you, Javier, to answer my demands. I conjure and bind you to answer what I will ask of you."

The silence was broken by the rustling of clothes. The sound was coming from the floor. Stanton was stricken, in disbelief, as the body's head bowed down, then slowly turned up toward the ceiling, like someone being gently woken from a deep sleep. As Javier's face rotated toward the harsh kitchen light, Stanton saw the good eye was still closed. The left side looked even worse than when he'd first looked at it. Unnatural. Not like Javier in life, but a mask made to look like his face.

As soon as it moved, he could tell something was horribly wrong. Skin was sucking in at the neck. It tried again. The body was trying to take in breath. The feet were bucking in desperation. The hands grabbed at the neck, but nothing was going to help.

James looked down. "You can't breathe, you're dead," he said quickly, trying to placate it. "Just hang on. Just relax."

"James! What the fuck?" Stanton shouted. His thoughts stumbled over each other, his heart thudded. *What did I expect? For nothing to happen, that's what I expected.* "What's going on? What did you do," Stanton demanded. Sweat prickled his head. "He's in pain. Help him!"

"No, just wait. I already told you it'd hurt him. This is all nervous system. Reflexes. Hang on."

Stanton crouched down and grabbed Javi by the shoulders. "Javi! *Javi!*" Stanton was gasping with him, in fear for his friend. "It's okay! Hang on. It'll be okay."

"Do *not* touch him," James cautioned, his tone was grim and forbidding. He pulled at Stanton's arm.

"I have to! Have to help him." Stanton waved James away.

"I'm telling you. Get *away* from him. I've got this."

Stanton leaned forward and put a supporting hand on the back of Javier's head. "Just hold on, Javi. It's going to be okay. It'll be over soon."

Dead Javier half-turned stiffly, grabbing Stanton's wrist and pinning it to the ground. Stanton tried to pull back with his arm, then his shoulder, then his whole body, but all his strength was dwarfed by Javi's fist.

"Jesus Christ, how are you this strong?" Stanton choked. He lost his balance, falling on his ass from the crouching position he'd been in. The body was still pulling for air. Calling on all long-failed organs to function, and growing increasingly more desperate. It took Stanton's arm in both hands and dragged Stanton closer.

Stanton looked into Javi's face. The one remaining eye was open. It was sunken, but it was Javi's. The eye pleaded to him for something he couldn't offer.

"I'm sorry, I can't help you. I don't know—"

"Stanton. The body is freaking out. The spirit is traveling back to the body. It'll be here shortly."

"Shortly?" Stanton growled. "He was my fucking *friend*. How long is shortly?"

James reached in to try and help. Javi's arm shot out, fingers outstretched. They clamped around James' necklace. The powerful fist yanked hard. James cried out and pitched forward. The black cord came undone, and the talisman landed with a tiny tap on the vinyl tile.

Javier let go of Stanton and grabbed James by the chin, fingers flexing hard against his jaw. Immediately on contact, James dropped like a dead bug. His back arched. Fingers curled and stiffened, his eyes nothing but fluttering lids over white-yellow orbs. His mouth opened wide in a silent scream.

17

"What are you listening to?"

Javier looked up at Corry, confused. He'd been listening to thrash metal for the past hour, wearing his headphones. He looked down to make sure they were plugged in. But they weren't.

How had he missed that?

He cleared his throat.

"Slayer," he croaked.

"That's your angry music. Everything okay?"

Her black hair hung in a loose ponytail that kind of contoured her chin as she tilted her head to the side.

"Yep."

He forced a smile.

It wasn't.

"Javi? Come on. It's been a week since I found out. Are we gonna talk about this, or no?"

He sighed. The last thing he'd wanted was to attract attention to his current mood.

"Please, we gotta talk about it. I've been sleeping really bad. I'm *so* fucked up about this."

"I just wish you'd have gotten tested back when that happened to you. You can't make things disappear by ignoring them."

Corry's eyes widened, angry tears welling up. She swallowed. "I didn't *ask* for this to happen to me. I just— I just couldn't deal. You know?"

"No, I know. My god, I know, baby. Me too. It's just— taking me time, that's all."

"I'm sorry if you got it," she whispered. "I'm so sorry. It makes me sick to think . . ."

"We'll find out soon," he said, quietly. Trying to keep his voice even.

It was quiet for a while. Her arms were crossed, her gaze fixed on the floor.

"You're the first person I ever told."

He tried to talk over his anger.

"I'm so sorry it happened to you. I am. I didn't know why you were seeing a therapist. I thought it was just regular stuff."

She shook her head. "I don't know what I wanted to hear. I just wanted more support. Like, I literally told *no one*. Not even my mom." Her voice got choked as she tried to say mom.

He didn't say anything for a while.

"What are you thinking?"

He felt angry, but like he really needed her at the same time. He didn't know how to express it. "I don't know. I don't even know." He rubbed his hair and stared out the window. "We'll figure it out. We always do." His throat hurt. It felt tight, like he was clenching it. He tried to relax, but couldn't.

He waited for her to respond. She was pensive. Still staring blankly at the floor.

"Was it anyone I knew, back there?"

"No."

"Do you think we could adopt?" he asked after a while of quiet. *She has to be wondering, too. I mean, it's our future.*

Her eyes flicked up to him.

"Not *now*, Javi."

She blinked rapidly, her eyes squishing in what looked like disappointment.

"Well, one day, maybe?"

"I *meant* I'm not ready to *talk* about that now."

She sniffed and pushed on her nose with the back of her hand.

He felt dense for asking too soon. Dense, and jealous that expressing feelings came so easy to her. He was taught to repress everything. Sub sadness for anger. That was all he was allowed to show. *If it weren't for that, I could probably help her more. I'd say the right things. Be better for her,* he thought and still, nothing.

So he sat and watched her. And she stood quietly for a long time. Probably waiting for some sort of reassurance.

"I'm sorry. I wish I knew what to say. But I don't."

The music hammered on between them. Sibling guitars wailed against each other as she left the room. An hour later, he heard the front door shut.

When he got up and checked the closet, her sleep-away bag was gone.

She finally texted him back that night. She needed some space. She was going to drive up to her parents' that night. He didn't know how to reply so he'd pushed it off for later.

***

He got the call a day later that she hadn't made it to her parents'. They'd found Corry on the side of the road. She was already gone. Police thought she must have fallen asleep at the wheel.

I'm why she left. I'm why she was tired. Why didn't I just talk to her? She needed me.

He hung up and blocked out all sound. He didn't leave the house. He pretended to forget everything outside.

One day, there was banging on his door. He heard his name being shouted, the last syllable higher-pitched; an open-ended question. His name was the one word that echoed against walls and walls of blank, gray thoughts.

After a few days, he ate and slept, a little. When he slept, he dreamt of her, motionless, her neck craned downward like she was concentrating on something. But the rest of her was just a big mound of wild black hair crushed against the steering wheel. He'd call out to her and beg for her, but not want her to respond at the same time. Eventually, she'd lift her head up slowly to look at him. And everything was crushed. Her nose pushed into her face, her eye sockets and mouth stretchy and bloated in a hideous death mask.

He'd wake up, his face covered in tears. Heaving up nothing. In those moments after waking, he felt he'd do this every night. Picture her and want her and look for her. But never find her. Not ever again.

***

A week passed. He woke up on the couch and looked at the clock on the wall. 4 a.m. His normal life suddenly rushed back to him. In an hour, he'd usually be getting ready to get the delivery truck and deliver fish to the restaurant. He looked over to the old glass-topped coffee table, littered with crumpled paper towels and used paper plates. He slapped a palm over his cell phone. He pushed the tiny button on the side with his thumb.

The battery was dead. He knew Stanton would have taken over his route, and decided to meet up with him at his first delivery point that morning.

His bare feet squished the stiff scratchy carpet and he rubbed his short black hair. He'd showered yesterday, but hadn't put any product in it, so it felt all fluffy. He decided he'd better go tell Stanton what was going on. He was pretty sure Stanton was the one who'd come knocking. He still wasn't ready to tell another person, sit through their reaction, assure them he'd be fine. But he knew he had commitments, and had to go back outside.

They knew each other well. He knew what time Stanton would be there. That he'd stop there first, hoping to run into the quietest sous chef. Stanton liked quiet people. But he had to hurry. Most mornings Jimmy was there, finishing up the dishes. For that reason, Stanton would be quick to drop off and leave. He planned to let Stanton know he'd be gone another week, and after that, he'd be back. He wanted to visit with Corry's family and see if there was anything they needed.

Javier grabbed his keys from the bowl by the front door. He pulled his boots on while standing up, working his feet in without untying the shoes. He grabbed his pack of Parliaments, pressing his keys against them to hang on to both. He brought the front door toward him to close it, his head leaned down as he pulled it 'til it clicked. He leaned into the storm door as he stepped down.

As both feet landed on the front stoop, he stopped.

It was super dark outside. Early-morning dark, as expected. But an unnatural stillness had taken hold of him. A strange quiet. A feeling of absolute dread. Of something there. Something in him was telling him not to look up. He heard a sound of scraping leaves. It was loud and sharp. Startled, he looked up to see no leaves. His eyes settled on his car. He could barely make it out in the dark; his eyes were adjusting.

Suddenly, he saw it.

A person stood in front of the driver's door. A person, but not. There was nothing to make out within the basic contour of itself against what lay behind it. The entire composition was just shadow. Darker than the early morning, darker than the night. It had no eyes, but he still felt it watching him.

Javi couldn't feel anything other than dread and disbelief. He stared and felt like he couldn't stop.

He scrambled. Fell. Hit the back of his head against the door. He lifted his arm for leverage to push himself up. The heavy old storm door banged into his side. The deadened pain held his wounds. He wasn't moving fast enough. It was getting closer.

Javier regained his footing to lift his backside off the stoop. He turned around to push himself up with his hands. He needed to get inside. And fast.

It was at his side. Pushing him. Lifting him. Terror washed over him. A sick, desperate longing wafted off the thing. Like it wanted him. Needed him. But not in any way he'd experienced. Not like women he'd been with. But like a hunger, like it wanted all of him. It wanted to eat the essence. The energy that held him up. The light that tethered him to this plane.

An impossible weight settled against his back.

Slowly, it was shoving him, hard, into the door. He struggled and swore, but in seconds, the side of his face, his head, his whole body was pushed up against it. He felt a pressure slide up his hand, down his fingers. It thrust his hand forward, jamming his knuckles against the bottom of the doorknob.

A frustrated hissing sound came from behind him. It banged his hand again into the doorknob. This time, much harder.

He shouted as the muscles in his hand worked to re-coil toward him, a reaction to the pain. But the grip on his hand was iron, and it didn't move an inch from where the thing held him. Hoping desperately to avoid that feeling a third time, he grabbed the knob. It relented—he assumed—because it was pleased with what he was doing.

Terror and adrenaline burned in him. He raced through his options. It needed him to turn the doorknob. In that sense, he was still in his own element and had an awareness of this location that far exceeded this creature's.

He tried to think through the fear. Through the disbelief, the impossibility of the situation.

He turned the knob and opened the door. It was trying to isolate him. It wanted to get him alone so it could . . . what? Have him?

It lurched awkwardly into the house, leading with a very large step in. He tried to assess where it was going to bring him. It held him there in the entryway. Then he felt it release him.

He stood still, temporarily in control of himself. He turned behind him. Nobody there. He turned back to the inside of his living room.

An unending darkness eclipsed his line of vision. Everything was quiet. He felt a crackle of energy, heard a loud hum, like a giant deafening furnace kicking on. Just when he thought his ears couldn't bear the sound to grow any louder, he felt it. A colossal force shoved him backwards, and his feet were off the ground. His head and upper back bashed into the front door, slamming it closed. His vision bleached completely, quickly. From the center, out. Like a white explosion. He lifted his head up, disoriented, his hand cradling the air around it, and shook his head to regain his senses.

A sudden, intense lethargy came upon him, and his mind tumbled into night.

***

He opened his eyes. The room was still dark. His mouth tasted like ass. He closed it, moved his tongue around. Didn't help.

The back of his head was sore. He was laying right on it, but was afraid to roll over. Afraid to exacerbate the pain. He lifted it very slightly off the floor. Nausea came immediately. He rolled onto his side and threw up. It was all over the wood floor, but some was on the side of his face. He groaned, wiped his face with his jacket sleeve.

He blinked. His eyelids felt heavy. The dark thing wasn't on him anymore. He prayed that it had gone away. But he lifted his head and saw it immediately. A humanoid shape right next to the TV. Almost looked like a human's shadow on the wall. The minute he looked at it, it floated toward him. Like it had been stationed there. Waiting for him.

"No," he croaked quietly. It wasn't going anywhere. He couldn't bear the thought of what this thing was going to do. Or make him do. He couldn't let it have him.

He forced himself up, slowly pushing the ground with both hands. *If I'm not in here*, he thought. *If I don't stay in this body, it'll have no use for me.*

He pitched forward quickly; a drunk runner at the starting line. His stomach lurched, and he gagged. His walk was quick but clumsy.

The dark energy prickled right behind him. Javi reached the kitchen, grabbing the threshold with his left hand, leaning all his weight against it. His busted head tipped forward into his other hand.

The loud humming sound began again. He didn't even turn around. He squeezed the ancient wood paneling around the doorway with both hands, gritting his teeth with the effort. He waited for the impact. Adrenaline rushed his concussed skull. His head throbbed with it.

A hard shove wracked his shoulder. He shouted in surprised pain as the old paneling cracked in his hand. He was airborne for a moment, a medium splintered chunk of wood in his fist. He fell hard on his right side, barely managing to keep his head from hitting the ground.

It was on all fours when he looked back at it, just coming back up to stand. It walked slowly toward him, taking its time. He reached for the oven handle, moving to hoist himself up. The oven door opened, and he fell down again. He looked up. The figure stood still, seeming to observe him curiously. He shoved the oven closed. He grabbed the edge of the stovetop, hoisting himself up. He reached into the upper cabinet, fumbling around until he felt the hard steel.

Quickly, he gripped the gun. Corry was the one who'd loaded it before they'd cut and run from the compound. He'd never shot it before, but he had to act fast. The thing was advancing on him now.

Just do it. Now.

He cocked the hammer back. The gun felt heavy and the trigger, stiff. He gripped it in both hands and pulled with all his strength.

The figure reached for his right arm. The one that gripped the handle.

NOW.

A boom rattled his skull. The kickback banged the heel of his hand, hard. His hands felt hot. The gun felt even heavier than before. He lowered the gun and stared at the thing. The goddamn thing still stood. Its hands had moved to its belly. Javier's breath came faster. It was hardly reacting.

Fuck, I gotta go. As Javier moved to the side, the thing looked up. It grabbed his forearms so hard he thought his bones would break.

No, no, no. He was afraid to look up. He couldn't. His chin was to his neck. His eyes closed. *Hang on to the gun,* he told himself, though he didn't know why. It hadn't worked when he'd shot the thing. What good would it do him now?

Something touched his lips, then spread across them. It flowed like liquid but was hard, like the thing holding his wrists. It opened his mouth, and surged up his nose.

"Aah," Javier cried out. He felt the pressure in his mouth now, too. It was filling him. Fast. Spreading through his torso. Soon it'd take his limbs. All of him.

It's going to kill me fast, or it's going to have me and stay there, he told himself. *I can't let it. There's no time.*

With great effort, Javier lifted the gun to his head.

***

He was weightless. The pain and fear dissolved. He was still in his kitchen but the floor had pulled away from his feet. He hovered there, staring down at it.

A translucent yellow flashed in front of him. It crashed its fist into the skull of the shadow figure. A ghost in a yellow jumpsuit pummeled the form into the ground with one punch.

"Corry!" he screamed.

"Javi!" she returned. He heard her voice and saw her face in double. They were like echoes.

"Go! Run!" she shouted, her eyes squeezed shut. The thing was moving. It grabbed her arms. Trying to pull itself up from inside the kitchen floor, where she had buried it with her fist.

He wanted to talk to her, to tell her he was sorry. That he loved her. He looked down at what he knew was his own body. It lay there on its side like it was sleeping, the gun an inch from the outstretched fingers. Blood flashed red, coating and cascading down the cabinets like too much paint. Bits of brain were stuck in spots to the doors.

"Javi!" she said again. "Now!" She was straddling it. Its arms traveled up hers, to her neck.

"No." He shook his head, looked down at his new form. Translucent. He was like her now, wasn't he? Maybe he could help. He rushed to her side, and crouched over its head, shoving its face back down through the floor. "No! Can it get you?"

193

"I think so." She paused. "It's trying to." She looked down at its hands. They grabbed her wrists weakly. "Step on its arms."

He did as Corry said, staring down at the thing. Watching the weird ridged matte-black hands flex helplessly against his transparent feet. He still applied effort to constrain it, but it was more balance than muscle. Evening out his weightlessness against the natural pull of the earth.

Where had the strangeness in all this been hiding? That reality gripped him, now. "I'm dead," he said to her. He was on the other side of his human life cycle. And somehow now that he died, he was stronger than this thing that tried to take him. He looked at the shadow figure, half in the floor, half out. "What's down there? Hell?" he asked his dead girlfriend.

"No," she looked uncertain. Then she looked in his eyes. Hers were solid black. "I don't know."

"How did you get here?" he asked.

She shrugged. "I felt something was wrong with you, and then I wasn't with my family. I was here. You're dead," she said, as if suddenly processing his earlier statement. She looked down at his body as she said it.

"So are you," he sobbed. He couldn't feel his face, but still. He felt like he was crying, hard.

"It's okay, we're okay," she told him.

"Yeah," he said. "We're something." He didn't know what else to say.

They looked at each other for a minute. He'd have to get used to her new form.

The ground rumbled. A quiet hummed melody filtered up from the dirt. But how could that be heard indoors? The song was not in any language, but it shook him. Told him the floor was nothing. A construct. Slain trees and smooth, hardened sludge. A temporary structure. Green criss-cross lines were gliding gently, slowly just underneath that floor. They slid to the side, vibrated, then pulled back up. A dance to match the melody.

The criss-cross lines stretched on and on. He followed them. A young person was alone nearby, and running. Separated from their mother. They needed help. Javier felt Stanton nearby, just past the child.

"That's the call," Corry's voice startled him. "The earth's calling you someplace. That's what happened to me right before. Before I showed up here."

"If I leave to do something, will we see each other again?" he asked. The very human, consuming pull he felt toward Corry was gone. He felt fondness, and wanted to see her again. But no drive to keep her near. He assumed she was experiencing the same.

"I hope so. I have to go back by my family. I was trying to find a way to tell my niece I'm okay without scaring the shit out of her. She can't stop crying."

"Okay. I hope you figure it out. Tell her I say hi."

Corry looked down at his body again. "Tell her my dead ex who just offed himself says hi. Now *that* would be fucking disturbing."

He smiled. "I'll miss ya."

"You too, Hedgehog." She smiled back and was gone.

James' eyes had never closed, but it was like a slide had been changed in his brain. He was lying flat on the floor of Javier's kitchen again. His head felt like it was full of cotton. A familiar feeling. His eyes felt dry, too. Like superballs packed with sand. He blinked repeatedly and lifted his head. A quiet groaning sounded to his left.

"Awh, shit!" The dead hand wasn't on his face anymore. Instead, it was squeezing the damned life out of his wrist. Stanton was crouched over the both of them, his face contorted in sheer panic.

"How long was I out?"

He sat up slowly. The hand unclenched ever so slightly, then released and moved to the dead thing's chest, like the arm was cradling itself. Javier's body seemed to be hunching inward, curling up.

"Uhm." Stanton's face stayed the same. His eyes wandered the room, as though he were trying to remember how to talk.

"You were right. Sweet kid," James nodded to Stanton.

"Nice kid? He never said anything. You just passed out." Confusion wrestled with the panic now. "I thought you were *dying*."

"Sorry, that must've been harrowing." James tried to show remorse on his face, but his wrist killed and he felt like he'd crawled into his worst hangover. "He pulled me into his memories. My necklace usually protects from that. But your friend broke it." He hoisted himself up quickly and retrieved his talisman.

"Do you mind?" he asked Stanton, extending the necklace toward him.

"Would *you* mind? Could you like fix my friend first?"

Stanton gestured down at Javi. Suddenly, he bent over, breathing heavily and pressing his hands on his thighs.

"You okay, man?" James asked quietly.

"No," Stanton whispered between breaths. He squeezed his eyes shut and was quiet.

"You're not gonna—"

"I thought I was. I think it's passing."

James patted Stanton awkwardly on the shoulder. "Good, good."

After a minute, Stanton stood back up. "So, about Javier."

"I promise you, I'm *about* to, but I need this on my person again before I restart, okay? Don't want to delve into another detour of this lovely young man's troubled skull."

Stanton eyed James sideways, then shrugged. "Whatever," he grumbled, leaning over to James and grabbing both ends of the string. "Is there no clasp on this?"

"No, it's just like a little rope thing. I tie it in a knot."

"That wasn't much of a knot. You were never *actually* in boy scouts, were you?"

"Ah, nope. I don't play well with others. Thought you could do better with your giant hands and tying all those boat knots or whatever."

"Boat knots?"

James laughed quietly. He grabbed a salt-shaker off the kitchen table and twisted off the lid. He muttered under his breath, creating a circle around the body with the salt.

He left an opening in the circle, and unearthed a bottle from his pocket. A little parfait of soil and tiny rocks. Sealed with a black skull and blood-red wax.

"What *is* that?"

"Oh, yeah. Sorry, I know it looks creepy. Just part of the ritual. Sacred soil and rocks. Helps guide his spirit away from the body again. I keep these on me just in case."

Stanton's eyebrows were furrowed. He stared intently at the bottle, not speaking. It was probably best not to know what he was thinking right in that moment. But there was enough strangeness flying left and right to assume the poor guy believed the bit about what the bottle was for. Hopefully he wouldn't think to research it later.

"That true?" was all Stanton said.

"Yeah." James looked Stanton in the eyes, challenging him. *C'mon, ask me more. I want you to.*

Stanton didn't say anything else. James removed the cork from the bottle and placed it between his teeth. He reached into his pocket, pulling out a string with a crystal pendulum.

"I need quiet for a few," he said to Stanton.

"Mm-hmm." Stanton watched him intently.

James closed his eyes and envisioned a strong rope stretching from the body to inside the bottle. He focused on his breathing.

"Who are you?" His mind echoed with the voice, more quickly than he expected.

"I'm called James," he replied, also in his mind.

"Why are you here?"

"I need you by my side. We're in trouble, and we'll need your help. I'm with your friend, Stanton."

"If you're with Stanton, I'll feel when you're in trouble. I can get there right away."

"Sorry, I don't do things that way."

"That bottle. You want to trap me in there?"

"In a sense. Let's just say I need you nearby. I've done this before. I'll know when it's the right time. Save your strength inside for when I call you."

"Why should I trust you? Why should I do it your way?"

"You sent the kid to Stanton to protect him. I promise you, they'll be fighting more than just shadow figures. I'll know. I'll call you when it's time."

"Okay?" The voice was hesitant. Then, resolute. "Okay."

"Follow what I've left for you. The pendulum will tell me when you're inside."

The rope was heavy in James' mind. It grew taut and shook. He opened his eyes. The pendulum swung wildly. He gripped the string on the pendulum as hard as he could. The vibrations grew tighter and tighter until the string was still and straight as an arrow.

James capped the bottle and moved it swiftly to his pocket.

"So, he's at peace now?" Stanton's eyes were watery.

"Yes, he's at peace."

Stanton stared at James, his eyes wide. "That was intense."

James sighed and wound the pendulum string around his hand and put it back in his pocket. "Do you have any questions?"

"When Javier touched you and you passed out? What was happening? You didn't just faint, you were convulsing. That's not just a medical thing?"

"Nope. I had a vision."

"So . . . in this vision, did you see what happened to him?"

"Uh-huh." James raced over the right wording. *This guy with no knowledge of magic at all prior just watched his friend come back from the dead, and now I have to feed him even more details.*

"Feel like *telling* me?" Stanton's face was growing red. James' heart kicked on faster. *Good thing I don't have an easy tell when I'm freaking out.*

"You wanted me to help him," James said evenly. "Right away. Didn't want to let you down."

"Okay, but can you tell me now what you saw?"

"Yeah."

Stanton widened his eyes at James. "*Well?*" His nose was flaring. He was fully incredulous.

James took a deep breath and held it. "He *did* kill himself. But to save himself from possession."

"Possession?" Stanton tilted his head back, looking hesitant. "Possession from what? Was someone trying to kidnap him?"

"Not a someone. A figure from . . . not from this plane."

"Okay. Can you just be more specific? I'm not into the same shit you are, obviously."

"I just don't know what you will accept from the story."

"You'll find out. Just lay it on me."

Stanton was quiet, staring at the floor while James explained it all. Javier leaving the house to go find Stanton, finding the shadow figure instead, being attacked, getting the gun, killing himself, and stopping the shadow figure with Corry. After he finished, Stanton didn't move or speak.

"Well?"

"So Javi was holed up in the house because Corry was dead."

"Yeah, and then after that, he was gone because—"

"—*he* was dead," they both said together.

"That part was kind of apparent before my little vision though?" James said sarcastically.

"No wonder he never showed," Stanton said quietly, crossing his arms and putting his hand to his mouth.

"Uh, yeah. We established that. He was dead." James was losing patience. "I think we need to pay some attention to the bigger issue."

"What, the shadow figure thing?"

"Uh huh," James responded, his eyes wide with impatience.

"What do you expect me to do?" Stanton asked. "I don't even know what that is. I didn't even know they existed."

"Well, who should I talk about this with instead? The wall? The five-year-old?"

"James? Try the adult who's the focal point of these types of visitations."

"Rachelle."

Stanton's reply was an exaggerated nod.

"Well yeah, at some point, I will. But when I do, I think I'm gonna try and rope you in with me."

18

Where in the blazing hell did everyone go, Rachelle wondered, puffy-eyed and tired on the couch in the front room. Rory came in and woke her up around two, and she'd been awake ever since. A morning glow crept in through the windows, but she'd given up on sleep an hour or so ago.

She held the weathered paper with Chad's handwriting in front of her. She'd folded and unfolded it a billion times. Re-read it, tried to make sense of it.

She'd planned to calmly ask where they'd been. But when Stanton and James finally showed up, she gave them her most dangerous withering glare.

"Where's Rory?" Stanton asked, his eyes skidding past her own the second he registered her expression.

"He's sleeping in my bed. He had a nightmare last night." Rachelle put her hands on her hips. "Where did you guys go? You look like shit, both of you."

"Thanks," James said coolly. "What's that paper you're clutching?"

"I mean, I don't know," she held it out to James. "Look at it. Tell me what you think."

James took it gingerly. "Where did you find it?" His voice was quiet, cautious. Unlike him.

"It was sticking out between the boards at the base of the radio, I had to be really careful not to rip it. It's in Chad's handwriting."

"Chad's?"

"Yeah. It looks like instructions. Like he was testing stuff when building the radio."

"That's a Celtic shield knot."

James raised his eyebrows; recognition leapt in his eyes.

"What?" Rachelle was hell-bent to find out why.

"What do you mean, 'what'? I'm still reading it," James said quickly.

"You went like this." Rachelle raised her eyebrows at James. "Like that had some special meaning."

"Oh, uh . . . I don't know. I think it's like a protective thing."

"What is?"

"A Celtic shield knot."

"Oh, sort of like your necklace?" *The thing you wear awake or asleep, showering or fucking? The thing that matches the one sitting in my purse?*

"My what? Oh that." James grabbed his necklace absentmindedly with one hand, held it, and let it drop again. "Yeah, I mean, I guess, sorta."

Rachelle stared at the necklace. "Is your necklace protective?"

James' eyes skipped across the ceiling. Rolling his eyes without rolling his eyes. "Yeah. It's like a superstitious thing, really, that's all."

"James, really?" Stanton prodded him, hands on his hips. He looked disgusted.

What the hell does Stanton know that I don't. And why are they suddenly best buddies, coming and going together? "You don't want to tell me," Rachelle said, annoyed. "Just admit it."

"No, it's not that, I—"

"Don't worry. I won't tell Stanton that you're a hippie dippie fucking witch or something."

"Yeah, thanks!" James said quickly. He took a sharp breath in.

Stanton was laughing quietly.

"Jee-zus!" Rachelle held her hands up, eyes flashing angrily. "I'm kidding?!" *What the fresh shit is so funny?*

"Sorry." James looked at her, his eyes softened.

Don't go for that. He's being smooth. Get answers. Rachelle shrugged at him. "Where did you guys come from with your ass feathers all ruffled??"

"You *don't* want to know," Stanton said, still swallowing breaths like an Olympian.

"What is it with you guys? According to you, I don't want to know *anything*. Maybe I shouldn't even leave the house? Are you worried I might break my ass or something?"

"Why do you keep saying *ass?*" James furrowed his brow and rubbed his fingers and thumb together against the paper. "I think there's like a second page to this." He separated another sheet from the top one and started to read it.

> TWISTING THE SPLICE INTO PROTECTIVE SHAPES = GOOD. CELTIC KNOT = BEST YET. NEEDS MORE WORK TO GET IT RIGHT.

> STORM IN THE AIR GETS QUIETER AS THE CELTIC KNOT GETS BETTER. BUT LAKE OF FIRE = FOR-EVER BURNING.

"Lake of fire . . ." Rachelle's quiet whisper was involuntary. Her whole body felt cold. The memories of Chad she'd always pushed away were bubbling up, uninvited. "What's that mean?"

"I mean biblically? It's hell. Does it ring a bell?" James gestured the paper toward her vaguely. His heart was galloping as he watched Rachelle.

"The last time I saw Chad, he said something about that. 'The lake of fire.' He said his dad was there. He was talking crazy."

She touched her eyebrow with her fingers and shook her head.

"Can you tell me more?"

James' eyes were trained on her. Waiting for her to feed him the info.

"You are very invested in this." Rachelle glared back at him.

"You got me there," he shrugged, twisting his lips to the side. "Listen, tell me this Chad story and I'll tell you what's been going on with me."

"I'll be happy to do that." Sarcastic emphasis on happy. "But be afraid of what'll happen if you don't live up to your end."

"I wouldn't dare doubt you. I'll do my best." He looked very serious. Not smooth serious, but dead serious.

Hopefully he could be trusted in the long run. She sighed. "I haven't thought about that day for years. At least you'll know I left for good reason."

***

They pulled into a motel and parked the car.

Rachelle licked her lips nervously. She was trying to escape the mood. Chad had stared out the window for the entire drive. At the stretch of desert. Staring through the mountains. Every thirty seconds or so, he'd repeated a sniffing sound. Each time, she had been pressing down the urge to react. To lash out.

After she parked, she turned to him.

"What's going on?" she asked him, then checked herself. Her voice had started out accusatory. Her patience had left her at some point on that silent drive.

"What do you mean?" he asked in monotone.

"Chad? Come on." She tipped her head, beckoning impatiently.

He sighed. "I need to go home," he said, looking at his lap.

Rachelle opened her mouth to speak, but disbelief stopped her.

"You realize we just got here, right?"

Her voice was growing louder. Her arms were crossed. She studied him. No observation came of it. No explanation.

"You didn't pack the radio, did you?"

"Yeah, of course. You asked me to, over and over. Then asked me if it was packed, over and over. I have it in my bag."

Chad shook his head slowly. "No. It's not here."

Rachelle closed her eyes and took a deep breath. "Why do you think I didn't bring it, Chad?"

"Because I can feel it's gone."

"You can—" Rachelle cut herself off and sighed again. Her eyes were still closed. That damn radio was absolutely in the car.

They sat in silence for a minute. "I know it doesn't make sense to you," he said quietly. "But I need that radio to feel normal." He paused. "It's a . . . weird issue I have. I know it's not normal. I know it doesn't make sense."

Rachelle held the bridge of her nose with thumb and pointer finger as she spoke. "Let's just bring everything in. We can look for it. We can check. I'll show you it's there."

"I really can't stay. It's not there. I'm telling you."

"Oh my god. Chad!" She started off speaking, and reached a scream by the time she got to his name. "You don't know. You can't know. You haven't checked. We haven't stopped since we left. I can *show* you that we have it. Will you believe me then?" Her voice was back to normal again. Now it had almost a soothing quality. Like she was talking patiently to a child. "And then maybe we can have a *vacation*. Maybe things can feel normal again."

He shook his head vehemently. "I thought getting away would help. I thought getting away from the lake would help. I knew it wasn't in the car but I didn't want to make you turn around. That was the wrong choice, though. I'm sorry." He wrung his hands slowly, and held them to his chest.

"Chad, I just wish you'd tell me everything. I don't know any of what you are talking about. Did you see a psychologist? Have you been diagnosed with something? Maybe they could help you with the radio thing. *Please.* If you tell me more, I can support you. Things can be okay."

"I've been dreaming about him again."

"Who?"

"My dad."

"You never told me about that before."

"He's down there."

"Where? Like, he died? He's in the ground?" Before when Rachelle had heard Chad talk about his dad, she was eager, relieved he was opening up. She didn't feel either of those things now.

"No. In the lake of fire."

"What lake?"

"They are torturing him, but it's like, practice. There's this bone they take out at your hips. It makes your torso swing down between your legs. It's like, how they train him. They think it's funny how protective we are of our bodies. They make little tweaks. They love how we react."

209

"Good God, Chad. Is this what's on your mind when you're freaking out about stuff? Like, uninvited thoughts?"

"No, he chose this. He gave me to them."

"To who?"

Chad grabbed Rachelle by the wrists. "We *have* to go home. They're coming closer. I can feel it."

Rachelle pulled her wrists away and held his hands. "Chad, I'm right here. None of this is real."

"We'll go. Drive fast in the opposite direction. Maybe they won't see us on our way back."

"Chad, *who*? I'm asking you who," Rachelle sniffled. "You're scaring me," her voice was choking out.

He shook his head some more and squeezed his eyes shut. His mouth was all screwed up. His voice was choked too. "I shouldn't have gotten involved. It was stupid. It was selfish."

"Involved? With me?"

"With you. With anyone."

Rachelle's throat felt tight. "Chad. I'm going to be fine. I love you. I'm trying to help. I want to stay. I want to help you."

"I'm sorry," he whispered. "You have to go. Drive away from me. Go get us some food or something. *Don't* tell me where you're going. I'm going to take a walk. Try to get lost."

"Chad, I—"

"Do it. Please. I don't want to hurt you."

"So, then what happened?" James asked.

"Well, I went out like he told me to. I looked for the radio."

"And?"

"It wasn't there."

"So what happened then? Did you tell him he was right?"

"I mean, no. I don't know. I ended up leaving soon after."

"But like, what else happened? You just left right then, got your stuff from your place in Cali, and moved cross-country?"

"I mean, what do you want? He freaked out on me. Had been, for a while. I couldn't raise a kid with him. I cut my losses and I left."

"Did you go back in the room and get your stuff? Did he do anything else?"

"He just scared me away. I didn't feel safe. I had to go. There's only so much a person can do for someone else before they have to just take care of themselves."

"Just seems kind of abrupt."

"Okay well, not sure you can tell me what you'd have done."

"You didn't try to get him help?"

"I did. I *begged* him to let me help. He wouldn't have it."

"Okay," James said quietly.

"You know what, I'm gonna go for a walk. You guys suck right now. Go rest from your little secret marathon you just came back from."

"I'm just here playin', mom!" Rory called from her room.

"Oh yeah, not you, Rory. You're my best guy."

As she walked toward the door, she saw Stanton and James exchange a knowing look. Her stomach sank. She didn't feel able to tell them the rest. She didn't know how to frame the memory anymore. Things were strange. And changing.

Where the fuck had they gone, and why couldn't they tell her? She shook her head, as if the questions could drop from her brain.

She reached the sidewalk and sped up. The thoughts she'd been batting away had been crawling back. She couldn't push them away anymore. *Fuck them. If they won't tell me their story, I won't tell them mine.*

***

"*How could it not be there?*" Rachelle grumbled the question. She was sitting in the parking lot of Pinnacle Peak, staring at the almost-mountain that looked more like a colossal stack of reddish rocks. Spiky plants shot up everywhere, biting the landscape; scores of cacti scattered across like big green sentinels.

He'd kicked her out of the motel room. She'd turned everything in the car upside down to find no radio. When she'd checked the room again, he wouldn't look at her. He stopped talking completely. She'd left him sitting at the end of the motel bed, arms and legs crossed. Grinding his teeth.

It hadn't been long. She'd driven for maybe five minutes to get here. She expected him to call her any second. To continue freaking out. So far, she hadn't heard from him.

Rachelle was still shaking a little. She rubbed her tongue across the bottoms of her teeth. She took a deep breath and tapped her browser app on her phone, looking up therapists in the area. Maybe someone could talk to him. Convince him it was safe to be away from his house. To be without his radio. Maybe she could still help him here. Get him away from himself and his obsessive routines. To see that the radio wasn't what he thought it was. That he didn't need it nearby to feel okay.

She ran through phrases in her head that seemed deep and encouraging. *Who the fuck are you kidding?* she laughed bitterly to herself. *You don't know what you're doing. You're not gonna be able to say any of this shit. You're being pretentious.*

She brought the phone closer to view her search results. *What's the difference between therapy and counseling?* She squinted and started to scroll through the names.

She almost dropped her phone when it rang.

Chad.

"Hey," she said tentatively.

She only heard a choked half-laugh, half-whimper. It continued for about twenty seconds.

She couldn't listen to it anymore.

"Chad?" she asked.

She began shaking again, trying to mentally prepare. Say something helpful.

"Wouldn't you know, they're following *you* now?"

"Chad, please," she closed her eyes, thinking. Not only did he make no sense, but his word choice was strange. Aside from the rambling. It was the expression. Not at all how he talked. And his voice was pinched. He sounded scared, yet threatening.

"I don't like what you've done. I *really* don't like what you've done—"

"I—"

"—or tried to do. You failed, you know."

"Chad, who? Please help me. I have no idea . . ."

"You know, without that radio? I'm a danger to you now. I'm damned forever, and you are as good as dead." His voice was getting harder.

Rachelle had no words. She sat, waiting to see what he'd say next.

"I'm not far behind, Chelle! They're bringing me to you!"

She could hear wind blowing past his mouthpiece. He was outside, somewhere.

"No!" she shouted.

The hang-up tone chirped in her ear.

***

She'd been jogging up the trail of Pinnacle Peak for ten minutes. The trail crawled up the side of the mountain like a folded snake, slinking between piles of rock and green brush. The red dust kicked up and clung to her socks as she walked. Every so often she'd glance down at her car, which grew smaller with each minute.

This is stupid, she convinced herself. *Why am I running? He can't really find me here, can he?* She looked up and tried to take bigger breaths of the thinning air. It appeared she was halfway up the peak on this narrow trail. She turned and looked down again at the shelves of the descending rocky path. Her shoe kicked some gravel. She watched it shower down, heard it spray the rocks and bounce off until it finally settled some fifty yards down from where she stood.

Where am I going? she asked herself angrily. *Why do I always get myself in these situations?* Was she heading to the top of that peak? What was she supposed to do when she got there? Just sit there and think?

Her thoughts were interrupted by the scraping of gravel above her. She turned around and looked up, shielding her eyes from the afternoon sun.

Her heart slammed in her chest. There was a man standing one path up from hers, looking down.

"Chad?" she shouted. "Where did you come from?" Her legs shook horribly.

She squinted at the man again. He looked like Chad. Same height. Same hair color. But different.

No. No way he could be up there. Above me. I left him there at the motel. I took my car.

"I'm sorry? Where did I come from?" he asked. His voice was hard. But courteous. No recognition in it, whatsoever.

"Oh my god. I'm *so* sorry!" she held her hands out defensively. "You scared me. You look like someone I know. I'm kind of going through something right now. Sorry."

She continued up the path. She was going to have to pass the man if she wanted to make her way up.

As she turned the corner to his section of the path, he turned to face her, blocking her passage. His hands were in his pockets.

"I came from the place where there are no trails," he grinned at her. His eyes glinted in the sunlight.

"*Why* would you go there?" she asked. The shakes were coming back.

"It reminded me of my home." He let out a short laugh. "I've never been this powerful! I feel like I've walked a hundred miles."

Rachelle's heart was in her throat. She was afraid to try to pass him. She didn't want to get any closer to him.

He looked like Chad, but the angles on his face were sharper. Pointier. Like another person wearing Chad's skin. The skin on his cheeks seemed stretched out, while his upper lip and eyelids sagged.

No way. No. Something is wrong here. This is him. It is, and it isn't.

The dry underbrush rustled in the wind. She tried to quiet the silent alarm clanging in her skull. Just. Stay. Calm. Talk it out. Make it make sense.

"Chad, is that you?"

She shielded her eyes.

"A hundred miles! Just to find you, Chelle! I would walk five hundred miles," he sang. "You know The Proclaimers?" He was smiling like he was in pain. His eyes were still shining. It hurt to look. She looked down at his feet, and saw the red dust absolutely covered his shoes, his pants, all the way up to his thighs.

"And I would walk five hundred more . . . Just to be the man who walked a thousand miles . . . .to fall down at your door."

She turned and ran back down the trail. She heard footsteps pounding the gravel. It sounded heavier than a person, but slow. Like he was fucking with her. She turned the curve to go back where she'd come. When she looked up, the person who looked like Chad had advanced one level down the zig-zag trail, but was standing completely still. Watching her. Gravel showered down the slope, skittered, then settled. She held her breath. *Why did he stop? What's he going to do?* Regardless, running seemed the only option. She tore her gaze away and kept running.

"Hey! Chelle! You gotta stay!" he cried out. He sounded anguished now, desperate. She kept going. She cursed loudly as she had to turn each corner to continue her descent. She glanced down. Couldn't believe how far she still had to go.

She slowed herself to a skid at another turn, but not enough. The rocks rolled underneath her shoes. She pitched to the side, her ankle bent awkwardly. One leg was stuck folded underneath her and the other one straight out. She lay still for less than a second, afraid to move, but knowing she had to. Her elbow felt bashed to shit but she forced her arm straight and pushed herself up.

"Why run, Rachelle?" His voice echoed down and through the place from on high. The tone had a feigned innocence that wrenched her stomach. "You wanted to spend this time with me!"

She made the mistake of looking up at him. He wasn't running. His eyes glowed brighter still. A white that seared like the sun. He stared at her before he jumped. He crouched down, then leapt a good ten feet to the portion of the trail below. He'd looked so sure of the jump. No thinking twice, no flailing.

Two more and he'd be with her. She could hear his breathing now. He was snarling, like a hungry dog. She'd been poised to run, but instead, she threw herself onto her side, pushing herself backwards over the edge of a shelf of rocks. She let herself hang over the edge, sliding until only her forearms hung on. She pushed her body away from the rocky wall, dropping a good three or four more feet to the next section of trail.

Landing hard on the balls of her feet, she scrambled against the red silt. She grasped desperately at the giant rocks.

From above, two hands gripped her by the jaw and pulled. Her neck snapped back, painfully. She angled her head up, trying to slip from his grasp. She shouted as she was pulled up to her feet. She grabbed him hard at the elbows, digging in with her fingers, to try and support her neck. To save herself.

He lifted her higher, then let go again. She shouted in alarm. He grabbed at her back, pushing his hands roughly under her arms. He dragged her up to his level.

"There you are," he whispered in her ear. He wrapped his arms around her middle. Cradling her. Crushing her. His skin smelled like Chad's did when they fucked. Pheromones and sweat. Paired with a musky outdoor odor. She kicked the air with her feet, tried to land on the trail to support herself. But he stood at the very edge, letting her float over the ledge.

"You're never gonna forget me, you know," he growled. His breath came out hot on top of hot. The inside of her ear was moist with his saliva.

"Forget *who*?"

She turned to face him, and spit. He blinked rapidly as it sprayed him. A splatter shone on his cheek, near his eye. He continued speaking as though it hadn't happened. She noticed.

"You'll tell yourself you did. You'll try to *cut* me out of you. But you'll just bleed yourself."

"I can't fucking *wait* to forget you," she said, almost out of breath. Her chest was pinned to his. She pushed at his hips with her hands, straightening her arms, so her own hips separated from his. She was gaining leverage while thrusting away from him. *He's gotta feel like he'll lose his balance,* she thought. *That's the only thing that'll make him move.* She'd lost all faith in Chad, or whoever this imposter was, but his countenance was stone. She'd spit on him and he hadn't even flinched. *I can work with this,* she told herself.

She put her arms around his neck and hoisted herself up, wrapping her legs around his waist. She squeezed hard, testing her grip on him. She looked at him and grinned, hoping it would throw him off, but knowing he'd come unhinged and was near impossible to shock.

Confidence, she told herself. *Fake it.*

Uncertainty flickered. Ever so briefly in his eyes. It felt like him for a second. Like Chad before the change. Then he was gone again.

That was all she needed.

"I hope you remember me, too," she whispered, still smiling. Tears were in her eyes.

Goodbye, she said inside her own head. In case she didn't see herself again. Her chest was pounding. Her neck was throbbing. Pure adrenaline. She married her hands together firmly at the nape of his neck. Her only obvious option.

She rocked backwards, hard and quick.

She felt herself falling. Somewhere, she felt him let go. She didn't feel pain as she landed. It was more like the world stopped short. And violently. She heard something big and heavy land, then roll, and land again, beyond her.

After that, a blackness.

She woke up curled in a ball, balanced somehow on her head, neck and shoulders. Like a dead bug.

I'm alive. She tried to feel joy. But pain was behind her eyes when she opened them. A bleeding glow coming on and off. Burning, then dying.

I should be dead. It started in her skull, and continued in a searing ache in the back of her head and neck. The vicious, unfeeling sun hammered down. She cursed and forced herself to sit up quickly. She looked down the mountain.

What happened to you? she asked Chad. He was lying on the last stretch of trail before the bottom. At least twenty feet down from where she'd landed.

She squinted at him. Invisible waves danced in the sweltering space and dizzying height between them.

Is he dead?

No fucking idea, she answered herself. *Not moving, though.*

Go, now! She pushed herself up to stand. She tipped to the side, leaning against the mountain wall. Bushes scraped and stung her legs. The ache was still there. Dizziness and nausea crashed over her. She squeezed her eyes shut and held her head as the world threatened to go dark again. She leaned there, waiting. Hoping for it to pass.

Cautiously, she turned away from the wall and shuffled down the path.

Get past him. Get to the car. She kept walking. Tried to speed up, but got too wobbly. Slowed again. She wondered if others would show up. See him lying there. Try to get her involved. Ask questions.

She studied him as she approached. He looked like he was sleeping; his face relaxed. Sweat streaked his cheeks, and wet the hair at his temples. It was so real, yet surreal. A minute ago, he was so threatening. Overpowering. Now he lay on his stomach, awkwardly crushing one arm with his body. She thought she saw him breathe, but wasn't sure.

No time. Keep going. As she hopped over him gingerly, she waited for him to launch up and grab her legs. He didn't. She continued down the trail. She glanced back one more time as she got in the car. He looked almost flattened, like roadkill. A pelt cooking in the heat lines that wiggled the air. As she pulled out of the drive, she saw him roll on his side, cradle his head with the heel of his hand. Rachelle kept going. She'd get out of this town, gas up, get some stuff and leave. She felt like she was abandoning him, but like she'd die if she stayed.

The feelings didn't mix. They churned in her stomach. She could almost taste them. Like ice cream and gasoline.

The next day, she found out she was pregnant.

19

James and Stanton talked quietly in the living room. They stopped as Rachelle opened the front door. She didn't look at them, just walked straight to Rory's door. Stanton raised his eyebrows. He nodded, grabbing his cigarettes and heading out the front door to smoke. James followed Rachelle into Rory's room.

Rachelle was crying, righting Rory's play table by the window. She kneeled on the floor, picked up the tiny chairs, set a plush action figure in one. Its head was bigger than its torso, so it tipped over the minute she let go. She looked at it, then looked away. A look of utter failure on her face.

"What's going on here?" James asked her, softly. He rubbed the back of his neck. His skin crawled and he wanted to distract himself from the feeling.

"Just was thinking about stuff while walking. It's none of your business, really."

"Okay, but don't you think it'd help to talk about it?"

"I could ask you the same. You're in my house, you're all up in my business. But you don't seem to want to answer any of my questions."

"I told you I—"

"Yeah, you're afraid. So am I. I'm afraid of what's happening in this house. I'm afraid of you being here but really only sort of. You guys came back here all disheveled and gasping for air like you just fell out of a fucking airplane. But I don't get to know. I'm just here, basically alone, struggling with my own shit." She sighed and gestured generally with her hands.

He wanted to tell her but he'd grown used to deflecting. And here, she'd given him a new thread to grasp.

He pulled that thread. "Why, what's wrong?"

Rachelle rubbed her eyes. "It's Chad. More happened than what I told you."

"What happened?"

"He tried to kill me. I tried to kill him. It totally fucked me up. I never fully let myself try to make sense of it. If the thoughts bubbled up, I'd keep telling myself it was him, but it wasn't, because the Chad I knew wouldn't do that. But now it's like there's this impossible connection. I've been attacked by a shadow figure. I've seen you . . . possessed or something. Eating dirt. Your eyes were glowing, then. Or flashing this bright white. His eyes looked the same that day. And now the shit that went down back then seems to be genuinely connected somehow. It's—"

"Impossible?"

"Sure, yeah."

"I'm glad you're telling me this."

"James." Rachelle glared at him expectantly.

"What?" He chewed at his bottom lip.

"I just told you about something I didn't want to."

Shit. "I'm glad you did." He pressed his lips together.

"Last time I'm going to ask. What's going on with you?" Her jaw was set. She pulled his collar aside, revealing the cord of his necklace. "Maybe you can start with telling me what that thing is."

James plucked at the cord absentmindedly. He remembered the day he tried to get her to wear the pentacle.

"Almost the second I met you, er, okay, the second time I met you, I was so into you. You know that. But I also never stop thinking about when you were just a work acquaintance. How you 'dropped' a necklace in my purse, then told me to keep it. Told me I should wear it. What *is* that? What were you trying to do to me?"

"Rachelle, I was *trying* to protect you. But I couldn't tell you. I couldn't tell you why." James closed his eyes. No way this was not going off the rails.

"Yeah you could. You *absolutely* coulda told me. That's how you treat someone you respect, that you trust. And now I don't trust you."

"I was being dishonest, okay? But for good reason. I don't know how to make it make sense so you know I was just trying to help."

"My god, James." Rachelle covered her face, taking in an unsteady breath. "Why? You've got to just tell me *why*." She sniffed and lowered her hands. Her eyes were teary but hard. "Please."

James sighed. He rubbed his hands together and sat down at the end of Rory's bed. He held his hand out to her and opened his mouth. He settled his elbows on his thighs, leaning forward.

"I'm here because of that radio." He pointed to the crystal radio sitting on Rory's desk. "Remember the day Rory turned it on?"

Rachelle knitted her brow for a minute, thinking. She was still sitting on her ankles on the floor.

"Yes. But how would you know? You weren't there."

James sighed. *Shit, shit, shit.* He stared at the floor. *Here we go.* "You're right. I wasn't. I came right after that."

"What are you telling me?" Rachelle's jaw hung open slightly. "When we met, you said you came here when you got a call about the podcast."

James bit his bottom lip. "No. I told you I got a call. I told you it *wasn't* about the podcast. That it was a long story. I'm telling you now: the call I referred to was a call from that *thing.* That"—he pointed to it—"radio."

"But that's a really weird coincidence, right? That when you moved, you changed jobs, and you wound up meeting me. And *I* had it. *I* had the radio."

James shook his head slowly. "Not a coincidence," he whispered, looking down.

"What are you *actually* telling me? You came here to get a job at my work, *because* I worked there? Why would you come all the way here for a radio?"

"I followed the signal. I didn't know the radio was what sent the signal at the time. But I used certain methods to figure where the signal hailed from."

Rachelle shrugged. Her face drooped. "How?" she asked, weakly.

"There had been talk of something like this existing a few years ago," James explained. "People like me, we seek out answers to life's more elusive questions. I met a guy. Anton." He hesitated. "He used magic. We could seek out frequencies to find others like us, to check out what kind of things others were doing. A bunch of us found each other and formed sort of a long-distance network on a message board. We picked up on this signal about five years ago. It wasn't the usual type. It wasn't natural. It was a machine, putting out strong frequencies. And there was dark magic. Satanic stuff, probably.

"This machine could open doors. Attract otherworldly creatures. Prompt the opening of a portal. If you could make them come at will, you could communicate with them. Bargain with them. Settle a score. Whatever. The signal would appear, but then before we could zero in on a location, there was this crazy noise. Or lack of noise. White noise, almost, that scattered it."

He rubbed his face.

"The thing had unspeakable value. Anyone who had this on their radar, if they were listening, watching, at the right time, could find a way to get to it. Back about five years ago. Then just like that, any trace of even that unidentified noise, was gone. Many gave up, but I didn't. I kept listening. I got lucky. I heard the call.

"I followed the signal here, and well, you know. I saw it was with you and Rory. I wanted it." James took a deep breath and steeled himself. "So I found a way to get close to you."

Rachelle walked quickly away from James, and stared out the window, arms crossed. She stayed that way for what felt like five minutes. Every so often, he'd hear her take a deep breath but couldn't hear her let it out. Slowly, she finally turned back to him, her head tipped; her eyes cast down to the floor. She held a closed fist to her paled face, seemingly deep in thought.

When she finally spoke, her voice was a whisper. "That's why you got close to me? Because of this thing in my house?" She sniffed. Chewed on her thumbnail. Her eyes finally met his and she continued. "How did you convince them to give you a job? A position that didn't even exist until you showed up?"

James sighed. "I'm sorry for that. For the pain it caused you. You deserved that job. I told you before, that job would have been yours, if it had existed. I didn't get it through the standard route."

Rachelle seethed. Angry tears welled up. She tightened her fists, looked down at them, and unclenched. "What the fuck, what the fuck." She looked up. "What *are you*?"

His gaze remained on the floor. He let out a small quiet laugh.

"I'm a witch."

He looked up at her, reading her face. He offered a pained smile.

He leaned over the edge of Rory's bed and reached for her hand. "You know how I feel *now* though, right?"

She stared at him, unmoving.

"Huh." James let out another small laugh. He held the rejected hand to his chest, watching her. He shook his head, tongue in his cheek.

She glowered down at him. Her voice was ice. "Why did you have sex with me?"

"Easy. I liked you."

"Yeah, yeah," she waved it away. "But why so quickly?"

"Rachelle, I liked you. I honestly care about you. A lot. How can you not know that? Feel that?"

"Whatever. Get out."

"No. I can't leave. Okay? You don't—"

"Yeah. I don't want you here."

"You don't understand. I *need* to find out how it works. This is for—"

"*Fine.*" She grabbed the radio in her arms and thrust it at him. "Take it with you! This thing has *completely* fucked us up. Who knows *why* it's still here, or what you want with it. Take it apart! I don't give a fuck. Just please, get out." The last word was a sob. "Please leave."

James looked at her sadly. He left, carrying the radio awkwardly like a load of firewood.

***

James dry-swallowed an Ambien and lay back on the hard motel bed, hands on his chest. The radio sat next to him on the nightstand. He had to figure out its history, somehow. It was like the thing was stuck on redial and kept breaching the expanse between their world and the underplace. Not just dialing, but opening a door where there wasn't one before.

At first he thought Chad had built it. But there had to be something more. Now he knew Chad was haunted by that place. And the note plainly said he was trying to protect himself. To quiet the "storm in the air." How had Chad gotten mixed up in all this in the first place? Where did the radio come from? Rachelle clearly didn't know.

James closed his eyes and mumbled to himself. An incantation, trying to open up his mind to all that had happened. He invited the universe to shed light on why this all was happening.

When finished, he stared at the popcorn ceiling, trying to create shapes with his mind out of the weird shadowy stains in the corner. He refocused and straightened his neck again, closing his eyes.

He moved past the red-black of his eyelids to somewhere the dark deepened. Whispers floated, unintelligible, past him. Just voices in a void. So quiet they couldn't reach or touch each other.

He floated. Blinked, trying to adjust his eyes, to make himself see something. The feeling of continually seeing nothing but darkness was something he'd never gotten used to. He still didn't understand where this place was, or what was coming next.

Ten minutes passed. His started to reel with the lack of action. As usual, he started to regret putting himself in this place of nothingness.

James grew concerned the Ambien would hold him in this state for hours. He laughed to himself, remembering he did this every time. He always saw something when putting himself in this mini-coma, but it never failed, he always started to panic when things didn't take shape immediately. At the idea he'd be awake while asleep and staring at blackness for eight hours.

Suddenly, he heard a rapid fluttering sound. Tiny wings propelling something along. He turned his head slightly. A moth flapped its way past his peripheral.

A moth, he thought. How in the fuck is that going to help me? He sighed to himself, staring at it. Get ready to be bored, he thought, frustrated. This was better than the blackness that preceded it, but not by much.

A chirping sound startled him from above. A brown furry-chested bat glided, its black wings spread wide. As it neared the moth, the chirping sound grew louder and faster. It slowed and righted itself, feet forward. Ready to grab the moth.

James' blood froze. He held his breath. He couldn't fathom why he felt such dread. Seconds ago, he was bored. And now, riveted. Poised for heartbreak. Staring at this poor stupid moth that didn't even seem to sense the bat's presence.

As the bat approached, a sharp, fast clicking came from the moth, right as the bat opened its claws to grab. The bat adjusted itself slightly just before closing in on the moth. An expert hunter, completely missing the target right in front of it.

The moth fluttered clumsily away. The bat looped around and tried again. Chirping. The sound speeding up. James began to feel the reverberations in his ears. To steer his gaze back to the moth. He almost felt the shape of it with his hearing. He could feel the panic too. The clicking sound came again. He struggled to focus, and this time the bat grabbed the moth. His heart raced. His stomach dropped, and the grip of death embraced him. Everything tightened; his chest, his heart, his throat. He was sweating.

James woke up on the grubby motel carpet. His pants were wet. Face, sopping. He lifted his head slowly off the carpet, the puddle of saliva slowly separating from his face. His hair and cheek were still soaked. Bright sunlight peeked in from between the old off-white blackout curtains.

James sat slowly up, holding his cotton-filled head. He thought through what he'd seen. He'd heard something before. The bat's chirping was called echolocation. This was common knowledge. They could hunt in total darkness this way. Reacting to how their chirping refracted off their prey. But it seemed like the moth's sounds had interrupted the bat's radar. Confused it somehow. Blocked it for a minute.

He stared at the wet spot on the carpet and wiped his sleeve against his face. His state of being left that embarrassing spot, and now he had to look at it. He thought about Rachelle. He was afraid of how she'd receive him when he went back, but he knew he had to go.

This was what he'd come for. To help. Whether she wanted it or not, she needed this information. She needed to know what he'd learned, or it'd never stop.

***

"Where are you going?" Anton asked.

"You hated me. You wanted me to leave." James stood at the foot of the burned-up car in the scant white glow of dawn.

"Don't get me wrong, I'm glad you're leaving."

"Shit. Tell me how you really feel." James kicked some loose rocks from the cement alley, gripping the strap of his old ripped duffel bag.

"You know what I mean."

"I don't."

Anton sighed.

"What I mean is, it felt like you were going to stick around sponging off me forever. Now that you're leaving . . ." He rubbed the back of his neck. "Just, let me give you a couple things, alright?"

"You mean like, drugs? That's not very wholesome."

"I'm not wholesome, Jamie. You know that. But no, not drugs. Hang tight."

Anton came back out with a gallon jug of water and a small pouch.

"What are these?"

"So from that rant after your crazy fever dream, I gather you're planning to run off and get yourself killed by all manner of ungodly creatures. Do me a favor and do some studying. Stick with that witchy group you've met. And keep these handy." He placed the pouch in James' hand. "No matter what, the life you've chosen is equivalent to playing in traffic. So you may as well learn what in the actual hell you've gotten yourself into."

James opened the pouch. "Hm. Shiny black rocks. Let me guess. Magic?"

"Obsidian. Some call it a wizard stone."

"For?"

"Protection, among other things. But I like to call it 'making the darkness your bitch.' You can illuminate it,

233

like a flashlight. Would do some real damage to all manner of hellish enemies."

"Holy shit." James laughed in disbelief. "This little bag of rocks?"

"Yep. Like bringing a bazooka to a knife fight."

James chuckled quietly. "And the water?"

"Oh. That's just for drinking."

James laughed again. A grin was stuck on his face. He'd had next to nothing in lieu of parents. This felt alien. Alien, and nice.

"Why are you helping me?"

Anton gestured at the air around him. "Really kid, does it look like I have anything better to do?"

***

James opened the front door a crack, then thought twice and knocked on the door, holding onto the handle.

"Rory! Are those clean or dirty?" he heard Rachelle yell from another room. Her footsteps made their way nearer the door.

"What, Ma?"

"Hey—" James said loudly, knocking again.

"These!" Rachelle shouted at the same time.

"Mom, what's 'these'? I can't see what you're pointing at. I'm in the other room."

"Ah, nevermind, I'll just wash it," he heard her grumble.

"Rachelle!" James said loudly. He leaned in the doorway.

Rachelle let out a quick scream and dropped the laundry basket, pressing her hand to her chest.

"James!" she shouted.

Her eyes flashed angrily, but then softened. He saw black smudges around them. She hadn't wiped off her eyeliner from the night before.

"Why are you back here?" Her question was mild. She seemed hurt, but hopeful. "I thought you just wanted the radio?"

"You really didn't hear me last night, did you?" James asked.

Rachelle sighed. "I heard you. I just don't believe you."

James came in and shut the door quietly. They knelt down and picked up Rory's laundry together.

"I think these are clean." He looked up at her. She was holding an undershirt. It was bright white and partially folded.

"Probably."

"I mean, yeah, I lied." Quickly, he handed her a pair of her own dark blue boyshort underwear wrapped strategically in some sweatpants, hoping she wouldn't notice. "But I told you the truth about *why* I lied."

"What you said didn't mean much after I caught you in a lie. The point is for you to tell the truth *before* I figure out a lie."

"Well, I guess I know that *now*," he said quietly.

"So, what? That necklace is supposed to be protective?"

"Yeah. I wear mine all the time."

"I know. I saw it on you. At first, it made me even more suspicious. Like you were in some satanic thing and wanted to like . . . conjure something with me."

"Nah, it's the opposite. I was trying to protect you."

He watched Rachelle's face, waiting for her expression to unclench. Waiting for recognition, or more questions to arise, relaxing her features. She looked stuck.

"I figured something out," he offered. "About the radio."

"What," she stated instead of asking.

"Well, there are places on this earth that are ancient; gateways to hell. But this one is like a man-made cellar door. I already thought it was a kind of summoning device. I felt it years ago, like I mentioned. But this one also splits the fabric that separates our world from theirs."

"Okay, but it sounds like you already knew this?"

"Well yeah, but I didn't know who made it and why. And what Chad had to do with it all. So I took the radio with me and did something. I get into this dream-like state. My brain creates an answer but I have to sort through the meaning. I think what I figured out is, Chad might've added to this radio, so that it protected *instead* of summoning. I think there's some signal it gave off at first. And maybe Chad altered it to harness that same power, but jam that signal. Like whatever it could do at first, it can now do the opposite."

"But it doesn't do the opposite. We're getting possessed and attacked. So, what do we do?"

"Well, I don't know. It belonged to Chad. He put that weird note in there. So I think we have to get in contact with him. Find out what he may know. Maybe the protective part of this thing is broken. You've had it for five years. Maybe it's crapped out. Or even worse, maybe we did something to it."

"We didn't though."

"We don't know that we didn't. You took it here with you and don't remember packing it. I blacked out and don't remember anything between standing in front of your house, and you staring at me in the back yard. Remember how my hands were all cut up? I have this memory in the middle of my blackout. Of scraping my hand up on a scouring pad in the bathroom. I don't believe that's real. I think they implanted it. I think, when they come, the activities likely center around them trying to take, or manipulate this radio."

Rachelle narrowed her eyes. "If you knew. If you *knew* this, why didn't you take it away? Hide it? Keep it from *Rory*, of all people?"

"I mentioned this. I wasn't sure it was the radio until now. But I suspected. Remember Rory commenting it kept moving on its own? Or the knock at the door when that shadow figure attacked you?"

Rachelle nodded slowly.

"Those were both me. I kept moving the radio. I'd followed the signal, but I wasn't sure what object it came from for sure. I didn't want to raise suspicion by interfering, so I'd move it. I'd observe where the activity happened after moving it. I've been staying in my car, as you figured out. Watching over you guys. Waiting for the right time to act."

"That was you who pounded on the door? You stopped that shadow figure from getting me?"

James nodded. His heart warmed, and started thumping harder. She was really, *actually* going to be cool with this. Maybe. He wasn't hiding who he was anymore. He tried to hold tight until he knew for sure.

"You know," Rachelle looked up at James. "When you told me you were a witch? That wasn't what I expected you to say."

James smiled. Small, at first. "What *did* you expect?" He couldn't help it. He was grinning now. His throat felt tight, and his shoulders, loose. Like a kid just starting summer vacation.

"That's just it. I don't know. There was just something very clearly weird." She kicked at the floor. It made a small scuffing sound. "I guess I was too distracted by what was going on to focus too much on it. Before I kicked you out, I was actually thinking you caused it, honestly."

"I've been wanting to tell you. *So much*," he said quietly.

She closed her eyes and leaned forward, toward him. She took a deep breath, then sighed again, like she was breathing him inside herself, then returning the carbon dioxide. "I gotta start the wash," she whispered, but didn't move at first.

"Rachelle, how much of those garments are already clean?"

"Probably most, but now I don't know which is which." She grinned at him, winked, then turned back and continued toward the laundry room.

20

She awoke slowly, a mass of sweaty hair plastered to her face. She parted it with her thumb, and observed James at her side. He slept with his eyebrows raised like some- one had surprised him, but otherwise he looked com- pletely relaxed, one cheek tucked snug into the pillow. She watched him with one eye, saw his torso fill lazily and relax, expand and relax. She hadn't realized until now just how guarded his posture was while awake. It was a nice change watching him like this.

Now, being awake, she tried to bat away the memory of what he'd asked her. He'd brought up Daisy. Re- minded her she'd seen Daisy, heard her voice on the way to Boston. Even warned her about the radio.

James said there was a way to summon her, enlist her to help. Oh how he'd insisted and oh, how she'd re- sisted. Eventually he'd dropped it and moved on to other options.

Before they'd fallen asleep they'd moved all the beds back away from the walls and he'd drawn those weird circles like what was on the necklace, with the names and pluses around it. She and Stanton made weirded-out faces at each other to lighten the mood while James chanted. She believed in what he was doing but it was hard to erase the three decades of her life spent thinking all this wasn't real.

She'd stared at him while he got chalk all over her carpeting, side-eyeing at all the weird items on her dresser. A shiny black rock, vials of stuff that looked like cooking spices but smelled like shit. She stared, and tried again not to think about Daisy. Where she was, what it'd be like to be ripped from your eternal rest. dragged back into the human world by your best friend who failed to save your mortal skin. Oh, and: welcome back to people and their fucked-up problems.

She'd tried to find the necklace he'd given her, but after emptying out her entire purse, it was nowhere to be found, which freaked her out. He'd told her not to worry and provided ample distraction. Like self-deprecating jokes about fancy warm bedrooms versus car-sleeping. They made good use of the edge of her bed before falling asleep. Her face flushed thinking about it.

Carefully, she turned her pillow upright and sat up, crossing her arms. Looked down at James again.

A dragging, scraping sound came from the bedroom door next to her. Wildly, she looked up and over, and saw the top corner of the door opening slowly. She looked down, expecting to see Rory.

A shape with two long, bent legs was crouching down, its strange deer-like snout tilted up, observing her. It hopped a bit as it walked. Its spindly legs almost completely folded.

Rachelle opened her mouth to scream, but her breath caught in her throat. Its legs lengthened. It looked like a deer with no torso or hind legs.

It reached her quickly, its hoof suctioning her face and mouth. No air or sound could get in or out. She struggled to throw her head back, but couldn't move. She tried to move one arm up to turn on the lamp but the other leg blocked her and muscled it back down against the mattress. It moved the other leg over to straddle her down into the bed.

All this was done smoothly and with ease, hardly making any movement to jostle the bed or wake up James.

From hell it came, were the words that flashed black, then red in her mind. Seething and horrified, Rachelle breathed fast through her nose, trying to alert James. The muscles in her arms and legs worked furiously, and to no avail. She couldn't move.

At least you can breathe. She squeezed her eyes shut, trying to focus on her breathing. Literally the only thing she could control. *James!* She screamed in her mind.

The moon glinted off its big black eyes as they pulled open wider. It was concentrating on something she couldn't see.

Two things that felt like fingers came out of the hoof, bent back, and slid up her nose. Again she tried to jerk back. They continued down her throat. Her muscles bucked again, and the thing pressed her deeper into the mattress.

She bit down on the unforgiving appendages.

Her throat was stiff with agony, warring muscles twitching uncontrollably. Everything felt wrong.

No, no. Nothing can go in this way. Get it out, get it out.

She begged, and she fought for many minutes. Then, even the darkness turned off.

***

Oh my god.

The stuck feeling released her. Her eyes opened. She felt her face. Nothing was there. She was still hyperventilating through her nose.

What the fuck was *that dream?*

She stared at James. Exactly how he'd looked in her dream. Eyebrows up. Mouth relaxed. Breathing slow.

Yeah, yeah. Real fucking *cute,* she thought bitterly. She was still pissed from the dream when her nasal cavity was being explored like a goddamned cave and he wouldn't wake up.

The feeling like she needed to get away from him itched like a bug in her skull. She had to go for a drive, and clear it out. James would just interrupt her moment of inspiration. Of self-actualization. A powerful song was just so in her head, and if he talked, she'd lose it forever. She just needed to be alone. To get on the road and figure out what it was.

She shoved back her hair and rushed in a frenzied tiptoe to the front door. She was pulling on her shoes when she heard sharp, angry whispers and rustling sheets from the bedroom. She felt panicked for some reason, like she couldn't let him catch her leaving.

Shoes half on, she quickly hobbled out the front door, shutting it quietly behind her.

She hopped to the car and pulled the handle.

Unlocked. She sighed loudly in relief. She gunned the engine and backed quickly out of the driveway without buckling up. When she turned forward again while moving into drive, she saw James running into the front yard in his boxers, waving and shouting something.

"Hurry Hurry Hurry!" she hissed at her car, gunning the engine.

He was approaching the curb, then he was standing there. His face was heavily shadowed. Disapproving and confused as he shrank alongside the car, then disappeared, behind her.

It felt weird passing Rory's day care without dropping him off.

A sound, a feeling, inside her was shouting. It made her picture a frog trapped in a fogged-up jar. It felt like it was getting quieter, losing oxygen. The feeling made no sense to her. She tried to shake it off and continued on to the building where she worked.

The parking garage was empty except for one car way in the back corner. She parked on the third floor, right by the door, and got out. She could still feel that weird shouting. She went to put her keys in her pocket and realized she had no pockets; she was still wearing pajamas.

The muffled screams became a whimpering.

Rachelle looked around as she crossed the threshold into her office building. She knew where she was, but she felt separated from the place. It felt surreal, as though she'd been gone for months. She wondered if it was because the place was so dark.

"Yes, that is why," she said aloud to herself. She jumped, startled by her own voice. That, too, seemed alien to her.

She was in the right place now. She knew she was supposed to go here. The next part had been hidden from her, but now it was being revealed. She couldn't see in front of her face. But she saw what she was looking for. Something moved with her, helping her navigate her way in the dark. The object she would need shone brightly somewhere inside her brain. Shiny and curved. Like a metal bow.

She reached the large open office area. It was different in the dark. The room was still, but there was a charge. Like a wind that didn't blow; it just built up pressure all around her. The pressure parted just in front of her. A figure walked up to her. An orifice on its face was open and pointing at her. She heard its soft shuffling footsteps come toward her and jumped back. This was the thing that had been guiding her since she'd woken up.

From hell it came, the thought repeated in her mind from that dream. Had that really been a dream? Not in the usual sense. Its influence had left her alone for a second, but it was coming to her again. A warm breath enveloped her face. It smelled like hot metal; like a shitty old space heater. A roaring sound surrounded both her ears, like a driving rain pouring over them. Something dense encased her skull. Something with weight. An invisible helmet.

***

Her eyes opened. She still couldn't see, but could feel everything in the dark room. She was sharp like the night.

And the night has teeth.

She could bite them all. She could take out the parts she didn't like of herself. Then get parts from the others and put them in its place.

The people she'd left behind. Chad and Daisy. They were hiding inside her. They had settled inside her bones.

How selfish that they will not let go.

Chad was in her toes. And Daisy, in her heels. She could cut them out. She'd replace them with her new friends instead. She had to do it now. And by the morning she would start fresh with her new parts.

And what will you bite with?

She could feel the tool she wanted by the window. The blade was left up by some careless person. It arched vaguely, like a sleeping lover. The crescent moon was watching. The moon made the corner of it glow.

Glowing as if to say hello.

Yes!! Ahh, yes. *Hello.*

***

James woke up swearing. Rachelle was gone.

He knew. He just knew. Before her fucking eyes glowed white at him from the windshield. In hindsight he felt he'd known before he woke up.

We broke the damn circle didn't we, he thought. I let myself get distracted.

But those details didn't really help right now. He had to find her.

They were coming up from deeper within now. From the underworld. From hell. The bad ones were coming. And it would only get worse and worse.

A quick thumping noise by the front door. Shoes being grabbed. The soft sound of a shoulder landing for balance as the shoes went on. By the time he got to her bedroom door to look, he saw her scramble out the front, like a raccoon caught scavenging by something much larger.

He'd run like hell, chasing her in his skivvies to the car. She'd looked at him horrified, as though escaping a murder house. By now, he knew that wasn't fully her, but that didn't stop the hurt mixing in with the fear and panic of losing track of her. *She's going to be hard to catch.*

Back inside, he yanked his pants on and hurried to her dresser, stuffing as much as he could in his pockets. He shook Stanton awake. Told him he had to go, asked him to watch after Rory. Stanton started to inquire, then seemed to remember the situation and told him to go.

He caught up to her car at the day care. Saw her tap an indecisive staccato on the brakes. Four or five flashes of red. It was 3 a.m. and black outside, but the muscle memory of this route must have thrown her. Then she turned and headed toward the office.

He tried to keep something of a distance between them, increasing it as they neared the parking garage.

To be visibly following her would be catastrophic. He tried to picture what one of those things would make her do to him if it detected him there. Him, or herself. Then he tried to *stop* picturing it. He realized he was probably minutes away from actually having to confront it. He had to wait until it was done traveling. He had to see what it was trying to do. To try and find out what it wanted. Figure how to get rid of it.

He parked on the same level of the lot, but three aisles over, behind a fat cement pillar. Most of the lights were out in the garage. This reminded him of the motion detector lights in the building. They were probably turned off at night. So no way to turn lights on once he got in.

Well, I'm fucked, he thought.

He didn't know his way around the building very well; only knew how to get straight to the office from the parking garage. He figured he'd go there first anyway. Check out the room he was familiar with first. No use stumbling around the rest of the building in the dark and getting lost.

Flashlight in hand, he climbed out of the car. Flicked the switch, dreading the sight of those glowing white eyes. He steeled himself as he headed toward the doors.

He reached the dark hallway, the flashlight highlighting very little other than exactly what the beam landed upon. The numbers on the doors told him he was getting close. So far every door was locked. Almost there.

The door to their office suite was propped open. The handle, crooked.

"Christ," he whispered under his breath. He touched it and it slid lower, hanging loosely. It made a small clunking noise that felt deafening in the silent darkness. He sucked air in through his teeth and his heart started banging away.

He stood very still for a few minutes, waiting for the silence to settle him. Nobody, nothing had heard him. Hopefully.

A scraping sound of metal on metal cut across the room.

James jumped. Another sound followed it; organic and humanlike, but he was caught so off guard he didn't know how to categorize it.

It repeated again. And again. A long scrape, and some kind of a groan. Almost a pleasurable one. But then high-pitched at the end, like a cry of pain.

The sound wrenched his stomach and his heart roared on, quick and heavy. This was unmistakably Rachelle's voice, but animalistic. He'd heard others like this, but this was her. *His* Rachelle. He took a deep breath. Swallowed. Turned off his flashlight. He caged his shouting insides and walked softly, flattening himself against the partition behind the front desk.

He closed his eyes and listened harder. The sound seemed to be coming from behind the other partition across the office, up against the windows. Immediately, he was able to identify the sound.

The paper guillotine.

James padded quickly through the row of cubicles to his left. He sidestepped to the area with the industrial paper cutter.

The moonlight had settled over Rachelle; her skin and eyes glowed in a gauzy haze. Her hair swung and shivered as she lifted the curved blade. Blood was the only color James could see. Drops ran down the silver-white blade as it sat, open-mouthed and waiting. Her shoulder muscles quivered. A shudder, trapped inside her skin.

Rachelle seemed stuck. Like he'd caught the act and it couldn't continue with an audience. A feeling like gunpowder stuck in a lit cannon climbed upon him and settled over his shoulders.

He realized it'd been some time since he let out a breath. He exhaled quietly.

The guillotine scraped rapidly down. A wet clunk, like a cleaver chopping a steak. He was closer now, so the cry was louder. He could feel her now as he watched.

Rachelle bent over her unmoving arm and groaned, the guillotine still closed on her arm. She cried out but seemed to quietly chuckle at the same time; a grated breath drawn in with little stops in between.

"Wake up. Stay with me. Feel it! You're missing out!" he heard it whisper.

Not realizing it, James had bounded over, closing the space between them. He wrenched open the blade and wrapped his arm around her waist, pulling her away from it.

"Rachelle, it's me. It's James."

Rachelle turned around slowly from within his arms, 'til their faces were almost touching.

"Yes, the witchy fuckboy!" Rachelle smiled.

Her eyes were big and black, like a deer's.

She tightened her good arm around his waist in return. He tried to check on her forearm but she hid it behind her back.

"How—" He could hear the blood dripping loudly on the carpet; two in quick succession every couple of seconds.

"I know it all," the throaty chuckle came back. "I knew you'd come for me. For her, I mean."

"Get the fuck away from her," James growled.

"How could I do what I don't want to do?" it laughed again. "I don't even know!"

"You won't have her. You cannot."

James felt like his insides were sweating. The sight of Rachelle being suppressed inside her own body was beginning to throw him.

"I'm telling you. You're better off heading back now," James replied steadily.

"I find it's much nicer here, actually. *Inside her*." It choked on the "r," like it was so excited it couldn't finish the thought.

A fury burned inside James now. It quieted the fear. He closed his eyes and opened them again. Whoever was within Rachelle grinned at him, open-mouthed and waiting.

He ducked out from her grasp quickly, unearthing the flashlight from his waistband, and a shiny black stone from his pocket. He took a deep breath and gripped the stone with the sharp black edges. He pressed his thumb against it 'til it hurt.

Don't fuck this up, you bastard.

Walking backwards, James gritted his teeth and opened his lips.

Light of protection,
Feel that I am pure of heart.

James continued his backwards walk, turning the flashlight on. The thing followed James in a mock zombie walk. Its smile stretched around the gums. It looked unnatural, like Rachelle's skin would crack.

Take hold of my essence,
And carry it strong.

He pointed the flashlight beam downwards, obscuring the obsidian stone inside his fist. He couldn't let it see what he was doing. The thing was getting closer to him now. Moving faster. He turned to look behind him. He was almost at the front desk.

My light is my weapon.
Follow its beam.
Find and then focus.

James held up the flashlight and pressed the stone to the lens. He pointed it at the eyes. The thing scowled and the eyes went from black to blinding white. It paused in its approach, letting out a quick shriek that went high and loud, and then seemed to quiet to the sound of air escaping. A pressure mounted rapidly in his ears.

He blinked hard to regain his bearings. When he opened them again, the thing was grasping at his shoulder. Shoving him up against the cubicle wall. He looked down at Rachelle's face. Her eyes sagged, pleading. Her cheeks drooped almost as if she were melting. Her eyes were black again.

Fuck! The flashlight! He'd let the beam move from her face. He tried to wrestle its hands loose but they held fast. He took a deep breath and braced himself, kicking it in the stomach. It loosened its grip but pushed up against him again with the good arm, bashing him back into the wall.

The partition rocked back against its metal feet. Quickly, James grabbed the top of the wall and heaved into it, along with the demon. He heard the welding fail; the metal foot cracked off the bottom of the wall.

The fall was short and quick. The wall crashed into the desk. He heard heavy things—printers and shit—crunch and slide off the desk and crash to the floor. He rolled off quickly, scrambling over the edge. He found the small triangle of space between desk, wall and floor. He crawled backwards on his belly into the shelter created by the chaos. He held the stone to the flashlight again and waited for it to find him.

Do it again. Restart at halfway through. This has to work.

He lay, waiting for it to enter. Flashlight and stone in hand. The vibration from the demon's mouth began again. He felt the silent screams, and then a strange croaking noise. He heard the drag and scrape of feet on the carpet. The sound was traveling around to the mouth of his space.

Something dropped to the ground, right outside the triangular opening. The shadowy face with the black shiny eyes peered in at him.

Flashlight on, stone on it. Its eyes were white again. The glow, a hellish luminescence. Fixed on him. He resumed his chant in a shout that numbed his vocal cords. He could only hear his own voice from within his skull; his eardrums barraged by the silent scream again.

My light is my weapon.
Follow its beam.
Find and then focus.

It crawled with an unnatural quickness. Shimmying its body toward him; undulating like a snake. It was on him again. Its head turning. Its tongue in his ear, interrupting the screeching. He couldn't hear his own shouts as he punched it in the forearm. The intensity in his ears was unbearable now. Something wet was leaking out.

Pierce the dark part
And rip it out.
Restore peace to this body.

Immediately, the pressure in his ears dissipated. Its exit flourished with a sharp pain, followed by a strong throbbing. He dropped the flashlight, pressing his hands against her shoulders, trying to hold her there until he was sure.

"Rachelle," he croaked. "That you?"

A long silence followed. He breathed heavily, shaking his head gently from side to side. His ears throbbed. Her face was buried in the alcove within his ribcage now. Her arms bent, hands on his chest. He definitely felt her abdomen moving. She was breathing.

He was pretty sure she'd be okay; She'd definitely need stitches. But disbelief tightened every muscle of his body. Even if he'd succeeded, he'd come so painfully close to losing her. He could hardly resist physically lifting her face to check on her.

"Chelle," he tried again quietly, his mouth dry as the fucking sun. "Are you with me?"

A long, shaky exhale. "I fucked up my arm," she said, matter-of-factly, rolling to her side. She held her it to her chest and hovered the other over it protectively.

"Well, the 'you' part of the equation is debatable. But yeah, we gotta get that looked at." James lifted his shirt over his head, then wrapped it gently around her arm.

"I was trying to cut Chad and Daisy out of my bones."

He winced at her. "How did that go?"

"I guess I didn't get far enough to know." Her laugh was a dry cough.

"Nope."

"Learned something about you tonight." She rested her chin on his chest, still squeezing her eyes shut, dealing with the pain.

"What's that?"

"Never knew you were pure of heart."

James laughed. "Yeah, it's just part of the chant."

"If it wasn't true, would the spell have worked?"

"Uh, I dunno."

255

"Were you scared?"

Another long silence.

"Honestly? For a minute, I didn't know if it was gonna work."

"How'd that make you feel?" She smiled knowingly.

James sighed. "Like you're my hero and I'd die without you."

Rachelle cough-laughed again, shaking her head. "So sarcastic."

"It's kinda true though. Had to make it sarcastic or I couldn't've said it."

"Ya did good, buddy." She shifted, patting his shoulder with her good arm.

21

Rory could see the smoke from very far. He smelled it before he could see it. The smell was old, like it'd been smoldering a longer time than the others. Muted, but musky. Like mothballs floating off an old person as they walk by you. He had no doubt they'd end up at the house that created the smoke. This signal that nobody else saw. That warning to stay away.

He wondered why they took him with. Why he couldn't have stayed home. Gaia and Stanton could've stayed home with him.

He was going to meet his dad. Most kids would get to feel excited. But not him. For him, everything seemed uncertain. And these days, threatening.

Rory watched James, who looked down at his phone. Scrolling mindlessly through some news app or something. He waited for James to look up. Eventually, he did. Rory saw the glint of recognition in James' eyes as he scanned the houses off the highway. Saw James steal a glance back at him. They held each others' eyes for a minute, then parted again.

He wondered if James'd been avoiding looking up on purpose. Rory wanted to ask him if it appeared as smoke and fire to James too, but he didn't.

He didn't know what he was going to do. Everything here made him feel very small. He smiled weakly at James. James maintained eye contact. James seemed to try to return the smile, but couldn't. His mouth was a hard line, but his eyes were soft circles.

Rory felt angry at first for the lack of reassurance. But then relieved he wasn't being lied to.

Are we going to be okay? Rory wondered. He wished he could ask these questions aloud. He felt cold, and tired. From traveling, and nerves. He shuddered. He felt James' hand on his. It was warm.

I like James, he realized. The thought surprised him.

22

The little blue house sat alone in a rural-looking area. The crumbled asphalt driveway stretched back a good twenty yards from the road. Behind it was the beach, big and glorious, the muted pinks of dusk coloring the mottled cotton clouds. Then a dark woodsy area off to the left.

As Rachelle pulled over and parked, she realized she only wanted one person with her. She had no clue what emotional catastrophe she was walking into, and that's who was there when she was all alone after leaving Chad. In these matters, Gaia always knew what to do.

"Gaia, can you come with me?" she asked. "I think I see him on the beach. James, can you give us a bit of a head start? And Stanton, maybe stay there with Rory until we come get you." Rachelle undid her seatbelt and stepped out, shutting the car door without looking behind her. Her eyes were riveted on the bony man in the stretched-out shirt. The familiar shoulders were rigid and set. But the stoop of them was new, at least to her. The gait was large and reaching, but a new limp had formed. Shuffle, step. Shuffle, step. She focused on moving toward it. Watching him as he watched the waves.

As Rachelle drew closer, she knew for sure it was Chad. His form was bent over and he kind of winced as he walked, like he had something up his ass. He carried a dingy off-white grocery tote on one shoulder. Despite whatever pain he was experiencing, he kept bending over, picking small items off the sand and placing them carefully in the tote. A few more steps closer and she could see they were seashells. He'd watch the waves after picking one, then stare at the ground. As if the waves were too much to look at, and he needed a little break after each time. Then his eyes would comb the sand again.

"Hey Chad," she said quietly, cautiously, hoping she wouldn't surprise him. He looked skinny and delicate. Like he'd been chewed through since she'd last seen him. His face was taut and pained, like one whose soul was wrenched with sorrow. It hurt her, even to look at him.

He didn't respond.

"Remember me?" she said, a little bit louder. What a stupid thing to say. What else could she say, though? Stupid was better than nothing.

"Hey." He squinted at her, again looking like he was in great pain. "What are you doing here?" He smiled at her, but only at the very corners of his mouth. It was like the rest of his face was stuck. Like puckered drywall. Pressed tight from the middle, out.

"We came to see you, and to ask for your help," she said, trying to make her voice soothing without sounding condescending, hoping they could somehow help him, too. Her stomach was starting to hurt with guilt and worry. Had he been here by himself all along? How long had he been in this state?

"I finish this, then we can go in," he said. His speech was muffled, like he had trouble moving his mouth. She looked closer, and his lips looked cut up. It must've hurt him to speak. This just kept getting worse.

"Hi, I'm Gaia," Gaia said gently. I'm Rachelle's friend. "Do you want me to hold that bag for you? It looks heavy."

"Yah, thanks," he said, again moving his mouth as little as possible.

"What are you gonna do with these?" Gaia spoke gently, like she was still assessing his character, afraid to make too much sound, or sudden movements. Rachelle glared at Gaia, frustrated by what she felt was condescension.

"She's just trying to help," Rachelle explained quickly to Chad. "She's afraid of freaking you out. It's okay." She touched his shoulder gently.

Chad's neck and shoulders went rigid. "I'm okay." He looked at Rachelle sideways without facing her. The cord of his neck twitched. Like his shoulder wanted to shake her hand off, but he was stopping himself. Rachelle felt queasy. She turned and watched the ocean, as though it were on her agenda. She pushed her hair back with her palms, trying to feel calm. Trying to shove back the worry.

Bad idea. The soreness from using her bandaged arm hit her in waves. Each little violence crashed over her.

Chad lying near lifeless in the dirt. James gorging himself with dirt. That fucking blade singing to her like a godforsaken siren. Violating her agency.

Stop, stop, stop. Her lungs only allowed quick little gasps. They were so close to finding out. But how much hope would they find in the truth?

She tried to retreat back to just the little simple things. The steps ahead. The walk to the house.

Don't, don't, don't, think about it. The mantra she'd started on the airplane came back. She'd avoid it until it was time. Her breaths were getting bigger. Nobody noticed her panicking. She picked up the pace to catch up.

"I'm cleaning up," Chad interrupted Rachelle's floundering thoughts, looking at Gaia.

Gaia peeked into the tote. "These are seashells though. Not garbage."

"It's refuse from the sea," he said, squinting at the bits of sun that glowed through the cloud cover above them. "I make use of them. Fractals."

"Huh?" Gaia squinted at him, holding her hair out of her face as the wind and sand combed through it.

"Fractals. They're everywhere. A pattern. A shape duplicating itself smaller and smaller. It helps temper the storm. Seashells have fractals. Snowflakes. Trees. Little trees too," he chuckled, remembering. "Cauliflower. I eat a lot of cauliflower. Don't know if it helps though, all crushed up in my stomach."

"Chad, keep in mind I just met you. I don't know your story. Do you think you could start earlier in the story so I can follow along?"

"I'm under attack."

He tipped his head as he looked at her, one eyebrow up. A genuine attempt at patience, but his right eyelid fluttered.

"Okay." Gaia was struggling with patience too. "By what?"

"You'll see when we get inside."

Rachelle walked backwards ahead of Gaia and Chad, toward the rear of Chad's house. She watched them walk together.

She tried to get used to this new hobble Chad had adopted. *It's not new, though*, she thought. She'd left him there. And look what'd happened to him. *Would it be any different if I'd stayed?* she asked herself. She didn't want to look back up at his weathered face. In her mind, though, she could see it. Like a waking dream. Staring at her. She thought about how he'd never be the way she remembered him. Chad, with the light in his eyes. Not ever again. She decided to look at Gaia instead.

Seashells scraped and clacked together inside the tote Gaia carried. The bag was banging heavily into her leg. The bottom half of it was soaked through, gritty with sand. Gaia's walk was uneven too, her gait weighed down by the odd collection.

Rachelle reached the old screen door first. She pulled it open and Chad grabbed it easily. He limped in after her.

The breeze followed them in. The back windows and the windows at the front door were open. The living room smelled like the outside. All the furniture was still where it was when she'd left, but nothing had been kept up. The rugs had dirt scuffs and stains. There was a small white plastic tub on the floor next to the couch, filled with water and . . . seaweed?

"What's in this tub?" Rachelle called toward the door.

"Kelp. It's soaking so I can weave it later."

"Weave it? Into what?" She tried to keep her tone light. She continued scanning the room until she saw something lying on the coffee table, by the windows.

"Jesus Christ, *Chad!*" Rachelle's heart roared in her chest, banging rapid-fire. She struggled to control her breathing. It had stopped for a second, and now it was coming too fast.

"There's a skeleton in your living room."

Rachelle gawked at it, her mouth open. She swallowed all the spit in her mouth, then realized she was out of spit.

It was brown, with mummified flesh across its eternally familiar shape. Silver hair still decorated its skull. Some strands had frayed out at the top of its head, and formed a clump. Like a little kid's Barbie doll. She scanned its body. It was covered in some kind of seashell chain mail . . . dress. She squinted, and saw what might be kelp. Impossibly thin. Painstakingly weaved through holes in the seashells, securing them into some weird vest for a dead companion. "Gaia," she hissed loudly, toward the door. "Do you think Rory's still in the car?"

"I don't know. Hopefully."

Gaia was still outside, on the stoop. Rachelle heard her kicking her shoes against the back step, knocking the sand off.

Rachelle walked up to the skeleton and stared at it. She heard Chad's broken shuffle. The floorboards squeaked by the back door when he walked in. She remembered that sound from when she'd nap in the den and he'd come in to wake her. He never let her sleep past forty-five minutes because he knew otherwise she'd wake up groggy.

"Chad, who is this? Who . . . did this?"

"It was me," he said quietly.

"You? No." Rachelle shook her head, in legitimate disagreement. "You didn't," she insisted, desperately.

"Well, me but, not. They made me do it." Chad struggled to get the words out. "They loved watching me with it. I've never felt them happier than that day."

"Who?" Rachelle looked up toward Chad.

"I call them the Shadows." He stood back a ways, tipping his head behind him, toward the kitchen. Two night-black humanoid shapes were blasted into the kitchen wall, next to the fridge. It looked like they were burned there. Rachelle squinted at them. It hurt to look at them. Her eyes stung, almost like she was staring at the sun. She shielded her eyes, then looked away again.

She backed up, bumping the coffee table. Something rolled, then landed on the ground with a thud and a crack. They turned in unison.

"Oh god, the head!" Rachelle shrieked, crouching down. Its jaw lay an inch in front of it, broken clean off the skull. She reached toward it, then rocked back on her heels, returning her hands to the tops of her thighs as she realized she was totally repulsed. Didn't want to touch it.

Of all things, chuckling came from the back door. James was there, leaning in the doorway, shaking his head.

"James?! Fucking *really*?" Rachelle cried out, looking up at him from the floor.

James held his hands out in surrender. "*So* sorry. Nervous laughter. I didn't mean to . . . I mean . . . is that *real*?"

"What do you *think*, bone boy?" Rachelle was so furious she couldn't think of a real insult. She turned and looked down at the head again, and back up at the body. A small decorative comb clung to a chunk of hair that hung awkwardly down near the collarbone. A tarnished silver thing with a shimmery blue butterfly set atop the tines.

"Chad, Is this Imogen? Immy?" she asked, incredulous.

"Yes," Chad responded, his voice sounding impossibly weak. "She came by a week after you left, to check on me. That's when it happened. I preserved her okay for about a year but then she started to go. But I kept her. I took care of her. And sometimes, when the moon is right, I'm able to bring her back. She freaks out but sometimes I can calm her down. Now she mostly gets that she doesn't have to breathe. That she doesn't have lungs," he offered. A small, sad smile was on his wrecked lips. Like he was nervously hopeful Rachelle would understand.

"That's fascinating." James looked deep in thought. "And what of these images in the wall? They can control you from there?"

"No," Chad looked down at the floor. "They live here with me. They mostly stay in the walls during the day. At night they come out through those entry points."

"Damn." James shook his head, rubbing his chin thoughtfully.

"Okay, you know what? Let's sit down for a little," Gaia said quietly to Chad. Rachelle caught Gaia looking furiously at James as she spoke. Rachelle snickered internally at this, but then righted herself, clearing her throat as she noticed Gaia had turned significantly paler since they'd come in. "When's the last time you had something to eat? Or drink?"

"This morning I had some glass," he said as he was shepherded to the easy chair.

"Oh good! A glass of what?"

"No, I ate some glass."

"Oh, for fuck's—" Gaia inhaled slowly. She took off her glasses, rubbing her eyes.

"They made me," Chad said again quietly, pointing to the shapes in the kitchen.

"So that's why your mouth looks like this," Gaia inquired. Chad nodded, licking the largest cut as though checking it was still there.

"What *is* this place?" she stage-whispered to Rachelle.

"It wasn't like this when I left." Rachelle's face sagged with guilt. She bit her lip and crossed her arms, looking nervously toward the kitchen, trying not to cry. James walked over to Rachelle and put his arms on her shoulders. She stiffened, and he let go.

"I'm sorry," he whispered to her.

She offered a stiff nod. *I just need some time.*

He settled for standing next to her, hands behind his back.

"Do they just stay in there, all day?" Rachelle asked Chad, eyeing the soot marks in the wall.

"Yeah, mostly they do during the day. Unless something gets them excited. They preserve their strength and wait for nightfall. They like to travel around the house and follow me sometimes. I think mostly it happens if I'm feeling anxious, or agitated. I can tell because I hear them knocking in the walls. When they knock, the lights go crazy." Chad sighed wearily. "Sometimes it helps if I sleep during the day. But then my nightmares wake them up, and they start with the pounding."

"Have you ever tried to get away?" Rachelle asked hopefully.

"Yeah, just once."

His exhale was laborious, like someone breathing through an old pain.

"Okay," Rachelle said, apologetically. They'd obviously caught him again. Brought him back. She was afraid to imagine what that'd been like.

"So, should I guess why you're here?" Chad said. His voice wavered timidly.

Hearing the stand-offish tone, Rachelle was eager to meet his gaze, but found his eyes were narrowed and watery.

She looked quickly down. "I'm so sorry I left." She kept her face impartial, but frantically pulled at some frayed thread off a decorative pillow.

"No, it's better that you did." Chad sat down slowly on the couch. "Are you guys together?" he asked, pointing to James.

"I guess sorta. Yeah." Rachelle looked James up and down while she spoke, appraising him. Wondering what Chad thought of her answer.

"Who's the kid outside? Are they yours?"

"Holy hell," James breathed, pressing his hands to the back of his head and turning away. "Do you want me to step out?" he asked Rachelle. Gaia made a move to stand up from the couch.

Rachelle stared at James, more over the situation than what he said. Then she shook her head imperceptibly at Gaia, who sat back down. The gravity of everything was bad enough. Emptying the room before she answered would be more than she could take right now. She decided she'd just go for it.

"No, Chad. James and I, we only met recently," Rachelle said, hesitantly. "I have to tell you something. About Rory."

"Okay?" his head tipped to the side in waiting. He was biting his lip. She couldn't tell if it was out of nervousness or just random. *Does he have any idea?*

"I just want you to tell me you'll be okay first—"

"Okay with what?" He furrowed his eyebrows, deep in thought. "I only asked about your kid. I've had plenty of time to get used to you leaving. Of course you'd have moved on by now."

Rachelle responded with a hopeful shrug, forcing herself to look him in the eyes. "Chad, Rory's five years old."

Chad's eyebrows raised. He jiggled his knee rapidly and twisted his lips to the side of his face. "So unless you ran away and got busy pretty quickly . . ."

"Yep," Rachelle whispered, nodding. She cleared her throat. "Rory's our son," she croaked.

The corners of Chad's mouth turned up, but his lips were still pressed tightly together, like before. Rachelle stared at him, praying he'd speak soon.

"Do you want to meet him?" she asked hopefully. She couldn't take the silence. Her insides were swimming and sick. Internally, she begged him to answer.

"No. Not now. Not like this." He held his arms out, looking down at his worn gray sweatpants and ripped white t-shirt. He chuckled quietly and shook his head. "I don't actually mean my clothes. Rachelle, I've been through so much. A lot of who I was, is gone." He shook his head slowly, running his hands through his longish unkempt hair.

After a silence, he took a long breath in through his nose. He swallowed hard. "What's he like?" he asked, eyes on the carpeting. "Is he—is he good?" He looked up, his eyes reaching Rachelle. "Is he a good person?"

"Yes," Rachelle breathed, returning his gaze. She got up and sat next to him on the couch. "He's a wonderful kid."

"So, not like my dad."

"Um, no." Tension unraveled from her body. She let out a short laugh. "Nothing like your dad."

"Good," Chad married his hands and held them, cupped, to his mouth. He smiled a little and looked at Rachelle. "Holy shit, we have a kid."

His eyes were still turned down at the outsides.

Rachelle frowned. "Do you blame me for leaving?"

"No. You were protecting yourself. And him. Do you still think I'm crazy?" His eyes floated around the room in thought. "Did you take the radio with you?"

"No. I don't think you're crazy. And the radio: I didn't remember taking it, but it turns out, yeah. I did take it."

His eyes narrowed again. "Is that why you're here?"

She nodded. "That's why I'm here."

"You turned it on," he whispered.

"Yeah, I—well, Rory did. He found it."

"So much for protecting you from my family's shit," he sighed. "What have you guys seen? How long have you been dealing with this?"

"Well . . ." Rachelle ran a hand through her hair. "A coyote. Or, hellhound?" She pointed to the kitchen. "Shadow figures, probably like those guys, at night? Um, possessions. James and me both."

James chimed in. "Not to mention Stanton's friend killed himself rather than allow a shadow figure to take him."

"Fuck!" Chad growled, pounding a fist on the couch cushion. He breathed heavily, shoulders heaving. He sat, still and quiet, for a while. James and Rachelle bowed their heads.

"What was his name?" he asked quietly.

"Javier," James replied.

"Yeah," Rachelle breathed. "A lot to unpack here, I guess."

Chad nodded slowly. "Who's Stanton?"

"A friend. He's outside with Rory." Rachelle rose from the couch, summoning Gaia with one hand. "Actually, we're gonna go check on him now. Sure you don't wanna come with and meet him?"

"Trust me, you don't want me to walk out the front with you." Chad pointed toward the kitchen.

"Do you feel that?" Rachelle asked, holding her arms out. Small tremors tickled her feet. *Oh, California*, she thought, shaking her head. *Just got back and everything's already shaking.*

"Is that an earthquake?" Gaia asked, turning toward a tapping sound.

Rachelle looked. The same three mismatched pictures were there, by the old oak TV stand, all wildly varying sizes and frame colors. A big gilded Victorian frame, and two rustic wooden ones. The tapping grew louder, faster. She focused on the painting she remembered most from her time here, watched it knock against the wall. A large ship with two masts. A sky, tinged with yellow, leaping up into blackness at the top edge. Waves roiled around the hull.

The tapping was coming faster now, and quieter. More like a vibration. "No earthquake," Chad said. "I told you. They're watching me. And now, us."

Three hard raps came from within the walls. The lights buzzed and flickered. The three visitors ducked down, hands over their ears. Rachelle saw Chad was just dipping his head slightly, eyes closed. Breathing heavily, but deeply. *It's like he's climbed into a dream*, she thought. *He's left this place.* She saw James observing Chad too, his face grave.

"Wow." Rachelle cleared her throat. Her heart leapt in her chest. "We'll be right back." She held tight to Gaia's arm, trying not to think too hard what all this had been like for Chad.

"Are you bringing it in?" Chad pleaded in a hoarse whisper.

"Bringing what—" Rachelle asked.

The banging came again, more loudly this time.

"Oh," she said. "Okay, yes."

She and Gaia exited out the front, clicking the door closed quietly.

***

When the front door shut, James searched Chad's face, waiting to come up with something to say. He couldn't believe someone had lived with this dark energy in their house for years. *Damn*, he thought. *Someone worse off than me. This guy will struggle with this the rest of his life, easily. If we all survive past today, that is.*

A chill settled over James. He couldn't tell if it was from outside, the monsters in the walls, or from within. He shuddered and crossed his arms.

He forced a smile. "You've got some shitty roommates, friend."

Chad rolled his eyes and nodded in response.

James pressed on. "Not to get all dark about it, but why do you suppose they haven't killed you yet?"

"I think they plan to, one day." Chad looked annoyed. "I'm gonna go change if you don't mind. I wasn't expecting company."

James sat down. Chad hoisted his bent body off the couch and shuffled himself toward the hallway. James looked around the room. Dirty rugs, the whole main floor covered in an outdated dark teal tile. The kitchen cabinets a beat-up dark oak. It looked like an old seaside shack. *I guess this is an old seaside shack. Or middle-aged.*

Chad walked back in. His hair looked wet and slicked back. His cheeks and nose were pink, like they'd been splashed with water and wiped off. His jeans had a giant hole in the knee. They looked loose—about to fall off. His black shirt hung off him as well. It seemed faded, like it had been washed thousands of times.

At least it looks like he's washed it, James thought.

"It's funny how this is the best I've got. Doesn't really fit me anymore," Chad admitted, shoving his hands in his pockets. "I used to lift when I was younger."

James smiled and nodded but didn't respond.

"So what are you, like, a sea witch, then?" James asked.

"A sea witch?"

"You harness energy from the sea." James gestured toward the seashell-laden corpse.

"I've never thought of it that way, I guess. My dad and I always had abilities. In the past few years, I've had to do some weird things to stay sane."

"Like what?"

"I don't know. Like, I go foraging for things that give off a vibe. That's how I came to use the seashells. I can feel this energy come off of things. I can feel when something's wrong, so I can stay away, at least back when I could go places."

"What can you tell me about your dad? Did he have these abilities like you?"

"Yeah, I'm pretty sure. He was a dangerous guy. He kind of put me in this situation. He's gone now, from this plane anyway. I thought he was dead, but now I'm not so sure."

James frowned. "Do you think he'd ever come back?"

"I mean, I can't think of a reason why."

"Chad, we are gonna need to go through this in more detail. There's a lot more to hell than just these"—he paused and looked at the kitchen, trying to force a smile—"shitty roommates."

Chad, while previously pale and gaunt, now looked like a ghost. "You mean I have to talk about them?"

James held his hands out defensively. "No-no-no." He paused. "Chad, I'm so fucking sorry for what's happened. For what's *been* happening to you. I've fought scum like this, and living like this longer than a day, I just can't even imagine. What I have to find out is how this all got started. And where the radio fits in."

At the word "radio," a rapid pounding traveled from where they stood. It raced along the back wall, toward the kitchen. What looked like black ink splashed across the window over the sink, plunging the kitchen into darkness. Then a clanging metallic bang traveled quickly from the window to the shadowy shapes next to the fridge.

"Aaaaahhhhh." A sound emitted from the shapes on the wall.

"Think they're coming out now?" James tightened his fists, trying not to back away in fear. It was all he could do to remain standing in that same spot in front of the kitchen. Hunger and excitement rolled from that darkened corner of the house in rapid silky waves. Their hunger flowed molten into his stomach, licking the insides like flames, and branched out. Moved past his stomach to envelop his whole torso, smoldering. He interpreted it as their whole being hungering for his soul. It broiled in his skull and cascaded out, then back in again. All his desires were throbbing. Flashing red, like they could feel more from eating him than he'd ever felt in his life. Like eating past his body weight in his favorite food. Fucking a consolidation of his favorite women. Lips, asses, sounds, everything. Hurting people who'd hurt him. Killing them. Slowly. Their blood like fertilizer, running thick like chocolate sauce. Blossoming in his mouth. All of this, at the same time. He rubbed his face, trying to focus on Chad as he answered. The room spun. He shook his head. Tried to clear it.

"I don't think so. But I uh, wouldn't use the r-word anymore. They really fucking hate that thing." Chad's voice was quaking. "Do you know some protection spells, for when Chelle and Gaia come back in?"

"It's what I'm here for."

James shivered, crossing his arms. He tried to inconspicuously bite the heel of his hand. Something, anything, to shift his focus from this. He tried to slow his breathing. He was sweating.

"You okay?" Chad asked.

"Yeah."

"I don't believe you."

"I bet you don't," James laughed dryly.

"It's a lot to get used to. Well, actually, you don't get used to it." Chad looked around the room and then rapidly changed the subject. "You said you had a vision?" Chad asked. "So you're a witch too?"

"Yeah."

"Are you part of a coven? Are those still around?"

"I doubt those will go away anytime soon. As far as humankind's concerned, they're rather ancient."

"Yeah I guess I sorta knew that."

"I used to be in one. Not anymore, though."

Chad sat gingerly back down on the couch. He gazed out the window. "I think my life would have really been different if she hadn't taken that r—that thing that she took."

James gestured toward the dark shapes again. "Do you think they made her take it?"

"I'm practically certain of it." Chad nodded slowly. "They can make you do things that you remember, or that you forget. Whatever their preference."

"Do you think they made her leave you? Or did they just sense she was going to leave and then got her to pack the . . . you know, the thing?"

Chad sighed. "I can't talk about that, can't think about that right now."

The "Aaaah" sound started up again from the kitchen. They could hear footsteps coming up the walk. Rachelle's muffled voice was unmistakable, even behind the door. Then a man's voice with her.

James' brain was prickling with warning. Those hungry feelings were trying to leap back up. "Any chance they don't know what she's bringing in?"

"I'm sure they know," Chad spit out. Then swallowed, hard. "You'd better start your magic stuff, *now*."

James turned his back to the door and faced the kitchen.

With the turn of the doorknob, a loud boom sounded from above, and all the lights went out. Rachelle pushed the door open, the scant evening light tossing her shadow across the doorway. Her eyes were wide on her shadowed face as she observed the dark room. She looked to Stanton, who held the radio.

"Should we do this outside?" Rachelle asked slowly.

Chad shook his head. "That would be even worse. If I put my foot at that threshold with you guys, I won't make it to the other side of the door. That or, they'd follow me out and"—Chad gestured toward the outside—"find the kid."

Stanton and Rachelle came quickly inside.

Stanton spoke. "Hey, I'm—"

"Stanton? I'm sorry about your friend."

"Me too," Stanton replied, matter-of-fact. "Wish we could apologize to *him*." He pressed his lips together, squinting, then changing the subject. "Hey, I can hardly see. Do you have a flashlight or something?"

"Or something," Chad said.

He closed his eyes and hummed. He held his hands out in front of him, fingers spread. Points of light appeared throughout the living room. Small, flickering points of light. Candles.

"You guys," Stanton said in a low voice, holding his hands out as though to steady himself. "I am *not* used to this shit, okay?"

"Fuck, man!" James took a step back, observing Chad. "You been holding out on me?"

"You just heard I revive the ghost of my dead neighbor to keep me company, and you're impressed by a little light job?"

"Fuck, dude," James repeated. "It's just quick thinking is all." He shook his head and smiled. "I'm a sucker for parlor tricks, I guess."

Stanton brought the radio around the couch and placed it on the scratched-up glass-top coffee table. Short high-pitched yelping came from the kitchen. Like dogs getting kicked or something. Stanton sidestepped, waving his arms wildly, as though trying to regain a balance he'd never lost. He returned his arms to his sides. He and everyone else laughed nervously. Everyone but Chad, who stared grimly toward the kitchen.

"Not sure why they're not rushing at us right now," Chad mumbled. "They must be waiting for something. They made it dark, I think so they can come out in the day. But they're still saving their energy."

"Looks like they even blacked out the windows?" Rachelle whispered.

"This is getting ominous," James said quietly.

Rachelle pointed to the radio. "Do you think you can make this work?" she asked Chad.

"I hope so. It *did* work, until you left me and took it with." He let out a short, angry sigh. "Did you guys fuck with it or something?"

Rachelle glared at him. Then she seemed to think it over, and softened her features. "I don't *think* we did."

"My dad's the one who built it," Chad explained.

"Yess!" James whispered.

Everyone stared at him. He'd tightened his hand into a sweet fist of victory.

"I mean, yess, he sure is the one who built it. Sorry," he whispered. "Just, that was my theory before we came here."

Chad raised his eyebrows briefly, then continued. "Anyway. It puts out an incredibly strong frequency. It fuses something like electricity with energy that acts as radio waves. It creates almost a battering ram that can tunnel through the earth. He used it to communicate with hell, the underworld, whatever. He used it in tandem with satanic rituals.

"I think he was always a fucked-up person. But I believe that when my mom died, it put him over the edge. He was afraid of death, but he had issues processing fear. It would make him crazy and violent. I've told you this before, years ago. Like that time with the air horn." He gestured toward Rachelle. She nodded.

"I imagine he wanted a way to not have to worry about dying. To him, this must have been the only thing he could come up with. So these guys I thought were his friends were other occultists. They'd formed this group. He worked his way to the top, like he did with everything. And he eventually got them to do what he wanted. To help him gain favor with demons. Inhabit the underworld."

Rachelle sighed loudly. "What did you find out that helped you form this theory?"

"I sort of walked in on them practicing their final ritual. They used me as an offering." He pointed a finger toward the kitchen. "After it was complete and he was gone, those fucks showed up and made me a prisoner in my own house. Well really, like it is now. I tried everything I could think of to get them to stop. I tore this place apart and found his plans from when he built the radio. After lots of studying and testing, I eventually was able to repurpose the energy the radio can create and use it as a protective force instead of what *he* built it for. For boring into the earth, summoning demons. Or the devil. Or whatever."

"Is there any way you can walk me through that ritual?" James asked. He made his voice gentle, soothing. He could see a hesitance in Chad's eyes. *Either he doesn't want to describe the ordeal, doesn't trust me enough, or both.* "Seeing the ritual will help me understand more of who and what we're dealing with."

"Sorry. I can't."

Chad shook his head.

James took the talisman off from around his neck and placed it gently on the coffee table, next to the radio. "I can help you. If you take my hand. I can see it with you. I'll put a charm on us so we won't feel the shitty feelings of that night."

"That really sounded too much like a sales pitch until you said shitty."

"I hoped that would work on you." James' mouth was a straight line, eyes closed. His lips started moving. After a moment, he reached his hand toward Chad's, like he wanted to shake. "Ready?"

"No," Chad said, though he didn't withdraw his hand.

"You can do it." James felt the promise of his words as he spoke. "You can go there," he said softly. "I'll be with you."

Chad's arm carried him through the final inches that hung between their fingers.

They touched, and James was thrust into the same house. In Chad's room. In the dark.

23

The minute Chad woke up, he knew his dad was gone. He could feel it.

Brock always came back in the mornings. But for now, he was alone in the house.

When he was younger, he used to cry when it happened. But he'd grown used to it. Sometimes, if he was scared, he called Imogen from next door. Immy, with the weird smells she brought over from her house. They came off her in waves whenever she made a big movement. Oily hair and cigarettes. She always brought her little wiry-haired dog. She'd come over and sleep on the couch in her oddly fancy clothes. The dog would sleep by the front door. Chad would hear the excited jingling when his dad arrived home in the morning.

He was fifteen now. Too old for that shit.

Chad got out of bed and walked carefully to his bedroom door. He peeked out into a dark, empty hallway. With his next breath in, a bonfire smell. But something was off. He smelled something else. He frowned, wrinkling his nose. *Was that burning hair? No, couldn't be.*

Chad wandered through the dark kitchen and looked out the back windows. The moon was hidden, but the snow still seemed to glow. He could see the point where the snow stopped. Where the ocean began. Then just deeper darkness.

He stared at the snow, and the darkness beyond. He checked the kitchen clock. Two in the morning.

He walked to the back door and looked out. Shivering, he listened to the rustling waves. Voices came from off to the left. A repetitive sound. A number of voices saying the same thing. Then quieting. Then saying the same thing again. Like a prayer.

He turned an ear toward the woods. It was coming from there. It had to be.

Why is he always out so late? What's the real reason? The fear inside grew like a brush fire. Licked him, like flames. He would not call Immy. A feeling arrested him, like if he went over by those voices, they'd know where his dad was. Maybe he was even with them. He could ask him to come inside. To come home.

I have to go over there, he thought. Where there was a fire, where it was light. Where someone could help him.

Chad returned to the house to retrieve his coat.

He emerged again into the back yard and followed the trail of smoke to the woods.

Chad pulled the hood of his coat far over his head. Icy fingers of wind still reached in and raked the front of his hair. The walk to the woods felt long. He told himself it'd feel shorter on the way back, and pressed on.

He remembered when his dad first found the group he hung out with nights. Chad was twelve. His dad said he met the guys at a bar, but his dad was never a drinker. He knew not to ask, though. His dad's explanations were usually a device. A means to prevent further discussion. Chad had learned by Brock's example not to seek further truth.

Anyway, his dad was happier than he'd ever seen him. The group got together twice a week. His dad wasn't any more giving, or active in his life, but he was easier to avoid conflict with.

It was an empty feeling, waking up alone in the middle of the night. At least before, there was a warm body nearby in case something happened to him. A safety net. A person who fed him and cared for him, even if it was in the most basic way.

The first night, Chad woke up terrified. He thought something had happened to his dad. He checked his bedroom, checked the living room. The kitchen. The bathrooms. What if he'd collapsed on the floor in there? No, nothing. After searching, and waiting, sitting on the couch in the dark hoping he'd show up, he walked over to Immy's and slept over there. He figured it's where his dad would send him when he was out anyway, so he'd know where to look. He left a note on the counter before he left.

He was shaken awake the next morning. His dad pulled him all the way home by the arm. He was tripping over his feet, struggling to keep up. To keep from falling down.

"You won't be doing this again," his dad had demanded. Not a request but a simple fact. "We need you here." He'd stuttered, then. "I need you here when I'm out. I can't have you scaring me. Thinking you disappeared, or were taken."

The best he could do was give a dirty look. *Bullshit*, he thought. He wondered what would motivate his father to act like he cared. Maybe fear of being arrested or something.

Chad wrenched himself from the memory as he reached the woods. The area directly in front of him was dark. He could just barely see where he was going from the glowing snow underneath him. He looked for the bonfire to orient himself. He was getting close to it. Dead branches reached out, pointing the way. Fleshless beckoning fingers.

He was nearing the bonfire. A group of men stood around it, evenly spaced.

Chad squinted at the scene ahead of him. Were they filming a movie or something? They looked like they had been placed by somebody. They seemed to be waiting for an order.

He heard his dad's voice. "Okay, now on to the next part." Chad followed the voice, and saw his dad crouch down to pull something out of a bag.

"Are we going to turn it on again tonight?" A high voice, across the circle from Brock. The man speaking was his dad's friend Ivan. A big guy with a bald dome, his remaining hair formed a horseshoe of sorts. Normally his voice was booming, confident. Chad thought he sounded scared.

"Yes, we have to get permission to proceed before the *next* dark moon," his dad replied shortly. "We've been through this."

"Are *you* going to do the talking again?" another man asked.

Chad didn't recognize him. A tall guy with long sandy blond hair.

"That's the plan," Brock said, sighing.

From the dark of the woods, Chad looked down at what his dad had pulled out of the bag. It was the crystal radio that his dad had started building a while back. He wondered what they were doing with it.

He watched as his dad pulled what looked like a screwdriver out of the bag. A screwdriver tethered to the radio by some kind of wire

"Hey Chad?" his dad's voice asked. Casually. Evenly. "What are you doing up?" As though Chad had just wandered sleepily into the living room.

Chad gasped and dropped his flashlight. He bent down to grab it. When he looked up, his dad's eyes were pointed right at him. The intense look that made Chad's skin prickle. He'd always considered it the "danger" glare.

How can he see me? Chad was sure the spot he'd been standing in was completely dark. Even if his dad had heard a sound, how would he know who it was standing there?

Chad's heart was beating up in his throat as he stepped into the clearing. He felt everyone look up at him. His face was hot.

He didn't like the way things looked. He didn't want to find out what that radio was for. He hoped his dad would just tell him to get lost. His skin was shrinking up. Curdling.

"What's that smell?" Chad asked. He had no idea what else to say.

"It's the bonfire."

Chad's dad was studying him carefully. He looked amused. Chad had no idea what he was thinking while staring at him. His stomach turned.

"I was just looking for you," Chad said lamely. "I couldn't sleep."

"Hey boss, any chance we do it tonight?" the tall man asked. Chad looked at him again. The man's coat was open. He could see a horn peeking out of the man's frayed v-neck undershirt collar. Part of some weird animal tattoo. "I mean, he's here, *right now*."

His dad looked thoughtful. "I was gonna turn the thing on now anyway. We can ask."

"*Who's* here now?" Chad asked quietly. Nobody answered him. His dad knelt down to turn on the radio.

Chad had heard enough. He backed away quickly and quietly for a few feet. Keeping an eye on his dad as he moved. He was about to turn and run, when he backed into a tree. Hit the back of his head, hard. He stopped for a second, disoriented, and then took off.

"Okay, Ivan? Paul? I guess you're gonna need to grab him. *Now*," his dad said. The urgency in his voice was a hungry growl.

Chad ran as hard as he could, skirting around trees. He heard the rustle of running legs. Crashing leaves and breaking branches. He cursed himself. The crashing was loud. There was hardly any distance between them.

Seconds later, a blow to the back, and he was on the ground, his face cushioned only by cold slimy leaves.

Someone was on top of him. His lungs hurt. They were stuck closed. He pulled and pulled for breath and there was nowhere for it to get in. He thrashed wildly but the pressure was too great. He shoved the hard dirt with his hands and his chest wouldn't leave the ground. His body allowed him short, loud gasps as the shock of the fall wore off.

"Get his arms," he heard Ivan's voice. Again, the deep tone was still there, but throttled. They pulled him up roughly, holding his arms behind his back. He thrashed some more, but they were older. Stronger. He felt bits of leaves on his face and moved to swipe them off, somehow forgetting that he couldn't. He groaned in angry defeat.

"What are you guys *doing? Why?*" He was beside himself. He couldn't fathom what all this was about. It seemed like they'd been planning this. But why did they hate him so much? What was wrong with him? He didn't think Ivan had kids. Maybe they'd talked his dad into it. He had fucked-up grades. He'd disappeared that one night. Most parents would ground their kids. But his dad didn't tolerate people fucking up. Maybe he'd finally had enough of him. He wondered if his dead mom was anywhere. If she could see all this. He wondered why nobody would help him. He felt the anger and sadness and confusion might kill him before these guys could. *Fuck them for doing this to me*, he thought. *Fuck this.*

Nobody answered him. "Bring him to the center," his dad said calmly. Chad made himself collapse, so they had to drag him. "It's okay," his dad said. "Just have him kneel."

They brought him to his knees in the center of the clearing, next to the bonfire, and held him there. He was so close to the fire, the heat stung his face.

Chad had an urge to beg his dad. To make him feel bad. Feel *feelings* for once. But he pushed the urge back down. Instead, he glowered at him silently. He waited for them to do more. So he could understand what all this was for. So he could start plotting his way out.

"We have to stay here to hold him," the tall guy pointed out. "We can't get in the circle for the ritual." Chad looked back at the guy his dad had called Paul. Paul looked down at him, like he was inspecting a fucking root he tripped over or something. Such a casual expression. What kinds of people were these? Chad had to look away. Fear and disbelief had him frozen and numb now.

"Okay, I'm gonna turn it on." His dad knelt down again, gripping the screwdriver. He jammed it into the dirt, burying it to the hilt. Brock twisted a switch on the radio.

A loud electric kind of buzzing sound surrounded them. Like they were inside and it had walls to bounce off of. Chad looked around at the circle of trees they stood within, trying to make sense of how the sound could behave this way.

Then a great cracking noise, like a giant tree trunk in the woods busting in two. Chad, startled, ducked down at the sound, but nothing happened. The electric buzzing continued.

A deep shadow issued from the dark of the woods. It crept from the bottom of the blackness, and climbed up the trees. It moved upwards, as if growing out of the ground. As it grew, it darkened. Arms and legs distinguished themselves. A head. It was sort of humanoid. But bent over. When it finally stopped growing, it was almost as tall as the towering redwoods.

Chad and the others had to tip their heads back to regard the creature.

"The boy is here now," the thing said. Its voice sounded electric, almost like the voice was being borrowed from the sound of the radio.

"Yes, we were practicing for the next dark moon and he discovered us in the woods," his dad said.

"This was not the agreement," it replied.

"I know."

His dad seemed to hesitate. Like he was gathering something. Courage? Or the right words to say whatever was next? "Because of this, we must request another favor."

"You wish to complete the transformation on this night?"

Another short hesitation. "Yes," his dad said.

"Time makes little difference," the thing said. "If you are prepared. If you do what we asked. We just need the boy. I have promised him to some others already."

"What will it be like for me?" his dad asked. "Will I have a body?"

"In a manner of speaking, yes."

"How will I get there?"

"You will be shown the way when the ritual is complete. I am here with you, but also, I am not. You must travel there yourself to fully cross over."

Chad's panic had been growing. Like an electric charge. Finally, it exploded out of him.

"Dad," he shouted. "Dad, what are they gonna do to me?" His throat was closing in terror.

"I don't know," he said evenly.

"You *really* don't care, do you?" He let out a choked sob. He couldn't help it. "This is really real," he told himself. "It's not a dream, is it?" He struggled, weakly now, against the men. He let his head drop.

Ivan leaned into him. The movement felt purposeful, but not efficient. Like it was meant to be comforting. Though it had the opposite effect.

"If you're trying to make me feel better, you can just fuck off," Chad shouted at Ivan. "If you wanted to help me, you'd have stopped this at *some* point."

"Shut up, kid," Ivan sputtered, clearly embarrassed by the attention Chad's outburst had put on him.

"*You* shut the fuck up." Chad turned and spit at him. Ivan tightened his grasp on Chad, twisting his wrist and pushing his arm into his back. Chad hardly cared. It almost gave him relief to release his anger at someone. It was somehow easier to direct it at Ivan than at his dad. Grief ran through him, hot like a fever. Numbness and pain wrestled each other. Chest pains. A final throbbing heartache after years of normalized neglect. His heart was a grenade. Looking his father in the eye would be equivalent to pulling the godforsaken pin.

"This boy," the giant shadow creature said. "This boy is very lively."

"I suppose?" his dad replied, sounding confused. "What do you mean?"

"*Your* request for *us* was unprecedented," it began. "So I propose something for you."

"I'm listening," his dad replied.

"We can keep the boy alive," the thing said. "My subjects can come here and have him. It would be like what you call a vacation for them."

"Whatever you want to do," his dad responded.

"Yes. His soul will remain within his body. They can play. When they want to come home, they will take his soul back with them. This is more fun for those like us. A rare thing. I can offer him to those even more deserving."

"Okay, sure."

"You may begin."

"We need the men in the center to hold him. Will that work?"

The thing waved its shadowy hand. "These are only formalities," it said, flippantly.

They resumed their chant. Like what Chad had heard in the woods.

> *We call on you, O shadowed crown;*
> *rend our restraints of flesh and bone.*
> *In hallowed shores beyond the tempest,*
> *temple of striated stone.*
> *Lead us to your sacred site,*
> *In shadow cast by rock of red.*
> *We'll follow 'til we find the place;*
> *the home where mortals go to die.*
> *In fealty, we offer the fledgling boy.*
> *Winsome leviathan, hear our cry.*

"Do you have the dagger?" Paul whispered urgently to Ivan between the chanted phrases.

They jostled him around as Ivan unearthed it. His heart began pounding again. The fear was surging out of the numbness that had deadened it. He struggled some more. He felt someone release one of his wrists. "Get his arm," one of the voices whispered. Another hand gripped it now. Paul was in front of him. Ivan was behind him, holding both arms.

Down, to the place where the hanged ones float.
Our pledge is our passage. This soul, our boat.
Cast your face upon us so we may see
your river paved with riches thick,
For which we all bleed.

His dad walked up and gripped his wrists. His hands were hard and warm, like stone. He tried to struggle, but it was no use; Ivan held him tight. The fear squeezed his insides, making it hard to breathe. His face scrunched up involuntarily, but he couldn't cry. He wasn't even sure who'd raised his sleeves, or when his dad pushed back his own. Ivan wrapped their wrists together in twine. Paul slid the double-edged blade flat between their wrists, turned it, and sliced.

"Aah!" Chad cried out.

At first it just felt like something thin and cold swiping across his skin. But then the pain shot up his arm. Deep and searing. He shouted and yanked his arms straight. His dad tightened his grasp on Chad's forearm. He glanced at his dad secretly. He was silent. Eyes closed. Paul moved the blade to their other wrists bound together and did the same, cutting both wrists again. He could feel the warmth of the blood. It tickled as it crept across his arms, then went cold in the night air.

Paul untied Chad from his father. It felt like half a dozen arms held on to Chad, someone tying his hands behind his back. The ropes were rough and tight. They touched his wounds and he recoiled, drawing breath through clenched teeth. Paul bent down to secure Chad's ankles, tying those together as well. They set him back on his knees. His cut wrists burned. He twisted his bound arms around to look at them. The red blood turned dark green and disappeared, like it was being sucked back into his wounds. He gasped at the sight of it. As the material disappeared into his wounds, the cuts seemed to heal back up before his eyes. A sour energy was jumping around inside him, starting at his wrists and radiating through his body.

Someone moved toward him.

Paul came at his face with the dagger.

***

Chad woke up in the clearing. He checked his surroundings quickly. He shuddered and pulled his hood up over his head, stuffing his hands in his coat pockets.

He remembered pulling his hood up on the way to the woods. *When did it come back down?* Everything rushed back to him, nearly knocking him over. His head was pounding. A strange pressure at the inside corners of his eye sockets. He touched the area. Both spots felt sore. His fingers detected raised skin. Like scar tissue. He rolled onto his stomach and pushed himself up to stand.

It was morning. The sky was gray. Everybody was gone. The radio sat in the clearing, exactly where his dad had left it. He already knew it hadn't been a dream, but this confirmed it. He could still feel that bad energy moving quickly around inside him. It was touching his mind now. It felt like he was watching a black movie in the back of his head, in fast forward. A movie with strange faces and unthinkable actions. Like knowledge of something, rustling around just behind a screen.

He moved toward the radio and put it in the black duffel bag, setting the strap across his chest and over a shoulder. It was heavy. He'd take it home with him. He'd learn about the thing. About how it worked. He would make it work for *him*. He didn't know where his dad was, but felt that he was gone. He didn't feel far, he just felt gone. Maybe whatever deal his dad made had gone sour. Maybe Brock was dead.

Good. Chad spit in the sand. He replayed what had been discussed last night. He expected something horrible was nearby, waiting to introduce itself. He looked around quickly. Nothing was visible. That sour energy he'd felt; there were two forces made of the same energy. They were far, down and away, but they were moving closer. Moving fast.

There was a ritual done with this machine. All these things were requirements for last night to have happened. Maybe there was some way to work against

296

these things with similar tools. He knew he and his dad could feel things. Sense things that others couldn't. That had to be a leg up.

He thought about how hard his dad must have worked to do . . . whatever the fuck this was. And to use his own kid like the missing puzzle piece; a fucking bargaining chip. So casually, too. *He wanted this like he wanted me once. Or my mom did at least, I think. I'll never know.* His heart galloped and his eyes stung. Well, his monster dad was still a person, just like him. Whatever he'd figured out to do all this, Chad could do the same to protect himself. He had to. He had no one else.

He was tired, sore, and cold. He blinked away the angry tears. Pushed back a sleeve and looked at his wrist. Faded scar tissue. He looked at the other one and saw the same. He touched it. It felt like the area between his eyes.

24

James woke up gasping. His lungs burned like he hadn't remembered to breathe. He felt multiple hands on his, and ripped his own away in confusion. His eyelids refused to lift. Much like trying to pull himself from a deep sleep. He lay still and took deep breaths. He focused his mind.

Slowly, he forced his eyes open. He was on the floor next to Stanton. Chad was lying on the couch, blinking. Looking equally disoriented.

"Who was touching my hand?"

Stanton was sitting next to James' head.

"You rolled off the couch during that Vulcan mind meld. You were about to let go of his hand. So I held both your hands together. Would that have interrupted the thing you were doing? If you'd let go?"

James just stared at Stanton. Trying to process the words. Clear the fog. "Yeah," he responded after a while. "Thank you."

Rachelle set the radio on the coffee table in front of Chad. "So right now, I'm guessing it's been doing the thing your dad wanted it to do? Attracting these skeeves from down under?" she asked.

Chad smiled at the characterization. "Yup. I think so."

"It seems like it opened a portal back where we live," James suggested. "I thought to destroy it but assumed that could do more damage. Make the monstrous beacon bigger, rip the portal open further."

Chad looked up at James. Sitting up now on the couch. "You're right, can't rule that out." He reached for the radio, his skinny fingers grasping the edges of the radio, sliding it closer. He slid his pointer and middle fingers against a small crack underneath the lightbulb-looking apparatus. A panel pushed open. Chad's fingers plunged inside. He shouted out, and retracted his hand, shaking as if to throw the pain from his fingers. He reached back in, slowly this time, then pulled a tangle of copper wiring out.

"What is that?" James asked.

"It was a splice. A joining of copper wires to connect a source of electricity to whatever needed to harness it. Normally you just twist them once to join them. But I'd twisted these into a Celtic shield knot."

He looked at James, then Rachelle. "I'm really not sure how they messed these wires up, though." The wiring was super thin, needle-like, and gnarled. Parts in the middle looked like they were braided perfectly, but the intricate pattern had been wrenched violently apart. Those thin wires pointed in all directions. Chad twisted his lips to the side, thinking.

"Ah, *fuck*," James was emphatic.

"What?" Chad asked.

James looked down, and sighed. "At one point, back in Boston, I was, uh . . . possessed." He looked up at Rachelle from behind his lashes. "Later, I had this memory come to me, where I was rubbing my hands vigorously on a scouring pad. You know, those sharp wiry ones?"

Rachelle and Chad nodded.

"I came to, and suddenly, I had this strong urge to go in the back yard and—"

"Eat dirt?" Rachelle finished for him.

James nodded.

"Yeah, your hands were bleeding after. We never figured out exactly why. I guess we were distracted." Rachelle put her hand to her forehead, raising her eyebrows.

James thought he saw her stifle a smile as she looked at the ground. *I think she's blushing.* Gently, he rubbed the scar tissue that remained on his hand from that night. Traced it from the heel of his hand to the space between his thumb and pointer. His blood surged in reply, and he flexed his fingers. The memories flooded back.

Behave, he scolded himself. His expression suppressed the avalanche within. He cleared his throat and turned back to Chad. Chad's voice came clearer as James returned his attention to him.

"Invented memories. That sounds familiar," Chad replied, quietly, turning away. He rubbed his face with his hands and turned back to them.

James sighed. "To think, I've been looking for the source of this signal for years so I can help out, and here I've scored a point for the baddies." He shook his head sadly.

"Fuck, indeed." Chad nodded humorously in agreement with James.

"Would it take a long time to fix?"

"It took me a long time to do it that first time," Chad said. "But I was doing a lot of experimenting. It took me maybe a year to get it to do what I wanted after my dad was gone. To use it to mostly keep them away. Maybe I can do it fast enough, if I can remember."

Chad stood up and headed to the kitchen.

"Any change of heart about your friend?" James asked Rachelle quietly. Their eyes were on Chad as he reached nervously into the corner-most drawer of the kitchen, keeping his body as far outside the kitchen as possible.

"Daisy?" Rachelle asked. "No way. The dead gotta sleep." She shook her head slowly, making a flat line with her mouth.

She hates me. He tried to push the thought away. *There's no time for this shit,* he scolded himself again.

Chad returned with a needle-nose and a spool of copper wiring. He did an apprehensive double-take toward the kitchen again before getting back to work on the splice.

James chanted quietly to himself as Chad cut some new wire, twisting it back into its old shape.

After a few minutes, James rose, still mumbling under his breath. He took a piece of chalk from his pocket and opened the back door. Drew a path from the door that opened up into the kitchen.

James sat back down and they all watched Chad work, waiting.

Eventually, Chad looked up. "Okay, I'm going to disconnect the power source for a second while I reattach the splice," Chad said. Yelping came from the kitchen again; this time louder; a chorus. Everyone ducked their heads. Chad scrunched down, covering his neck protectively.

A loud creaking sound now, as if every room of the house was settling at the same time.

"That's them," Chad rasped loudly. "James?! They're coming out now." He spoke rapidly, his voice a tight whine, throttled with dread.

The candles flickered wildly all around them, then stilled. The room plunged into silence. Then, a pulling. Like a force sucking at them. Starting at the mouth of the kitchen then circling slowly around the living room.

"Oh god. I just saw something." Rachelle spoke, and it sounded halfway between a sob and a gasp.

"What, what, what?" James whispered.

"I don't know," she moaned.

"Where," Stanton asked.

"It's here but it's moving. Around and around."

"You shouldn't've looked." James' head was bent down toward the ground.

"You gotta *do something*," she begged.

As James stood, his hands were fists. He drew them in front of his forehead, forearms flat in front of his face, elbows bent. *God, if I don't get killed for doing this.*

Javier, I call you.
As I once returned you to your body.
I held you near since that time,
I need you now to come beside me.

"Wait, Javier?" Stanton stood up quickly.

Follow the voice
you know to be mine.
In my hour of need,
I call you.

"What did you *do?*"

Stanton rushed at James, but was held back by the others. He wrestled against them, trying to free his arms.

Stanton landed an elbow to Chad's gut and wrenched himself free. He grabbed James by the shirt and hauled back to hit him.

A luminescent humanoid shape carried itself in through the back door in an easy, gliding motion, its legs still moving as though it believed it were walking. The movement was majestic, yet horrifying. James was afraid, but even more scared to look away. With every motion, a silvery light shone, then ebbed, shone and ebbed.

Its glow touched Stanton's cheeks and forehead. Shadows blackening the hollows: The eye bags, the frown lines. His expression lengthened, relaxing, as if dropping something heavy. He let go of James, and climbed off, staring at the transparent figure.

"Javier," Stanton whispered. The serene, disbelieving expression remained.

Javier looked at Stanton, offering an almost imperceptible nod.

"Who called me?"

His voice was quiet, hollow, *other*.

James opened his mouth to speak, but couldn't. The tornado of force that had surrounded them ceased. His stomach dropped. The phantom shimmering light from Javier illuminated two dark figures behind him. They were undoubtedly Chad's captors. And they descended upon the group.

Javi's light petered out, covering them in blackness.

And then the light returned.

They'd drawn nearer. The ethereal luminescence revealed the whites of two pairs of big, round, gaping eyes, polka-dotted with tiny red pupils. Mouths stretched into what looked almost like smiles, but rounder at the top, like they were about to take a bite of something. Their sparse teeth were brown and desiccated. Thin and pointy. Like large thorns. *Where are their bodies?* was the question that rang through him; an immediate and inescapable dismay. As his eyes focused, he realized their bodies were where he'd expect, only nearly invisible in the dark room.

When the light left and returned again, the demons flanked Javier on either side in approach.

"Javier?" James said sharply. "You got this?"

"Corry!" Javier's voice and tone was the same volume as before, but he seemed to throw it like an echo as he turned toward the back door.

Another ghostly figure rushed in and grabbed the demon closest to the door by the neck, wrestling it down, bringing it over her knee. It reached its hands up to grab at her face, but she pivoted herself away. It held tight to her chin, but didn't seem to be able to move her. It was snarling, then in between, laughing in quick nervous hiccups. The hyena-like laugh set James' teeth on edge. Its shoulders raised into hackles.

As though he'd been waiting for Corry to take action, Javier grabbed the other one by the shoulders. They locked arms and pushed against each other. Slowly, he lowered the demon down to its knees.

The humans watched the two glowing bodies, intermittently brightening, then darkening again, coming in and then out of sync. Corry was grabbing hold of the demon's arms, turning it, trying to push its chest against the ground. Pushing her knee into its back.

"James." The ghost turned to him, its ruined face flickering, on and off. The room darkening. "What now?" His energy was waning. His voice sounded weak.

"Chad," James directed. "Do that thing with the candles again." Teamwork, yes. We can do this. He can summon the flames, and I can draw power from it.

The candlelight returned gradually. Before long, the room basked in a shaky warm yellow.

James looked quickly down at his phone. "I can draw power," he mumbled to himself. "And I can harness it. But how do I draw, hold, then release?" James' brain was cramped by immediacy. The need for knowledge he didn't have. His mind flipped through things he could give people to do. But all the paranormals were busy, and all that was left were vulnerable humans. His shaking finger mistakenly punched the wrong thing. "What the hell is *witch cream?*" He rushed to close it and return to the spell he'd found. Fumbled with his phone. Dropped it.

He leaned over to grab it and looked up. The thing was flush up against Stanton's back. Holding his arms. Leading his hand to rip the splice from its connection to the radio.

The demon hand pushed Stanton's hand, forcing it to flip the switch.

"Oh fuck!" Chad ran over, saw that his splice was ripped from the radio again.

Peals of screaming laughter erupted from the demons. They shouted sounds that almost seemed like language. Three syllables. Repeated, over and over.

"What're they saying?" Rachelle shouted at Chad. "Can they speak? *Can they talk?*"

"Sometimes," Chad shouted back. He squinted his eyes, straining to understand.

"He's coming." Chad's whisper reached James in the dark room. "My fucking god. They said 'he's coming.'"

James chanted. Elbows to his sides, palms up, fingers outstretched. He closed his eyes, concentrating. Searching for the feeling. Letting it bubble up. Wrap itself around the words. They rushed out of him, deep-toned and thunderous.

> *Dark things what are not welcome here,*
> *You've made a home with your own sin.*
> *A nest of wood, a bed of plaster*

You've seen fit to dwell within.

I call you now, the souls of trees.
Of lime, gypsum, water, sand.
Take these beings. Hold them fast.
You've let these abhorrent angels last.
Lock tight your demonic contraband.

Fire within, fire outside.
Leave the places you are dwelling.
bring your rage, your force, your feeling.
Trap them in their place of hiding.

The flames from the candles sputtered. Smoke billowed. Flames shot out toward James' outstretched fingers, converging, then entering him. Somehow, he knew to curl his fingers. Flexing, letting it in. The heat became part of him. He felt hot, but like it belonged that way. The fire in him, outside him, was his to control.

He heard a scream. Someone shouting his name. Then a voice in his mind.

"Burn them all." The red eyes of the demons were fixed on him.

"Burn them all," they both said now, in unison. "Come with us." He felt the desire to follow their bidding. A small seed. Every second would give it space to grow within him.

Do it now, James ordered himself. *Burn them.*

"Yes," James heaved his shoulders slowly up and down with each smoldering breath. His breaths grew bigger and longer, until he realized no person breathed this way. All his organs were lungs now. They filled with smoke. The smoke and heat burned him. His insides tingled.

The humans moved away from him, coughing from the smoke. The sound was muffled. But he was the fire. He was doing it. He could hold it. Control it. He could breathe through it. He was powerful.

He flexed his fingers once more. Feeling . . . *good.* Some part of him realized he could only survive a few more moments like this. As a human, anyway. But the demons had promised him eternity. He'd felt that in their words. To be this strong, always. He could put down his little witch toys and change sides. He could be strong always, in body, and in soul.

Soul. He remembered Anton. Scolding him for doing too much. For wanting too much power. Too much knowledge.

"The sun, I'm like the sun," he growled. He felt the fire fill his eyes.

The world was hot. *The universe should be oranges and reds*, he thought. *Such a beautiful color. I could live eternally. A forever of sunrise.*

He squeezed his eyes shut. The heat licked him from inside. *This will hurt.*

He raised his hands, and released his fire. Used it to lift the two demons in the air. His fingers ached. He pressed on, still. His wrists, his arms, his shoulders shouted wordlessly. He moved them up higher, still. He pushed the inside of himself outward, toward the hole in the wall. The demons' wrinkled black eyelids folded closed and they screamed together. High-pitched and desperate. Two keening birds of prey. It felt like grating metal in his ears. The flames and smoke encased them, climbing quickly in brilliant waves of orange. Spreading. Their skin peeled and flaked, then floated into the air.

A sound of wood cracking issued from the kitchen. The smell of burning hair and sulfur seared his nostrils. The drywall and wood beams crumpled like wet paper at the black spots the demons had emerged from. A gnarled maw of wood and wall beckoned. Inside the wall, a thick, bubbling, black surface. He moved them closer to the opening.

"Keep pushing," James shouted to himself, not realizing 'til a second after that he'd spoken this instead of thinking it. Sweat seemed to congeal, a new, liquid layer of skin. *Maybe my skin's melting.* His thoughts were garbled, his muscles wracked with cramping.

One last shove and the demons were back in the walls of Chad's house. A thick, clumpy white substance dripped down from the top of the opening. The screaming carried on, growing muffled as the curtain of ooze carried itself down.

As the opening disappeared, the stream of fire slowly retreated back into James' fingers, back inside him. He felt hollowed now. Cold. Like he was nothing. No energy. No power. No anything.

I feel . . . he doubled over and vomited on the floor.

At least it's tile, he thought as he spit, trying to get the taste out. Knowing that was impossible. He leaned over and laid on his side. The tile felt warmer than his cold, wet skin. He shuddered.

"Holy shit, James. Are you okay?" Rachelle asked.

"Mm-hmm," he said, weakly. *She's worrying about you.* His burdened heart leapt, and he closed his eyes. *You did good, then.*

Nobody spoke. He lay there for a minute. Wanting to get up, but knowing that'd be a bad idea.

A sound, then. From behind the house. Like an amplified bull roar. An explosion, then a colossal crashing of waves.

Everyone looked at each other, eyes roving wildly, as though hunting for an explanation. Except Chad, who screamed and scrambled back against the couch, arms straight out, gripping the edges of the cushions.

James launched himself up. Ran to Chad, grabbing hold of his shoulders. He looked into his face. Something dark and green oozed out of his eyes, nose, and mouth.

"What is it? What's wrong?" James shouted. "Does it hurt?"

"What? No." Chad touched the substance dripping down his face and looked at it. "What the fuck? It's dark green."

"Yeah. Like that night. I saw it with you."

"Yeah," Chad whispered.

"Better out than in, right?" Tentatively, James chuckled.

"Right when we heard that sound, I saw something," Chad whispered. The skin on his emaciated face had gone pale.

"What? What do you see?" James shouted desperately.

"Him. He's here. Like they said."

"Who?"

"My dad. I see him, now. His legs." He moaned and covered his face. "They're growing!"

"His legs are *growing*?" James asked.

"At first all I saw were empty waves. Then a head. A long face and eye-holes. Then his legs were stretching. Longer and longer. Carrying him closer to the surface. From the bottom of the ocean. He's about to come above the water."

"Rory!" Rachelle cried out. "We need to go out there. Rory and Gaia are out there."

James, Chad, and Rachelle all looked at each other. They raced to catch up with Stanton, who'd already booked it to the back door.

***

Brock had been hanging. For days. Or in his old life, he'd have called it days. Shackled from the ceiling of the Big Room, in an enclosure of stone walls he could just barely see over. Ever since something happened with his old radio. Nobody had given him details; he had only overheard talk while they escorted him away.

A scrabbling sound echoed out of the still darkness. The fear that corroded him spiked with this new sound, but overall, it was constant. He'd learned to be one with it, like all the others here. The more time passed, the more he knew; there was no hope. No way out. The feeling that gorged itself upon whatever lived in his center was his home now.

There was always something happening up there at the top of this place. The top that he could only see when the white fire began spitting. When one of the beings here ascended to go through the dirt and enter the world above. To retrieve more humans that had earned a spot here. A blinding white light would envelop the creature.

It entered their eyes and mouth. Their eyes would glow with that white light.

He couldn't stop picturing what towered above him in the blackness. An inverted mountaintop, carpeted with moss. Gray-brown rock reached down, widening sharply with each shelf until it settled into gray-black walls of this cave-like underplace. Black striations dragged across the stone like a giant with knife-sharp nails had tried to mar it. Frayed tree roots hung down from the top. The white fire would twist with what looked like its own force, or wind. With it, the roots were like drooping willow branches; blowing violently in the furious breath of a storm.

Once these beings had swallowed the white fire, they would ascend up a branch, their eyes alight. Their hellish shapes pitched black shadows against the aged and dirt-mottled stone walls and disappeared into the green up above.

The noise continued, and seemed to be getting louder, though the constant echo made it hard to tell. Sometimes these creatures just came in to stare at him. Appraising him, or something.

He looked around him again. But nothing. There was no glowing now. The scuffing sound was drawing closer.

The echoes louder, and sharper. He guessed something had reached the walls of his enclosure.

A low voice that sounded like humming, and some sort of guttural other language.

"What?" he asked. The word came out high-pitched and quick. He sounded to himself annoyed and frightened.

"Are you searching for me?" The other voice was startlingly near. A voice that sounded like it was choking while speaking. The strange guttural sounds continued behind this voice. The location was on the wall opposite him. He heard a single scuffing sound. Then a landing. Feet touching down on the stone floor.

"Yes, I heard you coming." Brock knew his voice vibrated in fear, but ignored it. He used to lash out when frightened. Like on earth. There, his rage was treated like the roar of a lion; feared in return and—he felt—respected. But not here. Here, he was among lions. And he, the smallest and weakest.

"You have been here for some time but you do not speak like us," it said.

"I am learning," he said, concentrating on keeping his voice even. "It is harder than any human language."

"You do not try very hard," it said. "You should be honored to be among us, but you do not show it."

Brock decided not to answer.

"Your foolish little radio has been turned on, after your human offering fashioned it into a device to block our influence. Why your disciples did not think to destroy it once you had established contact and secured your place here is incomprehensible."

"I'm aware of this," Brock's voice cracked in his attempt to sound composed. "It has been pointed out to me already."

"Your arrogance is astounding. We have allowed you to join our ranks, and you complain that we point out your mistakes. Do you not wish to become acclimated with our kind?

"Yes, I do."

"So far, you have done nothing but cause problems."

"I see your point. I fail to see why you should need to repeat things that have already been said. If you are tasked with giving me some sort of news—"

"You will speak only with respect." Its voice was a loud effortless growl that seemed to shake the small enclosure. "The time has come to retrieve your little radio."

"Will I return to the surface through the um—"

"—through the cliffs?"

"Yes, up there?"

A low hum came from the creature. Like a generator trying to kick on.

"No," it said slowly, drawing out the "o."

The sound was low and long, like a monk's otherworldly chant.

Brock's fear spiked again. "How will I go?"

"That passage is reserved for those of honor who retrieve the human dead. Somewhere between this underplace and the passage to your world, the worms or the mud-wraiths of the deep would eat you."

"So... how would I—" Brock started, swallowing his annoyance with the creature's flair for the dramatic.

"Only *we* can gain passage through the oldest of trees. Those ancient trees whose roots reached our underplace, then died. They crack easily. We seize them, without need to ask, for they danced away years ago. Their vacant bodies bend to our will. We break them, and then, with very little work, we are their marrow."

It was then the white fire came. The sound was like a blowtorch, but deafening. Brock squinted in the blinding light, then opened his eyes slightly, focusing back down on the creature. A hideous thing that appeared to have a long snout like a horse, the barrel chest and gangly legs of a deer. But only two. No torso or hind legs. It smiled. Or what Brock imagined must be a smile. Its long snout split completely in two, opening like two blades of a pair of scissors. Its jaws were lined with long rows of broken teeth. Like brown, cloudy glass shards.

"You do not need to stare. I know that I am beautiful," it said evenly. It continued with its instructions. "The sentinels who are with your son are creating a passage for you through the earthly sea. You will find the radio, and return the way you came with the radio. If you do not come back, or you come back without the radio, the ocean will drink you. And the ocean is *always* thirsty."

The creature laughed. Though it sounded more like an "ahh." Like it'd surprised itself by making a joke.

"How does this work when I cross over? Will I be a spectre? A shadow figure, like the sentinels?"

"As you exit the water, you must pull earthly materials from what is nearby to fashion a body. The portal will bring you to the place where you resided in your human life. The storm will fuse your parts together, or"—the monster shrugged—"it will destroy you."

Brock furrowed his brow at the flippant warning. "How will I defeat them?"

"That is your problem to solve."

"I want to be large. As tall as the trees. Like Satan when he appeared to us in the woods. He was majestic. Fearsome."

"That was but a shadow of his true self. He was merely communicating. He did not need to get around. To fight. That is not advisable."

"I'll get you your radio. I'll destroy those who tried to fight us with it."

"In this place where horror is art, I must say my bets are hedged against our kind for the first time, horrid Goliath. Either way, the show will be glorious and I will not miss it."

***

They came out to an angry sea. Dark waves seething against a darker sky.

"Rory! Get away from there!" Rachelle shrieked. Gaia and Rory stood at the beach, staring up at the waves, mesmerized.

"Look mom!"

Rory pointed at the sky.

Rachelle gulped in a breath. She rejected the desperation in her body and shouted over the crashing waves. "Get *away* from the water, Rory. It's dangerous." She gestured sharply to Gaia to get Rory back to the car.

"No, not the water. Look above it! That red rainbow!"

Rachelle stared in the direction Rory pointed, but all she saw were fast-moving, black roiling clouds. She felt, rather than heard, a deep humming. Like she'd gone deaf, but knew that the earth was singing. A song of death. Of an entry. "I don't see anything." She bowed her head, turning to James. "James, can you see it?"

"Send Rory back by the house," James responded, slow and steady. "It's dangerous. I hope, knowing that, you will still agree to come with me."

"Where?"

"We'll start with wherever we heard that crashing sound."

"How bad is it?"

"Don't know." James bit his lower lip. "It's definitely something though."

25

Rachelle sped after James, kicking up sand, trying to catch up. He'd started a path up the coast toward the trees. The others had gone inside the house. She heard a huge splash as something emerged from the sea, a few yards past the shore.

James was closer. He must've seen more. He stopped immediately, arms out in front, as though the splash had taken his balance.

"What," Rachelle sputtered as she got closer, not even forming the question.

A pair of legs met at the top. A triangle made of rotting, gnarled driftwood. Its gait stuttered unsteadily as it reached the shallows. James grabbed Rachelle's bicep, pulling her next to him.

"Don't touch it. Don't even go near it," he whispered. "Don't let it know you're here."

She turned quickly at the clatter of hollowed wood. More scattered driftwood from the beach shook slightly, then dragged along the sandy floor toward the legs. The wooden pieces gathered, thickening them.

Rachelle started: "It's heading to—" James shook his head slowly.

Not now, he mouthed.

The figure headed toward the woods along the beach, driftwood climbing up its form. The wood piled up, and a torso materialized. It gathered speed, tripping every few steps. Righting itself. Once there was a considerable distance between them, James motioned for Rachelle to follow.

"I can see flames on the water. I think there's some kind of portal there," James whispered. "That thing came from underwater without a body and is having to build its own. The more materials it gathers, the stronger it will be."

"So you think he's heading to the woods so he can grow?"

"Yeah, and I think the flames are what Chad described in the note we found."

"The lake of fire," she breathed. "What the fff—" Her jaw hung there. "Are you sure we should let . . . *it* . . . grow like that?"

"I don't know if it's Brock yet. I need to watch what it does. If it is him, I need to know what kind of entity he's become. What his abilities are. And the longer it doesn't know we're here, the better," he replied, looking only slightly sure of himself.

"But once it's finished building itself, you think it'll start looking for—"

She trailed off. She was afraid to say "radio" after what they went through in the house. She rephrased: "For what it came here for?"

"Yes, exactly," he said. "So for our sake, I hope it's not Brock."

"Who else would it be, really?" she rasped.

"I mean . . . it's *probably* him."

Rain burst from the sky. The cold wind of the storm had intensified since the figure had emerged from the ocean.

They were almost at the woods now. Their hair already sodden, pasted to their heads. They wiped the driving rain from their eyes.

The creature had grown arms, shoulders, a head. The branches of colossal, dead trees bowed around it, groaning at the joints, as though they'd been grabbed and ripped down by an invisible force. Tiny fingers of wood bent and severed themselves. They hurtled toward the monster like bullets. They reached its body and writhed in a frantic jerky way. Stop-motion worms, entering the openings on its body.

A huge branch severed at the trunk, bashing into the creature's gnarled belly. It doubled over, absorbing it. Thickening, growing. More branches assailed it. Malformed and crooked, it grew, then reshaped until it was almost as tall as the trees. More cracking as the branches tightened themselves to the now massive humanlike form they'd created. Two holes like almonds opened in its skull.

The eyes. They glowed with fire.

"Oh god," whispered James. "Can you feel that? Coming off him?"

Rachelle let out a scream. It looked down at her casually.

A great sound like crackling flames emitted from the head of the thing.

"Thou shalt have no other gods before me," it thundered. The crackling sound continued. It felt like laughter.

"Kind of a shitty excuse for a god if you ask me," James shouted through the rain.

"You think you are pious, little magician?" the voice went on. "I've watched you. You use magic, just as I do, to try and alter what comes next. And you do so poorly, if I might add."

"So what are you saying? Being better than me means you're golden? Setting a low bar for yourself, my friend."

Rachelle's stomach flipped. She rubbed her face. *We're in mortal peril and he's started a pissing contest.*

"You don't know where I've been. What I've accomplished."

"I'm good at guessing. I can tell you think you've done better. You talk like one of them now. You know? Like you're thousands of years old. How much of you is left in there? How's it feel to sell out, body and soul? Is it as fun down there as you thought? Staying up late? Eating ice cream from the carton?"

The giant thing that was Brock slowly moved to its knees. It hauled back its great arm to swipe at James. Rachelle followed James as he ran from the clearing, into a grove of trees.

"You missed us up here, didn't you?" James taunted. "Well, it's too fucking late now," he shouted behind him as he ran. Rachelle ran ahead of James. She turned to check on him. Saw him trip on a giant root, but he righted himself and kept running. Brock's wooden hand came down, trees slowly parting. Tipping back, their twisted roots exposed. The ripping of the ancient trunks was so loud, her ears seemed to give up comprehending. Rachelle covered her ears, and they ached just the same. After a minute she gave up covering her ears, used her arms instead to keep her balanced as she ran.

"Any ideas?" James spit out, the question quick and tense. Rachelle stared back at James, terrified at the prospect that he didn't have a plan. His eyes were wide and they darted around.

"Don't know," she shouted, panting as they ran, dodging trees. Branches dragged across foreheads, narrowly missing eyes. She had to speak between the colossal footsteps. This felt too certainly like the end of the line for them. "Don't know any spells for this?"

"Nothing's coming to mind," James replied. Another earth-shaking step. "Feeling existential right now. Was lovely knowing you, though." His terrified eyes didn't match the casual way he'd spoken.

Something connected, hard and heavy, into Rachelle's calves. Immediately, her feet left the earth. Her back and head bashed against the hard ground. The pain in her head blossomed like thorns in her skull. She sucked in air through her teeth.

The crackling fire sound coming from Brock intensified.

"Couldn't run long, you must have known." Brock's booming voice shook her skull now. It was impossible-close now. Surreal.

She could think of no response. Instead, spit and let out a screaming groan. She looked down at the ground. Couldn't look at this creature, at how she was going to lose to it. To lose her life and give it the pride in having taken that life was more than she could handle.

Nothing, she thought, straightening her body. Lying on the forest floor. I have *nothing. Nothing.* She stared up at the canopy of living branches above her. The luminous flower moon gazed at her through the dead and living branches, the bunches of leaves. *Life,* she thought. *Please. I don't want to leave you.*

Look down, came a whisper. Somewhere in her mind. Daisy's voice. *Look down, my little seashell. I have a flower for you. It's named the same as your supermoon.*

Rachelle sat straight up, holding her head. She looked around. Nobody there except James, bent over, hand resting on a tree, panting and looking helplessly into her eyes.

There's magic in these woods. Find it. Use it.

She scanned the ground. There. A cluster of moonflowers, vines climbing up a nearby tree. The petals stood open. White pinwheels, drinking the moonlight.

"Moonflowers," Rachelle shouted to James. "Can you do anything witchy with that?"

"Moonflowers?"

"Yeah! I think Daisy talked to me. She said it's named like my supermoon. Tonight's the flower moon."

The giant dried wood thing cracked and popped as an arm swung down and picked up James. They were out of time. A shout, followed by a strangled cry. Rachelle looked up, horrified. He was going to squeeze the life out of James right now. In front of her. And then he was going to do the same to her.

"No!" she screamed.

Grab it, grab it now! Ignoring her aching head, ignoring everything, she lengthened her body and bent over, snatching up as many of the white bell-shaped flowers as she could get.

"James!" she screamed.

The moment she looked up, her torso was encased in the giant fist of wood. Pushing her ribcage. Crushing the breath from her body. "James," she shouted, but her voice hardly made any noise. He was bent over the other fist, his head and arms spilled over limply.

"My god," she whispered. "James?! Are you alive?"

Yes, my dear, the voice that sounded like Daisy's said. *He's playing.*

"Now you're going to tell me where this radio is," the booming voice rattled her once again.

"Is that why you're here?"

Rachelle forced herself to laugh. She was shaking with fury. *If this giant fucking log is going to laugh as it kills us then I'm going to at least try to piss it off.*

"So you need something, huh? You didn't come back just because you felt like it? You're on an errand?" She kicked hopelessly toward James. She wanted to hand him the moonflower.

"Tell me what you are doing."

"Checking if he's dead." She tried to force her voice to be matter-of-fact. She could feel the joy it took in their misfortune. James' limp form was devastating her, but she persisted.

"You wish to see him better in this condition," it said, and brought its gnarled fists together, bringing Rachelle closer to James.

Quickly, Rachelle gripped James' hand and thrust the flowers into it.

"Plant it, James," she screamed. "Make it grow. Make it live. Make it hurt."

She watched him closely. She'd clearly felt his hand close on the flowers. She watched the vines and the clump of dirt sag in his fist. He didn't move.

"Pathetic," the voice said casually. "A basement magician, and now a gardener too?" He squeezed her again. Rachelle tried to suppress a grunt as her breath was forced out of her. The wood was solid, unforgiving. "I will crush your friend and then you will tell me where the radio is. If you don't, I will crush you too, and go find Chad."

Brock's screaming white eyes looked down at James. A loud, dry, cracking echoed through the clearing—outer branches from Brock's arm were coming loose. They slithered, jerky again, breaking themselves with every movement. One small branch reached up, then splintered.

The cracking became a chorus, as the pieces split, traveling down Brock's arm.

When they reached James, his head was still lolled to the side. He squinted in anguish, bent his forearms up and crossed them protectively against his chest. The cracking wood was still moving, encasing his midsection now. James' head rolled to the center. Rachelle thought she could see his mouth moving.

When the wood grew still and quiet, Rachelle could make out a strong, but shaky voice.

> *Flower moon,*
> *rouse these blossoms*
> *that bloom under your gaze.*

> *Moonflower,*
> *Give this dead wood your seeds.*
> *Grow.*
> *Curse its death with your life.*

A rustling sound was coming now from James. His head still bent down. His speech had tapered off to a whisper. Rachelle didn't want to speak. Didn't want to force James to betray anything. Didn't want to satisfy Brock.

Something is happening. She searched desperately for the source of the sound. Her heart was leaping in fear. Fear, laced with a blind burst of hope. Was this sound something of James' doing, or Brock's?

Skinny green vines were growing, wrapping around the wooden branches holding James. They moved quick and shaky, like a time-lapse. Rachelle blinked as they spread up Brock's arm, stopping at his elbow. Little green buds emerged from the vines in threes, wrapped into points like tiny tridents. As she watched it, her soft squishy innards were growing edges. An architect etching her flesh with a blueprint from the inside out. A whole-body war tattoo.

"Huh." The monster looked casually at his arm. Nothing else seemed to have changed. He lifted the arm with the new growth, still gripping James easily. Brock pulled at the vine with his mouth. It was coming back out from between the branches in sections. With three separate motions, he tore the vines from himself. Most of them fell to the forest floor.

"No," Rachelle whispered. "Fuck. No!" She looked to James. He was whispering to himself again between gritted teeth. She felt helpless. Helpless and doomed.

"Yes." The giant bent its face down toward her again. "He won't be trying that again." Rachelle pushed against its fist, trying. "It isn't any use," it said. "It must feel like a loss. But, be useful. Tell me what I want to know."

Rachelle squinted up at him. A strange green glow seemed to be coming from beneath his impossible smoldering eyes. From his mouth.

"Yes, it is not an easy decision, but—" He paused, tilting his wooden head, as though considering something himself.

"But you know it's the—"

Rachelle watched in awe. *What's happening?*

"How strange," he said, and tipped forward slightly. The hand holding Rachelle swayed and started to loosen. She leaned back and inhaled. She could breathe deeply again. The soft smell of dirt rushed over her, twisted with the sharp, fresh scent of new growth. The smell of green.

James spoke one word. "Genius." Her chest swelled.

They swayed again. James crashed into Brock's chest, crying out. He still couldn't move from being wrapped in branches. He struggled to free his arms, but nothing moved. He kicked at the thing's torso, missing by yards.

"James!" Rachelle screamed and reached for him as she drifted further away.

Brock swayed again. The hand that held Rachelle seemed to loosen again. She slid down, almost falling out. Locking her teeth together, she grabbed for the ledge just before his pointer finger. Groaning, she pulled herself up and straddled his hand.

Another bigger sway as gravity fought to take the weight of its body off one foot. A giant "boom" as the other foot moved and stumbled, overcompensating for the loss of balance. They were vibrating. It was all Rachelle could do to hang on. Brock had caught himself just in time.

Her shoulders, her chest, her aching arms screamed in protest, as she dragged herself up, scaling his bicep, and pulling herself up onto his shoulder. Her belly was against it. She hung on, desperately.

The giant face turned to her. Her heart was in her throat. She shuddered violently. The blinding white eyes stared at her. The bright light screamed against the inky dark, but somehow, the expression looked deadened. Like he wasn't all there anymore.

The giant maw hung open. She couldn't help but look down into the green glow. She swore she saw the corner of a giant white moonflower flute deep inside him. Waiting to see the moon. Waiting to open itself.

She turned away and squeezed her eyes shut, trying to force away the breathlessness. James was bundled up in driftwood. Stuck still at the giant's chest. There was going to be one chance to help him. If Brock stumbled while she jumped, she'd fall and be dead. She'd have to make her leap.

Don't think. Just go. She gathered herself up into a crouch, and immediately launched herself down.

She opened up her arms, and tried to grasp James at the shoulders on her way down, but she slid and landed on the wrapping of dead branches. She shouted out in pain. Her arms were around James, and the wooden bindings that held him. They were hard and unforgiving. Even harder to grasp. She pushed past the pain in her fingers, and hoisted herself up, so her arms were around his shoulders.

"Ah!" he shouted out, sucking in air between his teeth. She moved so one armpit was positioned over his shoulder, and she pulled desperately at the bindings with her fingers.

"Is it working?" he asked, still gritting his teeth. "It's so tight." He winced as he tried to move.

"No—" she started. They were tilting again, this time violently.

"Hang on," he shouted.

They heard the collision he made, and they landed immediately after. It felt like the *ground* was hitting *them*. Rachelle peeled herself back up.

"Fuck," she heard James groan in pain. She turned, and he was facedown. His arms still stuck, but the wood around his elbows had fractured in the fall. The giant wooden creature was lying on the forest floor. Eyes and mouth still open and glowing. A long "aaaahhh" was emitting from its mouth, but it didn't stir.

"Come on!" Rachelle screamed, pulling James up by the wooden bindings. They took off toward Chad's house.

26

They rushed in through the back door, Rachelle gulping for air. James headed straight to the kitchen.

"A little help?" He gestured toward a block of kitchen knives.

Rachelle moved to the knives and crossed her arms, thinking.

She turned to Chad.

"Chad? Do you have—"

"In the garage," he said, getting up slowly, exiting out the front.

"What's he getting?" James asked, hesitant.

"Hedge clippers, I think," Rachelle said, furrowing her brows in thought. "At least that's what I was going to ask him for."

"Mom? Are you okay?" Rory asked quietly.

"He's been scared," Gaia said.

"I'm okay, honey," she said, too scared to hug him. Didn't want him to feel how hard she was shaking. She hid her hands in her pockets and tried smiling reassuringly.

Rory looked pale. "What's James got on him?"

"It's uh. Like, pieces of trees?" Rachelle looked at Gaia, then at Stanton. "We should get Rory far away from here. Brock is back. James hurt him but he's still making sounds. He wants the radio and he's going to have it unless we physically stop him." She plunged her shaking hands deeper in her pockets. "I thought we were gonna d—" She held her knuckles up to her lips, inhaled shakily and exhaled. "Nevermind." She tried to keep from crying.

Rachelle tried to change the subject. She turned to James. "What did you do with that spell?"

"Moonflower seeds. They're potent."

"You're kidding."

"We," James stopped himself. "I mean, people ingest them to get a cheap high," he sighed. "If you know where to find the flowers. But it's dangerous. People get hallucinations, but they can also totally lose their grip. Or get really sick. Someone I knew ended up in a coma."

"Ah," Rachelle nodded. "So that's why you said—"

"Genius," James finished the thought.

"It's not gonna last, though," she stated for confirmation.

"I mean, I can't pretend I know how moonflower seeds affect a giant demonic tree, but probably not."

"Yeah," she nodded. "I guess I knew that."

"Speaking of genius, how did you know about the flower moon?"

"I dunno, I'm a space girl." She smiled nervously. "Like a Spice Girl but with space. But ultimately, Daisy made the connection for me."

"Daisy?" Gaia asked, incredulous. "Not your friend? Your friend who *died?*"

"Yeah," Rachelle said quietly, clearing her throat. "She talked to us. Helped us slow that thing down."

"Damn," Stanton whispered.

"Exactly." Rachelle bit her lip. She looked at the door impatiently. What was taking Chad so long? Her mind floated back to the forest. Maybe learning more about what they'd done to Brock could help them. "So, Daisy told me about the flower moon. But does that track in the supernatural realm? I mean, humans named it that, right? And same goes for moonflowers?"

"From my experience, it does seem like the universe likes our little human coincidences. I think of it like Skinner getting excited when a pigeon scores a pellet. Like someone or something rewards us when we notice things or make connections."

Everyone looked up as Chad came back in through the front door. He held a lopper with long handles. The blades were curved; perfect for cutting branches, but they were covered in rust.

"Did you check if that thing opens?" Rachelle asked.

"I, uh, nope." Chad looked down at it, holding it in both hands, elbows out to pull it apart. Nothing happened. Chad pressed his lips together, straining. He let out a loud breath, giving up. His arms relaxed. "Uh . . . Stanton?"

"Yeah, I'll give it a try."

Stanton walked over and took the tool from Chad, then brought it over to James.

"Aren't you gonna test it first?" Rachelle asked.

He pulled it open as he reached them in the kitchen. "It's not broken, just stuck," he said to Rachelle. Carefully, he severed each branch from around James' body. They dropped heavily to the floor.

James stepped away from the pile of branches. He moved his arms from his body slowly, sucking air between his teeth. Stanton and Rachelle stepped back and looked at James' arms.

"You okay?" Rachelle asked. His pale biceps held fingerlike bruises and scrapes where the branches had been. His skin was still indented. Her face felt suddenly cold as she pictured how it could've gone if the thing had squeezed just a little harder. The sound of snapping bones echoed cruelly in her head.

"I mean, I don't think anything's broken." James' voice was wound tight. He shook his arms out slowly. He watched Rachelle intently. "Are *you* okay?" he asked her.

"Yeah," she whispered.

"Chad?" he asked, without looking away. "Can we borrow your little seashell blazer?"

"What for?"

"I am gonna need Rachelle's help to finish off this tree chunk. You said it worked to protect your neighbor's body."

"You want me to wear that?" Rachelle's mouth lifted in disgust, looking at the body. Nausea rolled through her, and her throat constricted. Sweat crept across her forehead.

"Are you coming back out to help me? If it might protect you, I really want you to wear it."

She looked to the ceiling in thought. Their escape had been so narrow. Her heart was leaping. A hot, sick feeling sat in her stomach. "I suppose it wouldn't do for us all to just run, now?"

"I think you know the answer to that."

They were really going back out there. "Yeah. Giant tree demon-person who is here just for a magical radio we must protect. Got it."

"So you'll model the shells for us, Chelle?"

"When you put it that way, it just sounds soo tempting." She tried. If only they could skip to a time where playful jokes were actually funny. They were all just going through the motions. She tried not to think of how all this might end.

***

Rachelle walked out the back door to a horizon folded in fog.

She groaned, turning toward the woods, where they'd left Brock. Listening intently for some kind of movement. The rain was gone, but still hung in the atmosphere with a sick kind of humidity. Like if she only concentrated, she could see droplets suspended in midair.

The seashells hung loosely from her shoulders, tapping each other with her movement. It was awkward, uneven. She'd already had to adjust it twice to keep it from sliding off one shoulder; the other side was tight.

She walked directly toward the ocean, unsure of what they were going to do. James had done some protection rituals in the house. He'd focused mainly on her strange seashell chain mail. But it seemed they were both hoping she'd pull something out of her ass—or Daisy's dead ass—at the last minute again. His only advice was to stay near the ocean, the place where he felt the seashells—her supposed protectors—would harness the most power. He'd spent a little too much time googling chants. Reading off his phone as he went. The internet research was enough to fracture her confidence in him. To put a tremble in her step. There wasn't much choice but to press on. They were out of time. Out of options.

She was trying to wrestle the noise from her mind when something outside interrupted her.

Boom. A sliding step. *Scrape. Boom.*

Her heart roared to life. As though it had been waiting dormant for this moment.

"He's up," James called to her, from a few steps behind.

Shit, she thought. She hoped the others were safe. Stanton, Gaia and Rory would be in the car now, driving away from what would ensue. Chad had stayed behind in the house. He wouldn't allow the radio to be in the car with Rory, knowing that's what Brock was after.

We can offer to destroy it. While he watches. Then maybe he'll let us live. She pushed the heels of her hands against her forehead, working to breathe in the heavy air. She turned around, shoulder to the ocean, and waited for the goliath to emerge from the fog-choked forest.

The fog parted. Or the monster parted the fog. Something looked off about the gnarled dark form. More so than before. The white eyes were set wider apart, and uneven. There was a tinge of green in there, like Rachelle had seen emanating from its throat. It seemed to be heading straight toward her. She twisted her feet in the sand, and stood her ground. Her hands became fists. Her mind raced through what to say. What to do. What would carry them to the other side of this moment. She waited as it drew closer. The earth-bashing sounds grew in volume. The ground began to absorb the vibrations his steps were causing. The nerves in her ankles leapt up, zapping throughout her body. She tried not to focus on that.

"Your friend saying anything?" James mumbled.

"Nope," she said.

Brock was nearer still. She could see what looked off. Two giant moonflowers had blossomed upon his gnarled face where its eyes had been. One much bigger than the other. An eerie deformity. The faint green glow sat behind these eyes. Its gait was uneven, as though it were a little drunk. It stumbled a half-step every few feet, then continued. As she looked at its feet, she realized they had scrunched up; they were no longer flat. It reminded her of applying water to a straw wrapper as a kid. Watching it twist up like a snake.

She took a deep breath. She was never good at shouting. Her friends used to laugh at her voice when she got mad.

"We can destroy it for you," Rachelle shouted, her voice screechy and uneven. Her hands cupped around her mouth. "If you let us live!"

Brock stopped in his tracks and stared at her.

"It must come with me." He turned quickly toward the house and headed in that direction.

Rachelle faced the house in turn. The blood leapt in her temples. She and James stared silently.

The thing marched toward the old blue house on the beach. When it got there, she saw its waist was as tall as the house itself. It lifted a foot and bashed the roof in. A chaos of splintering wood echoed across the empty beach. Brock had to hold onto his bent leg to get the foot back out. He stood for a moment, steadying himself. Then kicked at the same spot again. Its whole leg was inside the house now. A quick shout echoed from within the house, and a groan.

"Chad," she uttered, her breath gone from her now. She held onto James. "No," she whispered. "No, no, no." She shut her eyes and bent her head in mourning. She sunk immediately to the ground, enveloped by the feeling.

Another sound pulled her back up. The worst possible sound.

Another voice. Another scream.

Rory's.

The second she heard it, she was up. Screaming and running full blast toward the house, feet sliding in the sand. "Rory!" his name wrenched out of her. "Rory!"

The tree reached in and grabbed the radio.

"Leave him there!"

Her voice was a hammer. A command, burning from the inside of her. Exploding out.

"Leave him there and we will let you go."

The force of that promise, and the truth in the phrase rang in the heavy air like an echo. Her body was empty. Everything blurred except Rory.

It looked down. "Is this mine? A grandson?" it asked, ignoring her warning. It reached into the house again and lifted Rory out. Another more frantic scream.

"Mom," he said. His sobs broke his speech. "I'm sorry."

He was supposed to be far away from here. How had they let this happen? Rachelle steadied herself, picturing herself as an immovable stone. Blood, water, muscle, bile: All of it, solid. She willed her face to harden. She addressed Brock, not looking at Rory. "Put him down and I guarantee you will leave us unharmed."

"Unharmed," it chuckled, turned, and headed back toward the ocean, carrying the radio and Rory.

James ran up to meet Brock. He hurled his chant, anew, up at the thing. Hands out, fingers spread.

Flower moon—

"Unharmed," it boomed over James' voice. It turned the word over slowly in its mouth, lengthening the "a." It lifted its colossal, gnarled foot high off the ground, hovering for less than a moment.

Rachelle knew it was too late even as she lurched forward in a desperate run. The giant foot stomped James. She heard a surprised shout, cut short as the thing twisted its foot, crushing him in the sand.

"Mom!" Rory shouted again, his middle held tight by the monster.

"God," she whispered. "No." Rachelle had no more breath in her lungs. She tried not to look at what she couldn't undo. At James lying there, crushed. Tried not to think about Chad and what had happened to him in the house. To forget what she'd felt when being squeezed by that fist, knowing Rory was feeling that right now. She followed as the monster waded into the ocean.

She was the cold now. The cold was her. Her arms, her legs, her middle, the back of her neck. Every part of her cringed. The water held her back. Made her feel desperately behind. She'd never felt so hopeless. So out of time. Footsteps sounded behind her. A glowing circular shape with blurred edges sat ahead of the thing. There was something inside it; something big and dark. She couldn't make it out. A portal? Rory's head was barely above the waves. He reached for her. Then she could only see his fingertips.

Focus on your surroundings. It came out of the water. Is it going back in? Taking Rory and the radio to hell with it? Her hands were fists. *I have to fucking slow it down,* Her mind was shouting now. *This is it. If I don't do anything else in my life. It doesn't matter. This is it.*

"Repeat after me," Daisy's voice was in her ear again. "Finish what James started."

Rachelle's next words were a hoarse shout. She could hardly hear herself, with Daisy's voice, and the water in her ears. But she let her words be an earthquake inside her.

Flower moon,
grow these blossoms
what bloom under your gaze.

Moonflower
Now it's time.

Take what's yours,
Completely.
Eat your dead.
Crush
Cultivate
and multiply.

Brock went under. Rory with him. She filled her lungs, and went down, swimming in big, hurried strokes. Rory was crushed between its arm and its torso. His eyes were closed, cheeks puffed out. His hair flattened, then floated up on its ends with Brock's every uneven stroke.

Rachelle pulled on his arms, and his eyes burst open. She couldn't stand the fear in them. The pleading. He was stuck fast. She looked toward the bright circle in front of them. A giant green grid pattern slid sideways around the circle. Slid sideways, then shook, and slipped back in place. As she stared harder into the circle, she saw big dark rocks with black striations that resembled scratch marks.

She looked back down at Rory. A green glow emanated from the cracks of the wooden creature. Vines wrapped around its arms again. She grasped Brock's torso and grabbed his other arm, trying to lift it. To get Rory out.

Is it starting to give? She didn't dare admit this to herself fully. She pushed again. She could swear she was feeling something crack between its arm and torso.

Its wooden foot kicked her in the gut. Stars blossomed in her face. When she could see again, Brock's misshapen white flower eyes were boring through her. Everything felt slowed down. It reached for her, letting go of Rory and the radio.

A loud splash sounded from behind Rachelle. She turned as somebody swam past her, pushing her back. Moving her just out of Brock's grasp. The person headed straight for Rory. She screamed angrily, a high-pitched muffled sound, circled with giant bubbles. She grabbed for their shirt. Her brain snapped back into place. Blue jeans. Blue fleece. Stanton.

A harsh pressure built quickly in her ears again. A sound like the whooshing of a seashell. At first, it was unintelligible rasping. Then it formed words:

> *Worry not,*
> *it's only*
> *the fisherman.*

Rachelle held her hands to her ears. The spot nestled right against her ear canals was dry. Like air bubble earbuds.

> *He found*
> *a waterway.*

Same way I
found you.

Again, it was Daisy. Even past the inhuman rasping. The way she lengthened her "r"s. The way she threw her whole being into the word "you." Like she cared for nobody else but whoever shared that moment with her.

The beauty in that ethereal sing-song voice twisted her guts in sorrow and awe. How she missed the Daisy she knew. The one who lived and breathed. And she knew she'd do the same for her, in life or in death. *Thank you*, she thought. And hoped desperately Daisy could hear it.

He's allowed passage.
He knows not our secrets;
He only knows
What he needs to do.

Stanton pointed at what looked like another shaking grid. A second one to the right of the first one. Instead of rocks in this one, she saw a dark horizon.

"Safety," Stanton mouthed, pointing to the grid with the second ocean. He was taking Rory to safety. He pointed to the radio. "Get it," he mouthed.

Listen to Daisy. He knows what he's doing, she told herself. She swam over and grabbed the radio. *This will distract him. He'll let Stanton leave with Rory.*

The thing grabbed Rachelle, then immediately let go. It threw back its head with a high, inhuman scream, jerking its hand away. She looked down at herself, where he'd touched her. The seashell vest was looped over her biceps, but covering her chest and stomach. It was glowing green, too. Brock looked down at his hands and arms. The vines thickened. Growing faster this time. Leaves sprouted more stalks and again more leaves. These are fractals too, she thought. They raced up his torso and covered his shoulders. Tightened around its wooden form. Over its shoulder, the second portal flashed a bright white. Stanton and Rory disappeared.

Wood snapped as one arm severed, then the other. Connected now by the fat tendrils that ravaged its body. The vines bunched up, and bound around the arms, wrapping them back into the torso. More cracking as they twisted, snakelike around his middle and crushed inward with loud rapid-fire fractures, like a boot stepping on bubble wrap.

Then with one final loud ripping sound, the head came clean off.

A giant white moonflower blossom appeared in place of Brock's wooden skull, which floated slowly away.

She wanted to rejoice and collapse at the same time. She started abruptly back for the surface. Her lungs burned. The muscles of her throat were spasming. Trying to open. To pull for air. She started a desperate half-stroke upwards with her free hand. She looked for the surface and saw only darkness above. Something from behind grabbed her bicep and pulled.

***

Stanton ripped a path behind Rory, toward the little blue house. The backdrop had looked so mundane the first time he'd walked through that door. All he'd noticed were the scorched grass and rusted lawn chair, plastic straps at the seat ripped to hell.

Now, it was different. Curdled black clouds swallowed the sky. Dead branches half-cracked and hanging, still managing to scrape the skyline. Fog engulfed almost the entire beach and forest. The sound of waves crashing on the shore. Rapid fire, one after the other, as though the ocean were trying to empty itself.

He kept picturing Rory's eyes wide open as they drove away from the house. Like his brain'd been stuck or something. It'd worried Stanton, but he was still shocked when Rory threw open the door and jumped out.

"Rory!" Gaia had screamed. She'd barely gripped his jacket as he exited. Stanton had shouted at her to let go, for fear the kid would fall too close to the car.

"Shit!"

He'd slammed on the brake pedal and pulled up and away from the curb, fear ramming his horrified heart. He'd braced himself for the worst. The Worst being the lurch of tires over a human speed bump. When the car came to a full stop, he shoved the gear shift into park and took off down the block, toward the ocean.

The kid was already halfway to the house. Cutting across the grass, turning, heading toward the front door. Stanton saw Rachelle standing out back, at the coastline. She was facing away from them, looking to the woods.

He still wasn't even close to the house when the infernal tree thing reached it and stepped through the roof.

Stanton changed his trajectory, turning away from the house as he saw where the thing was going. Stomping away, holding Rory and the radio. He watched it crush James.

"Goddamnit!" He ached to arrive. To catch up and help.

Almost there. Chest burning now, he followed behind Rachelle. As she entered the waves, he was still too far behind. She shouted something right before he lost sight of her. Her weird dead person's vest started glowing. The waves were restless. Choppy. They looked black and glossy. Like a watery obsidian. Two glowing spots leapt out at him in the black water. The one to the right was a brighter black. It shimmered at him. Then flickered. As though it were sentient, and commanding his attention.

His gait slowed as he splashed clumsily, heavily, into the frigid water. Its chill covered and entered his body, hardening his skin before the water so much as reached his knees. He dove in, his body fighting him, trying to float atop the surface. A large wave came out of nowhere. He hadn't even seen it gathering. It pushed him, ass-down, back onto the sand.

As soon as that wave joined the ocean again, the water flattened. No waves. No ripples. Nothing. He shuddered violently. Little bubbles were suspended in place.

His mind twisted and turned, trying to recall some explanation for a phenomenon like this. His heart kicked him, and hammered faster. *Why do I feel like I'm supposed to go in there? Like this is an invitation?*

He waded down quickly. The water didn't feel cold anymore. The moment he dove in, he saw that goddamned demonic driftwood let go of Rory. Again, he looked to the two large glowing spots in the water. The one to the right was a dark beach. *His* beach. The place he fished at before he got a bigger ship and moved to Boston. Good Harbor Beach in Gloucester. He remembered he'd gone back to fish there for a day right after he'd first met Rory. The day he'd seen the other beach in the water. The beach and the moving grid.

He squinted, trying to focus on the hole in the water. On the beach he knew. The sky was just barely tinged yellow, coloring a small part of the coast. He saw it now. The grid, shuddering over it. Then sliding, and settling up again.

As he noticed the grid, a female voice rang out. Clear as a bell, but under the water. Frantically, he looked left and right. He saw nothing.

> *The sun here set,*
> *But it has risen. To you,*
> *the sun is at the center.*
> *Now's the time where you can enter.*
> *Take the boy, and now, cross over.*
>
> *Enter the hole in the water.*
> *Follow the path of the rising sun.*

He didn't recognize the voice, but felt he could trust it. *Is that Daisy person talking to me?*

He pulled himself toward the kid. The most important thing was to get Rory to safety. As he reached Rory and grabbed hold, he heard an eerie sound. A high-pitched underwater shriek. He turned to Rachelle, her eyes bugging out in fury, her face pulled up in a sneer. "Safety," he mouthed to her, pointing to the opening. He pointed to the radio and swam for his fucking life. Rory clung to him. He was shaking. Swimming took more effort now.

Stanton hesitated when he reached the hole in the water. His stomach lurched. *Am I really just going to enter this thing? What's it going to feel like? Are we going to die?*

Rory's face was screwed up and hardened. Stanton imagined Rory couldn't go another second without breathing. He didn't have a choice. It was either commit and do this, or swim to the surface and risk Rory getting grabbed again.

Rory nodded, very slightly in encouragement.

They held each other around the waist. One more stroke and they'd be there. Their free arms pointed forward into the world-hole. He felt them being propelled forward, as though being vacuumed out of the water.

***

He was startled out of his shock by a childlike whine that quickly grew deeper. A tortured moan. Then an acrid stench. Sulfurous. It burned his nose.

Stanton started to remember.

He'd been swimming toward the hole with the dark beach. But this place was bright. Impossibly so. And cold. No, hot. So hot he felt frozen. He was slick with sweat. Or thicker. Like his skin was melting.

Keep going, the voice rasped urgently. *Move like you're swimming. And don't stop.*

Stanton looked down at Rory, and immediately regretted it. He saw blackening hair. Curling up. Smoking.

Then, the bright swallowed his sight. He could hardly open his eyes.

Now! The voice was angry now, its otherness alien and terrifying.

Startled into action, he swam with one arm. His eyes were swollen shut and burning. He tried to aim straight. Vertigo wracked him. He was as much right-side up as upside down.

He pressed every muscle as he swam. Arms, legs, pelvis, abs. No air seemed to move past him. He didn't know if he was getting anywhere. The smoke tickled his nose. He coughed, but could only hear it within his own skull. His throat was scorched.

He'd observed enough. Now his mind was making room to wonder if this was it. And if it was, would that be so bad. The boy buried his face into Stanton's chest. He felt Rory's rapid breath, sticky-hot on his skin. *If his breath is hot within all this heat, he's basically breathing fire. Just let it end,* he thought. *He's suffering.*

A shadow materialized over the brightness. Like someone had placed a hand over his closed eyes. He tried to pull them open again. More burning. He squeezed his eyes tighter in response.

Into the cooling darkness, they fell. Whatever came with that darkness seemed to immediately settle itself against him. It felt wet and cold. But the real kind of cold. He tried to breathe. His lungs rejected it immediately. He was coughing water from himself, into more water.

Rory. His mind was stuck. His eyes shut. He felt him there, still. *Are you okay?* Stanton was still coughing. Trying desperately not to inhale between coughs, though water had already gotten in. Again, slimy seawater entered his mouth. His nose and throat burned; eyes stung. Rory and him were floating. Stanton's brain still obscured up from down. With each cough, his lungs felt like they were shrinking. A few more coughs and he'd be out of oxygen.

A shift. Rory was pulling Stanton now. As they moved, his mind flipped. Suddenly, he knew they were going to the surface. His mind and body were centered. He was convinced that what was down in California had somehow become up.

They must've been close to the surface. The air embraced his face. The atmosphere entered his mouth and nose. He coughed again, violently. Expelling the seawater. The ocean hugged his ears. Water streamed from his mouth in rivulets. Rory dragged him until the sandy beach met his body.

"Are you okay?" Stanton managed, then coughed some more.

"—eah . . ." was all he heard as his coughing subsided.

"Yeah," Rory repeated simply.

His voice felt stretched thin. Fatigued. "Where's my mom? Where are we?"

Stanton was lying flat on his back, arms out. Waves licking his legs. He tilted his head up, chin to neck. Saw the sun peeking up. Its rays were fingers. They touched the clouds.

"Gloucester."

"Where's that?"

"Home. We're practically home."

"Oh. Is it all over now? Is my mom okay?"

"I hope so. We'd better find out."

***

Something grabbed Rachelle by the shirt and pulled her; violently, suddenly, from the water. She felt her body become heavy as she emerged. Her bare legs and torso dredging up clumps of wet sand. Her entire back was exposed, her shirt hiked up violently as the surf passed beneath her. She hung on dearly to the forearm with one hand, radio still under her bandaged arm. She used the rest of her strength trying to keep her body from dragging on the ground. She kept trying to look up, but couldn't move her head. Her legs burned as the sand grains dug across her skin.

"I'm so lucky I found you." A familiar voice. Choked with emotion.

Her heart stopped, then leapt in staccato. She strained her arms, her back, her neck. Righted herself roughly, gripping the taut forearm with both hands.

"Jesus, *James?*" she shouted.

He came to a stop, a few feet from the shore. His eyes looked incredulous.

At what? she thought. *My response?*

His eyes roved back and forth, plucking words like stars from the night sky. "Jesus James. That's not my name." His smile was warm; his eyes were moonlit, shining.

"You were dead!" The word stuck in her throat. A small un-cried sob. She dropped the radio. Used his body to pull herself up. She hugged him, hard, feeling the full length of him with herself. There was time for this now. There was space for this feeling. She couldn't believe it.

His eyes searched hers. Invitation, swimming with relief. His face came closer, and they kissed. Her sea-wet lips slipped across his own. His mouth was gritty with sand. She kept stopping to re-center. With each return, Rachelle tightened her grip.

After awhile, he stopped. He breathed heavily, like he'd forgotten to for a while.

"Not dead. I think I broke my hand though?"

"Your hand? That's it?"

"Disappointed?"

"Shut up!"

Rachelle swatted at him, gave him a look of disbelief. "How are you alive?"

"I think it was that moonflower spell in the woods. When he came out of the woods, his feet were all gnarled, like the moisture from the seeds curled them up. I guess he missed all the good stuff when he brought his foot down on me."

"I can't believe you're okay."

"It's funny, I thought you hated me. "

"That's ridiculous." Rachelle stared in disbelief. "Why?"

"I dunno, maybe you're a bit terse when you're scared?" He smiled, but his eyes were drawn down at the corners.

"Maybe." She smiled back cautiously, taking his good hand. "I'm sorry. I *definitely* don't hate you."

A scraping sound across the sand broke the quiet of the beach. The shadow things dragged Chad's body out from the ruined house, scrambling together, appearing to struggle with his weight.

"Oh god, what are they doing to him? We have to help." Rachelle grabbed James by the arm with both hands, pulling him. "He's like a stick! How is he too heavy?"

"Human life has a weight to it. They can't always just manipulate it like that. Especially if—" James stopped, and sucked in a breath.

"If what?"

"If the soul is getting ready to leave the body."

"What—"

"Chelle, he's probably dying," James said quietly.

She hadn't realized he was still alive. The idea of Chad still in pain settled heavily upon her now. "Is there any way we can help?" Her speech hiccupped, unable to hurdle over the sob. She let go of James and covered her mouth.

She watched his face as he looked over at the ruined man and the demons. "Please don't look," he said, hanging on to her. "He's practically in pieces." Tears gathered in his eyes, and he scrunched up his nose. When he spoke again, his voice was choked. "They're going to give up. They won't be able to carry him to the water. They know they've lost him."

"Why are they trying to take him anyway?"

"They've got him in their veins. Like a drug. Like Chad said, they've been feeding off him, but letting him live so it could continue. They're gonna be hurting for a while without him." He covered half his face with his good hand. "I know that hurt. It's damn near impossible to let go."

"Oh."

"Plus, they've lost his soul. Lost their hold on him from the ritual five years back. They can't bring him down there after we restored him. So he'll be at peace."

"Oh. That's good." Rachelle still shook her head, looking down. She knew it was good, but couldn't feel that good inside herself.

The demons gave up and floated toward the ocean. They stared as they passed. James and Rachelle watched them float down into the waves. They were still dark, but looked like ghosts now. Transparent figures that lowered into the ocean, disappearing before they were fully submerged.

Rachelle and James walked over to Chad. He looked stretched out and distended. If possible, skinnier than he'd been when Rachelle had left the house. His whole chest cavity seemed to fill with each breath, then almost cave in with each exhale. As they approached, his eyes peered at them through the slits his eyelids allowed. He opened his mouth slightly.

"Are there crickets where you are?"

Rachelle tried to breathe steady. *Look him in the eyes. Keep the life inside them.*

"Crickets?"

"Crickets. I can hear them, but it's so rare. The ocean drowns them out."

"Chad, we've got to get you to the hosp—"

"Shhhh, listen."

"What—" Rachelle started, but stopped herself.

They were quiet. Chad lying on his back, his hands folded awkwardly at his chest, and Rachelle crouched over him, her hair spilling down. Straining to hear what he was hearing.

"No waves," he whispered. "No waves, but also no crickets. Too quiet. Like me."

"What do you mean?" she whispered back. She was crouched over him now. Her hand rested gingerly on his elbow.

"I'd found your new number. Had it for years." He smiled, shaking his head. "But I told you, I told you to leave that day. You did so good. I couldn't fuck it up."

"We almost killed each other," she said quietly.

The words were hard to say. She'd had to push them out.

"Did either of us really have a choice?"

She thought hard. "No." Some sort of weight lifted from within her.

"So, there it is. It's only that."

"I—" She stopped again, not even sure what she was going to say.

"You did what you had to do, and so did I, and that's how it is. I have to leave you now. But you guys saved me. So wherever I go, I'll be better off there than where I was before."

"I love you ya know."

"Yeah, I know. Think of me while you grow that kid, huh? Tell him about me sometimes."

"All the time."

"I should be so lucky. James seems good. He'll help."

"Damn, that's noble of you."

"Well I wanna kill him too, but I'm stuck here, dying, so I'll just play the hero." He laughed quietly. It came out soft, like three small coughs in quick succession.

"Aw c'mon. You're not dy—"

A loud gasping rattle startled Rachelle, rocked her back on her ass and hands. He was pulling for air, or for life. His hands were pressed to his chest, fingers touching his throat. Somehow he was already gone. This was just his body taking longer to get the memo. She kept watching him, guiltily praying for it to end. She felt like she was the only one to look. To really see him, so she shouldn't look away. She knew it'd take seconds, but it felt like forever. After a while of that godawful sound, his hands relaxed and fell to his sides. Elbows bent, fingers wilted. His head tilted to the side. Like he'd fallen asleep.

James touched her shoulder gently, then let go. Rachelle touched Chad's hand briefly, then stood up and hugged James.

"How do you feel?"

"Sad. And, a little sick." Rachelle said. Then covered her mouth and looked up at James. "I mean . . . I loved him, I just meant—"

"I know what you mean," James said. His voice was somber but eyes were turned up, almost smiling. "Reminds me of when you knocked that guy over and we had a big laugh about it." He shook his head playfully. "*So* insensitive."

"Let's bring him in the house, and find Stanton," Rachelle whispered to James. "He took Rory somewhere. To safety. I don't know where."

"How do you know?"

"Daisy told me in the water. He used a portal or something."

"See? I told you she'd come help us again."

"No you didn't, you just asked me a million times if she'd left us any more breadcrumbs because *you* were out of ideas!" Rachelle hit James playfully on the back of his hand.

"A million?" James smiled. "Try two?"

27

Rachelle opened her eyes. Something smelled like spoiled food. Sour and strong. Her throat constricted. She retched and covered her mouth. Coughing, she took a gasping breath in.

Phew, she thought. *Really thought I was going to barf on myself in bed.* The candle by her bedside flickered wildly. She must have passed out and left it burning. Didn't explain the smell though.

A humming sound started as she leaned toward the nightstand to blow out the candle. A face appeared above the candlelight. Pale, with white irises and black pupils. The mouth was wide open and black. It looked like it was rotting from the inside.

How can an opened mouth hum? was all she could think to ask herself.

Her chest locked up, a hunk of iron. She stared at the face, unable to move. A pale, bony hand reached for her. It grabbed her by the chin and pulled her roughly toward the candle. She shoved the hand away and screamed, trying to lean back away from it.

A moan escaped the black mouth. It was quiet and grew progressively louder, until it reached the back of its throat and gurgled. The smell intensified.

She gagged again, then screamed. "James!" She felt behind her in bed but nothing was there. "James! Where the fuck are you? Help!"

The handle jiggled loudly. The door swung open, and hit the wall with a loud bang. The ghost disappeared immediately.

"Where were you?" Rachelle cried out.

"Are you okay?" James stalked into the room, his face concerned.

"Yeah, I'm fine!"

"You're fine," James repeated back, unconvinced. He rubbed his eyes slowly, surveying Rachelle with a furrowed brow. "You screamed my name, though?"

Rachelle ignored him and pushed on. "Where *were* you?"

"Couldn't sleep so I moved to the couch and turned on the TV."

"Oh." Rachelle buried her face in the pillow.

"Wanna tell me why you were screaming?"

"Nope."

"Oh, hello. How did this get here?" James gestured toward the fat white candle at the bedside.

"Oh uh," she shrugged, trying at a smile. "I found it. It's yours right?"

"Well, if you found it, you found it in my trunk. So yes, it's clearly mine."

Rachelle tried to laugh it off, halfheartedly. "I mean, yeah. I went through your stuff."

"Soo," James raised his eyebrows.

"So, what?"

"So! What do you want help with?"

"I'm not sure you want to help me. Plus, I got scared. It wasn't how I imagined it. I thought I could handle being haunted."

"What, because you spent the past couple weeks wrestling with hellions?" James smiled and shook his head. "Trust me, this isn't something you just get used to."

"No?" Rachelle asked. Then decided. "No. I guess not."

"You don't have to be afraid to admit it."

"Admit what?"

"You were summoning your ex-boyfriend, weren't you?"

"How'd you know?"

"I mean, who else is dead who you'd want to suddenly see? Your great grandpa? Your favorite pope?"

"Maybe both?" Rachelle smiled mischievously.

"I don't think bringing Chad back will help you, him, or Rory," James said. "I've tried magic for personal reasons myself. Lots of times. It never once turned out the way I needed it to." He looked sideways, remembering. "Actually, always made everything worse. Anyway, don't you remember how adamant you were about not conjuring Daisy?"

"Well yeah, I do. And I know all this now. He smelled like garbage and tried to grab me."

"That's funny. Took me a lot longer than one try to figure that out."

She rubbed her face, which was burning red. "Honestly, I told Gaia my idea and she made me promise not to do it. But, I don't know. It was killing me. I just had to." Un-cried tears burned in her eyes. She touched James' arm. "He looked really bad," she whispered. "Is he . . . okay?"

"I mean, he was probably at peace until you ripped him back over here with my necromancy candle."

"Yeah but, is he okay now, again?"

"Should be, yeah."

James smiled and leaned over Rachelle in bed and kissed her. He felt warm all over from sleep. Smelled like detergent from the afghan on the couch. Detergent, and himself.

She breathed him in and sighed. He'd forgiven her already. "*You* smell much better," she said, her speech muffled. Lips still pressed against his as she spoke. She grinned. Her chest was getting fluttery again. If Chad was really at peace, she felt like she could finally be happy after so much fear and struggle. Rory was good. James was all right. The radio was safe at Stanton's. He'd insisted they keep it at his house, away from Rory. He still came for dinner every Tuesday night after work. *Everything's just so sweet. So sweet it's almost sick.*

James drew back a little and smiled. "Hey, I've got one up on Chad. I'll take it. My next challenge is being enough of a dad to Rory to stop you reminiscing about his real dead dad." James sat up. He leaned toward the nightstand and blew out the candle.

"You're an asshole." She slapped him gently on the cheek.

"Welp, was being a little too moral for my own good. Gotta counterbalance it somehow."

"You've got problems."

"And you love it."

"Yeah. I do," she smiled again. "I do."

About the Author

Lauren lives in a suburb near Chicago with her spouse and two young kids, and her very loud drum set. *Kill Radio* is her debut novel. Her short fiction can be found in anthologies like *In Somnio* (Tenebrous Press, edited by Alex Woodroe), *Beyond the Levee and Other Ghostly Tales* (edited by Peter Talley), and *Tales from the Clergy*, an anthology inspired by the band Ghost (edited by Mark Scioneaux). More information can be found on her website at www.laurenbolger.com.

Acknowledgments

Thanks to everyone who helped me keep writing. Maybe this stuff can happen for some in isolation, but I don't think it could have for me. What I'm saying is I need lots of help.

Thanks to awesome mentors like my friend Peter Talley, and my high school teacher Doug Koski, for seeking out people who love doing this writing thing, and being encouraging and wonderful. Thanks to Peter for reading an early draft and chatting about family and life and fun Horror stuff!

Thank you Alex Woodroe, my amazing editor, for editing the original manuscript for submitting. Her understanding, and championing of an author's intent with their story, is just deeply unmatched. She always knows what to do, and talking these things out with her is just super enjoyable. She makes it fun, and she is a wonderful human.

Alan Good, honestly, same. He is fantastic at his job, and his support and trust are everything. He has made so many hard-won dreams come true for a whole lot of us, and he treats us authors wonderfully. He works hard to make everything great, and working with him is the best experience. A true freaking pro.

Thank you to my amazing writing group, and Mike James, for the critique, support, friendship, pet pics, music swapping and very, exceedingly funny jokes.

To Evangeline Gallagher, for being so patient, easygoing, and cool to work with, and for the end result, a cover that absolutely slays.

Thank you to Laine Lesley for beta reading that early draft and for the encouragement and fun chats.

Thanks to my mom, Heidi Sakol, who has always been so willing to read my stuff even...before, when it was...less good. And my dad, Jerry Sakol, who spent so-o-o much time on the phone with me talking about crystal radios and splices and the funny ever-elusive line between technical correctness and "spooky magic."

Thanks to my mom and dad-in-law, Sue and Dan Bolger, for being so sweet and supportive and frankly for reading Horror, period. Muhuhaha. :)

And, rather importantly, thanks to my husband Marty and my kids, Hannah and Ryan, because they are my everything. Thanks for letting me talk about something that's not technically your thing in the same ways it is for me. Bonus thanks for being hilarious, awesome to be around, loving Horror and books, and laughing with me even when I'm insufferable. You support me because you are loving caring wonderful people and I can't take that for granted. I love you so, so much.

Other Titles from Malarkey Books

The Life of the Party Is Harder to Find
Until You're the Last One Around, Adrian Sobol
Faith, Itoro Bassey
Music Is Over!, Ben Arzate
Toadstones, Eric Williams
It Came from the Swamp, edited by Joey R. Poole
Deliver Thy Pigs, Joey Hedger
Guess What's Different, Susan Triemert
White People on Vacation, Alex Miller
Man in a Cage, Patrick Nevins
Don Bronco's (Working Title) Shell, Donald Ryan
Fearless, Benjamin Warner
Un-ruined, Roger Vaillancourt
Your Favorite Poet, Leigh Chadwick
Sophomore Slump, Leigh Chadwick
Thunder From a Clear Blue Sky, Justin Bryant

malarkeybooks.com

CPSIA information can be obtained
at www.ICGtesting.com
Printed in the USA
LVHW101629080423
743794LV00006B/8